Malcolm Richards crafts stories to kee͏͏ ͏͏uessing from the edge of your seat. He i͏͏ ͏͏several crime thrillers and myst͏͏ ͏͏ ͏͏e PI Blake Hollow ser͏͏ ͏͏vil's Cove trilogy, ͏͏of his books are s͏͏ ͏͏ ͏͏d raised.

Before becoming ͏͏ ͏͏ ͏͏iter, he worked for several years in the ͏͏ ͏͏ education sector, teaching and supporting children with complex needs. After living in London for two decades, he has now settled in the Somerset countryside with his partner and a Miniature Schnauzer called Sebastian.

Author website: www.malcolmrichardsauthor.com

Books by Malcolm Richards

PI Blake Hollow
Circle of Bones
Down in the Blood
The Dark Below

The Devil's Cove Trilogy
The Cove
Desperation Point
The Devil's Gate

The Emily Swanson Series
Wish Me Dead (prequel)
Next to Disappear
Mind for Murder
Trail of Poison
Watch You Sleep
Kill for Love

Standalones & Shorts
The Hiding House
After Midnight
Prey for Night

PI BLAKE HOLLOW BOOK THREE

Malcolm Richards
THE DARK BELOW

First published in 2023 by Storm House Books

Copyright © 2023 Malcolm Richards

The right of Malcolm Richards to be identified as the Author of the Work has been asserted by him in accordance with the Copyright, Designs and Patents Act 1988.

All rights reserved. No part of this publication may be reproduced, stored in a retrieval system, or transmitted in any form or by any means without the prior written permission of the publisher, nor be circulated in any form of binding or cover other than that in which it is published and without a similar condition being imposed on the subsequent purchaser.

All characters in this publication are fictitious and any similarity to real persons, living or dead, is purely coincidental.

ISBN 978-1-914452-46-8

www.stormhousebooks.com

For Ida Oftebro

1

The first signs of spring came early that year, with clear blue skies and a pale yellow sun that shone over the drab concrete of Porthenev Harbour. Although winter's stranglehold was loosening, the air remained crisp and thin, slipping beneath the folds of Blake Hollow's long black coat as she climbed out of her car and shut the door. She shivered, slid her hands inside her pockets. At the other end of the half empty car park, a tall, silver-haired man stood next to a white transit van. Dressed in dusty overalls, heavy work boots, and a donkey jacket that had seen better days, he appeared strong and healthy despite nearing retirement age. His bare hands were currently wrapped around a cup of takeaway coffee, warming them against the cold. As Blake approached, he opened the van door, leaned inside, and took out a crumpled paper bag and another cup of coffee.

'Your mother insisted I bring you breakfast,' he said, holding out the bag. 'Says you're wasting away.'

Blake rolled her eyes. 'She knows I don't do breakfast.'

She accepted the coffee and brought it to her lips. Ed Hollow stared at the paper bag in his hand, shrugged, then removed a sugary pastry and bit into it. 'I'll tell your mother you ate it anyway.'

Blake turned her back on her father to peer up at Porthenev. The fishing village was hundreds of years old, consisting of small white cottages that clustered together on a sloping hill, their windows watching over the harbour and the ocean beyond. It was Blake's first visit to Porthenev, but it reminded her of so many other Cornish coastal towns nestled between towering cliffs. She had already researched the place, learning that what had once been a thriving community built on the back of prime pilchard fishing was now a ghost town for half the year. Tourism, second homes, and holiday lets had sent local property values soaring, which had resulted in not only pricing local people out of the area but doing serious damage to the fishing crews' livelihoods.

The seafront cottages that had once been home to generations of fishermen and their families had all been snapped up by property developers and converted into short-stay summer rentals and seasonal gift shops, forcing the current cohort of fishermen to live further from the shore, even in other towns and villages. Worse still, younger crew members, who were needed to work on the trawlers, were growing increasingly scant, because who could afford to live in a town where the cost of living was three times higher than the local average salary? Which meant several of the remaining fishermen had no choice but to set out on solo trips that yielded fewer hauls of fish and put their lives at greater risk. Add to the mix the growing tension between locals and second home buyers who left their dwellings empty for most of the year, and you had a village that had become a boiling pot of frustration, resentment, and a begrudging dependency on tourism.

Standing in the freezing car park, Blake could taste the uneasiness in the air. She sipped more coffee and turned back to her father. 'Shall we get this over with?'

Ed nodded as he swallowed the last bite of pastry, then tucked the paper bag inside his jacket pocket. There were grains of sugar caught in his stubble that Blake decided could stay there. She was annoyed her father had insisted on accompanying her to Porthenev Harbour, using the excuse that he had been friends with the harbourmaster, Jasper Rowe, for years, and it was he who Jasper had reached out to in the first place. Blake believed his presence had more to do with a need to protect his daughter from a harbour full of grizzled old fishermen with wandering eyes. But what he hadn't accounted for was that in Blake's long career as a private investigator she had dealt with all kinds of violent and unsavoury people. She could handle a few surly fishermen with her eyes closed. And yet, for the sake of their fragile relationship, she had agreed to let her father come along.

Exiting the car park, they walked along a stony path, passing a row of empty cottages and closed shops, until they reached the main harbour. A long granite pier stretched out into the green water, while an angular seawall to the right enclosed the harbour in the crook of its arm. High tide had come and gone two hours ago. Now the water was restlessly ebbing and flowing as it gradually receded. Most of the larger fishing trawlers were already at sea, with only a few smaller boats left behind. The stench of fish guts hung thickly in the air, making Blake grateful that she hadn't eaten the pastry.

She cast her gaze over the rest of the harbour. Stacks of lobster and crab pots lined the quayside. A row of net lofts stood behind them, filled with fishing nets and related equipment. Over to the right, two industrial-looking ice plants towered over the cold storage units where trays of freshly caught fish were stored before being taken to market.

At the top of the main slipway that sloped down to the harbour water, a fishing trawler named *Laura-Lynn* had been hauled up and secured. A large, ragged hole was visible in its side. Standing next to the trawler was a group of men wearing yellow waterproof over trousers, dirty jackets, and rubber boots. None of their faces had seen a razor in weeks. The men looked up as Blake and her father headed towards the harbourmaster's office, which was tucked in next to the storage lofts. One of them nodded at Ed, while the others stared, unsmiling, at Blake.

'Friendly bunch,' she muttered.

Ed knocked on the office door then pushed it open. Jasper Rowe was waiting inside. The office was a single room, not much more than a shack, but Jasper kept it immaculately tidy, the paperwork on his desk organised neatly in trays and the noticeboard on the wall symmetrically arranged. The harbourmaster got to his feet as they entered and shook hands with Ed. Unlike Blake's father, Jasper Rowe was a short man, but he was stockily built with thick white hair, a silver beard, and smiling eyes that reminded Blake of a friendly sea captain featured in a TV ad from her childhood. He had a weathered, outdoor complexion, and as he shook Blake's hand, she felt the roughness of his skin borne from years of working at sea.

'Good to see you, Ed,' Jasper said, in a heavy Cornish accent. 'Nice to meet you, Blake. Your father speaks highly of you.'

Blake glanced at Ed and arched an eyebrow. He avoided her gaze.

'I was about to offer you coffee, but I see you already came armed,' Jasper continued. 'Please, sit.'

He took two wooden chairs from a stack in the corner and set them down on one side of his desk. Once they were all seated, Blake got straight down to business.

'So, how can I help?'

A frown rippled over Jasper's forehead. 'I expect your father already filled you in.'

'All the same, I'd like to hear it in your own words.'

The man scratched his chin. Ed automatically did the same and discovered his sugar crumb coating, which he quickly brushed away before glancing at Jasper and Blake to see if they had noticed.

'The boys outside will tell you more,' Jasper said, 'but it all started a few weeks ago. Just a bit of graffiti at first, on one of the boats. We assumed it was kids from the village, bored and playing up. There's not much for them to do around here. Still, it's no excuse to vandalise private property. Anyway, the paint came off easily enough after a good scrub, and we thought it was over and done with. But then a couple of days later, the net lofts were broken into and some of the nets torn up. After that, it was the cold storage units. Someone tampered with the refrigerators, so that was thousands of pounds worth of fish gone to ruin.'

Ed shook his head in disgust. 'Youngsters have no respect these days.'

'We don't know it was youngsters,' Blake said, shooting him a look before turning back to Jasper. 'What did the police say?'

'Oh, they came down and had a look around, took out their notepads and pens. But that was about it. They said the same thing, that it was probably just kids mucking about. Said they couldn't do much beyond asking around, and that if anything else was to occur we were to get in touch.' He blew air through his nose. 'Fat lot of good that did.'

'What about cameras?' Blake asked. 'CCTV?'

The harbourmaster shrugged. 'We don't have anything like that. We're not some fancy port like Padstow or Falmouth. Anyway, that seemed to be the end of the trouble for a few days. We thought whoever was behind it had been scared off by the police. But then, a week later, it started again.'

'What happened?'

'This time it was broken windows and smashed lobster pots. By this point, the men had had enough, so a group of them camped out in the harbour the following night to see if they could catch the bastard.' He glanced at Blake. 'Pardon my language.'

'I've said a lot worse. Go on.'

'Well, they waited and waited. Nothing happened. A few more days went by, and then Albert Roskilly and his crew came to take his trawler out in the early hours, only to find someone had put a bloody great hole in the side of it. Now she's out of action. You probably saw her on the slipway as you came in. That's Albert's livelihood gone right there, along with his crew's. Don't know if or when she'll be seaworthy again.'

Blake glanced at her father, whose face was pulled into a scowl, then back at Jasper Rowe. 'Please tell me you went back to the police.'

'We did,' the harbourmaster said. 'But again they said they couldn't do much about it.'

Blake sat up. 'I can understand that for a bit of graffiti. But for sinking a fishing trawler?'

'They said without us having any security cameras or witnesses they didn't have a lot to go on.'

Jasper was quiet for a minute before solemnly shaking his head.

'Do you have any idea who might be behind all this?' Blake asked.

'At first, I put it down to rivalry, some disgruntled fishermen with empty nets trying to thin the competition. The waters around here were overfished for years, and although the fish are coming back, it's still not how it used to be.'

'And now?'

'Now, I'm not so sure. These attacks feel personal to me. Like someone's bearing a grudge.'

Blake thought a grudge was possible; the repeated offences, and the scaling ferocity of it all certainly felt like a vendetta.

Jasper regarded Blake from across the desk. 'So, I've told you what I know. Do you think you can help us? Do you think you can find out who's doing this? Because Albert Roskilly and his boys can't afford to lose another day at sea, and the other crews are worried their boats will be next. These men, they don't have much, but they're willing to club together to pay your fees. But I want it to be worth their time and their hard-earned money.'

Blake leaned back on the hard seat. Her father stared at her, his cool eyes unblinking.

'I'll talk to Albert Roskilly before I answer that,' she said.

'You passed him when you came in. He and his crew are repairing nets just outside.'

Blake rose from her seat. Ed did the same. 'No, Dad. You stay here and catch up with Jasper.'

Her father opened his mouth to protest, but a sharp look from Blake made him sit down again.

'I'll be back soon,' she said.

2

Closing the harbourmaster's office door behind her, Blake buttoned her coat up to her neck and began a slow approach towards the men she had seen earlier. They had climbed up from the slipway and were now gathered at the foot of the pier, busy repairing a large fishing net that was unrolled and spread across the ground. They hadn't noticed Blake yet, so she took a moment to observe their surprisingly nimble hands fashioning intricate knots. The oldest of the men was a stern figure of average height, with salt and pepper hair and steely eyes. Blake guessed him to be in his mid-fifties, but his sea-weathered appearance made it hard to be specific. What was easy to see was his confidence. This man was the leader of the group, which meant he was almost certainly the trawler captain, Albert Roskilly, that Jasper Rowe had mentioned.

Working next to him, was a younger man who looked to be in his late teens. A tall and stringy figure, he had pallid skin and blonde hair that protruded like straw from beneath his black hand-knitted hat. His sparse beard was little more than fluff and he had a nervous energy about him, his eyes constantly flitting between the other men, then back to his slim fingers as they worked on the net.

The third man was early thirties, broad and powerful-looking, with a square jaw and a straight nose. He wore a black and yellow striped woollen hat, Cornish rugby colours, and had emerald green eyes that creased at the corners as he talked. He was an attractive man, but Blake could tell from the way he held himself that he was very aware of the fact. Suddenly, he glanced in her direction and those green eyes turned as dark as seawater on a stormy night. He muttered to the other men. All eyes turned towards her.

Blake felt a flutter of uncertainty as she drew closer. She had met men like this before. Men who believed they were still in charge of the world and that women were subservient. She held her head a little higher as she came to a halt in front of them.

'Morning, gentlemen,' she said, ensuring her voice was confident and even. 'My name is Blake Hollow. I'm a private investigator. I'm assuming you know why I'm here.'

The older man straightened, wiped his left hand on his jacket and extended it towards her.

'Albert Roskilly,' he said in a gruff voice. Blake shook his hand, which was icy and calloused. He nodded to the young boy next to him. This here is Ewan, and that's my son, Conrad.'

Blake nodded at them both. The young man,

Ewan, stared at the ground, while Conrad took a moment to appraise her, a leery smile spreading across his full lips. Blake was surprised to learn he was the older man's son; they looked nothing alike.

'I didn't realise there were girl private detectives,' Conrad said, flashing his eyes at her in an unsubtle attempt at flirtation.

'Well, what can I say? We *women* get up to all kinds of things these days.' She peered down at the fishing trawler that had been hauled up the slipway. She could see the hole in the side of the boat now. It was large and ragged, like someone had taken a sledgehammer to it. She turned back to Albert Roskilly. 'Is that your boat? I heard someone tried to sink it.'

The fisherman's eyes darkened. 'That's right.'

'Can you tell me what happened?'

'Not much to tell. Some bastard put a hole in it one night last week. When we came in the morning, the tide was in and the boat was already half under. If we'd come any later, she would have been lost to us.'

'How long until it's back on the water?'

'God knows. We're still waiting for the insurance company to send someone out. The repairs won't get done until I know they'll pay up. I can't afford to take out another loan if they don't.' He nodded at the other men. 'This is my crew. Until we can get that boat seaworthy again we're all suffering. We've got mouths to feed, bills to pay.'

'Little Ewan doesn't,' Conrad said, elbowing the young man. 'He still lives with his mummy and daddy, don't you, Ewan?'

The young man was quiet, staring intensely at his feet.

Blake had spent less than a minute in Conrad Roskilly's company, but she already knew him well. She had met his type before—a misogynist and a bully, the type of man who got off on belittling those he saw as weak and vulnerable, undoubtedly to cover up his own deep-rooted insecurities and fears. She ignored him for now, focusing her attention on his father.

'No one saw anything the night someone tried to sink your boat?' she asked.

Albert shook his head. 'You spoke to Jasper?'

Blake told him that she had.

'Then you already know about the graffiti, the nets, all the rest.'

'It sounds like whoever's responsible has done quite a number on the harbour. Whose fish got ruined in the cold storage? Yours?'

'Mine, and a few of the other boys' catches as well.'

'Any other boats attacked apart from yours?'

Albert shrugged. 'Not to my knowledge.'

Blake's eyes wandered back to the damaged trawler. 'Have you had a problem with anyone lately, Albert?'

The man narrowed his eyes. 'I mind my own business. Try not to have a problem with anyone.'

Conrad was staring at Blake again, that smug smile only serving to irritate her.

'What about outside of the harbour? No strange phone calls, anonymous threats?'

'Not me,' Albert said, then glanced at the others. 'Ewan?'

The teenager shoved his hands inside his jacket pockets and shrugged.

'Is that no?' Blake asked.

He shook his head.

Conrad jabbed the boy in the arm. 'He's not used to talking to girls. Probably too scared he'll squirt in his pants.'

'Leave the boy be,' Albert said, a warning tone in his voice.' You'll have to forgive my son, Miss Hollow. Sometimes I think he was born with fish guts for brains.'

'What about you?' Blake settled her gaze on Conrad. 'You seem like you could easily make a few enemies.'

The smile faded from the man's lips and his eyes widened in mock innocence. 'Me? You must be mistaken. I used to be a choir boy.'

'John George Haigh used to be a choir boy, too.'

'Who?'

'The Acid Bath Killer. He murdered a bunch of people and disposed of their bodies using sulphuric acid. He also thought he was a vampire.'

Conrad stared at her, momentarily speechless.

Blake suppressed a smile. 'So no run-ins for you, either?'

'No,' Conrad said.

'So, we have smashed windows and damaged nets, sabotaged freezer units, graffiti, and a hole in the side of your boat. Has anything else happened I should know about?'

Conrad cleared his throat. His expression was serious now, as if he had finally accepted Blake was here to help. 'There's one more thing. The night after the boat was hit, me and some of the other lads camped out again in the harbour, in case that fucker came back to do more damage. It was getting late. We were cold and about ready to give up for the night. But then I thought I saw someone creeping around one of the other boats. We tried to sneak up on him, but he must have heard us coming because once we reached the boat, it was like he'd vanished into thin air.' He smiled grimly. 'That was when we found the blood.'

Blake shivered as an icy chill swept across the harbour. The fishermen hardly seemed to notice it.

Conrad continued. 'It was on the side of the boat. A large cross painted with a finger. "X" marks the spot.'

'You're sure it was blood?'

'Looked like it to me.'

'Whose boat?'

'Tom Mathers',' Albert said. 'He's at sea right now. Back in a few days, I believe.'

Blake's gaze shifted from man to man. 'And this happened last week?'

'My boat got hit Wednesday night,' Albert said. 'Police came around again the next day and did nothing. Conrad found the blood on Friday. Mathers and his crew camped out Saturday night in case someone decided to put a hole in the side of his boat. But nothing happened. They took her back out yesterday.'

Blake peered at the harbour and the swelling sea beyond. 'Bored teenagers might spray graffiti on a wall or two, but they don't sink boats. Which is why you should have called the police back when you discovered the blood.'

Albert Roskilly scowled. 'What was the point? They'd already made it clear they weren't going to lift a finger. That's why Jasper had the idea to get hold of your dad and bring you down here. So what do you think? Are you going to catch this bastard for us or what?'

Movement to her left made Blake turn in the direction of the harbourmaster's office. Her father stood at the window, watching silently. She heaved her shoulders then turned back to the fisherman. Conrad looked at her indignantly, while Ewan continued to stare at his feet.

'It's an "I'll look into it but I can't promise anything",' she said. 'I work by the hour, and I expect to get paid regardless of the results. I won't waste your time or money either. If I can't find any leads, you'll be the first to know. Does that work for you?'

Albert nodded slowly, mulling the words over, then held out his hand. Blake shook it.

'You've got yourself a deal,' he said.

3

The sun continued to shine over an increasingly cold day. A breeze had rolled in from the ocean, whistling past corners of buildings and toying with the colourful bunting that hung in neat rows over the cobbled streets of Falmouth. A thriving port with a rich maritime history, the town was a popular tourist destination, with each holiday season bringing a flood of new and returning faces, excited to visit such attractions as Pendennis Castle, built in the 16th century on the orders of King Henry VIII, or to attend annual flower shows, sea shanty festivals, and sailing regattas. Falmouth was also home to one of the country's most celebrated creative universities, and its vibrant young students could frequently be seen brightening up the town as they traversed from pub to bar to art gallery, in no particular order.

Today, the streets were relatively quiet, as was the way of most Cornish tourist towns during the off season. Blake had returned to her cramped and crumbling third floor office an hour ago. Its gradual degradation was a constant irritation, especially when she considered how much she was paying in rent each month. But she supposed the views of the Prince of Wales Pier and the pristine white yachts floating on the waters of Falmouth Harbour, the third deepest harbour in the world, almost made up for it. Just how long she could continue renting the office was a different problem entirely.

Since returning to Cornwall eighteen months ago, and despite having run a successful company back in Manchester for years, Blake had been forced to rebuild her private investigation business from the ground up. It hadn't been the easiest of beginnings, despite cracking two major cases in the past year, one of which had almost ended her life and left her with permanent scarring and lingering nerve damage in her right hand. But she was getting more walk-ins now, as well as a few regular insurance fraud gigs and the occasional case working for Ivy Trevara, a lawyer who had helped Blake's father out of some trouble in the recent past and had been impressed with Blake's skills and experience. Yet even though money had started to trickle in on a semi-regular basis, she was still living from case to case.

Times were hard. The country was neck-deep in a cost of living crisis, with inflation levels at an all-time high. Food, fuel, and interest rates were all on the rise while wages had stalled. Blake's monthly rent for the office had already seen one increase, and now that she had finally moved into a home of her own, she could not afford to withstand another.

Perhaps it was better to give up the office altogether and save the money. But Blake was not about to start inviting potential clients into her home; her privacy was paramount, and so was her security. Nor did she think meeting clients at a coffee shop was a better solution; Cornwall was a sparsely populated county, and with a handful of other private investigator agencies already established long before she had arrived, an air of professionalism was of the utmost importance.

Sitting at her desk, she leaned back in her chair and stared at the thin crack slowly dividing the ceiling. At least she had the Porthenev job now, which she supposed she should thank her father for. And hopefully Ivy Trevara would have something for her soon. There was also the option of taking on a second, temporary job of a different nature until things improved. Bar work, perhaps. Or serving tables in a café. 'Beggars can't be choosers,' her mother would say. But Blake wasn't begging in the streets just yet. Besides, a job like bar work would involve making small talk, which was one of her least favourite pastimes, unless she was trying to extract information.

Blake checked the wall clock: 12:32 p.m. She had requested the harbourmaster Jasper Rowe compile two lists for her. The first, a list of names of all fishing crews and corresponding trawlers who used the harbour on a regular basis. The second, a list of dates and approximate times of each incident, along with the names and contact details of those who had been directly affected by the ongoing sabotage. Jasper agreed to have the information ready for her by tomorrow morning. Before that, Blake needed to return to Porthenev Harbour to initiate the main part of her investigation.

Surveillance was an integral part of any private investigator's toolkit, but what the movies didn't show were the long, mundane hours in which you staked out a house or an office, or followed by car or on foot, hoping for a small slip or reveal that got you the evidence you needed to prove the target was a fraud, a liar, or a cheat. The Porthenev case would require only static surveillance for now, which could be murder on the spine and an endurance test for the bladder, unless you had a few technological tricks up your sleeve to help. Which Blake did.

She drummed her fingers on the desk. It was a long wait for this evening with little to do to pass the time other than research the history of Porthenev Harbour while drinking copious amounts of coffee. Because that was the other gift Blake had been rewarded for years of undercover surveillance: a caffeine addiction so intense it would probably kill her long before old age did.

4

Darkness fell at 6:27 p.m., shrouding Porthenev Harbour in a murky veil. With lighter evenings still a month away, the only illumination came from the window of the harbourmaster's office. Inside, Jasper Rowe tidied the paperwork on his desk into a neat stack, ready for his return in the morning, then reached for his coat hanging on a stand in the corner. Blake watched him from the shadows. She had arrived an hour ago and remained in her car, watching the last of the fishermen and harbour workers leave for the day. When hers was the only remaining vehicle in the car park, she had made her way to the harbour, carrying a black backpack and a telescopic ladder. From the backpack, she had produced a pen light and four micro security cameras, each no larger than an inch in diameter and with a magnetic strip on the back. Three of the cameras were now fixed in place, one high up on the external wall of the ice plant, one above the door of the cold storage unit, and one attached to a baluster next to the quay. Together they would provide Blake with a decent view of the harbour; perhaps not full coverage, but enough to capture anyone skulking about after hours with the intention of doing harm.

There was one camera left to attach. Picking up the telescopic ladder, Blake was about to head back to the car park when the light from the harbourmaster's office went out, momentarily plunging her into darkness. Jasper Rowe emerged with a lit torch in his hand. He locked the office door then turned in Blake's direction, illuminating her in a flash of bright light.

'Sorry,' Jasper said, as she shielded her eyes. He lowered the torch, pointing the beam at the ground between them. 'You got them fancy cameras all set up?'

'One more to go.' Blake said, following his gaze as he searched the darkness of the harbour. 'They're really small. You won't find them. Which is kind of the point.'

'Run on batteries, do they?'

'That's right. And they're motion activated, which means they only record when they detect movement. Cuts down the amount of footage to review and extends battery life, but I'll still need to come back and change them in a couple of days.'

'The things they come up with these days,' Jasper said. 'Won't be long before we have flying cars and fish that catch themselves.' The harbourmaster chuckled then fell silent as he peered into the shadows again. 'Well, let's hope we catch this troublemaker sooner rather than later, eh?'

'Speaking of which, you should get those lamps fixed,' Blake said, pointing to two overhead lights that hung over the quayside. 'You're making it very easy for our culprit to get around.'

'Oh, right. I'll get on to it.'

In the harbour basin, the tide was low but restless, lapping at the hulls of awkwardly leaning boats that reminded Blake of beached marine life. The ocean breeze was sharp as razor blades on her skin. She shivered. She had been working without gloves for just thirty minutes but could no longer feel her fingers.

'Well, one more camera to go,' she said.

Jasper nodded. 'Right on. I best head home before the dog gets two suppers tonight. You planning on camping out here tonight?'

'For a little while.'

'You'll be all right down here on your own?'

'I will.'

The harbourmaster hesitated, shifting his weight from one foot to the other.

Blake smiled pleasantly, dousing a spark of impatience. She couldn't decide if Jasper was more reluctant to leave a woman alone in the dark, or have another stranger prowling around his harbour, unsupervised. Perhaps he would feel more at ease if she showed him her illegally obtained can of pepper spray, or reminded him that he had in fact hired her to be there.

'I'll be fine, Jasper. I'll call you tomorrow once

I've reviewed the footage. And don't forget to send me those lists.'

'You'll have them first thing.' He frowned. 'Well, I'll leave you alone then. Don't stay out too long in the cold. You'll catch your death.'

He said goodbye and walked away from the harbour, twice turning to look over his shoulder. Blake shook her head as she removed the pen light from her jacket pocket and switched it on. Returning to the car park, she saw Jasper was already climbing the hill that Porthenev stood upon, the beam of his torch bouncing off the pavement. She followed the light for a short while, until it and the harbourmaster vanished behind a row of houses, continuing the journey towards his home. Blake glanced around the empty car park. A steel litter bin sat at the far end in the left corner. She headed towards it, stooped down, and attached the final camera to its side. It wasn't the securest spot, but it would provide an excellent view of the only entrance and exit to the harbour.

With all four cameras in place, she hurried back to her car, slipped the key into the ignition and set the heaters to maximum. It seemed to take forever for hot air to blast through the vents, but when it did Blake held her frozen hands up, then flipped them over, as if she were barbecuing meat. When she could at last feel her fingers again, she pulled her phone from her jeans pocket, tapped the screen, and opened the security camera app. Thirty seconds later, she was staring at a grid of four live streaming video feeds. Despite the darkness of the harbour, the quality of the night vision was crystal clear. And so it should be, she thought, considering how much the micro cameras had cost.

Her gaze moved from image to image, settling on the bottom right, which showed her vehicle in the car park and the entrance to the harbour. Lowering the window of the driver's door, Blake gasped at the chill rushing in then stuck her hand out and waved. She watched the image on her phone screen, saw her hand wave a second later. A slight delay in the live stream was perfectly normal. She drew her arm back inside and raised the window again, feeling a sudden vulnerability. She shrugged it off as she tapped on each of the four feeds for a full screen view. All cameras appeared to be working, but she wouldn't be satisfied until she'd performed one last live test on each one.

Pulling the keys from the ignition, she stepped out of her car and hurried through the car park, back towards the harbour. The cold clawed at her exposed skin as she hurried past the net lofts to stand in front of the harbourmaster's office. She waved a hand then dropped her gaze to the phone screen, where a second later she saw herself repeat the action on camera feed #1. She moved on, this time standing at the quayside. She raised her hand then dropped it, stared at the screen. Camera feed #2 was running smoothly. Finally, she made her way past the cold storage units until she stood before one of the towering ice plants. This time she raised a middle finger, saw the screen version of herself retaliate, then gave a satisfied smile. Sometimes it was the little things that kept you going.

Her eyes sought out the slipway, where a few

smaller row boats with outboard engines had been pulled up for the night, and the *Laura-Lynn* sat at the top. In the darkness, Blake couldn't see the gaping hole that had almost sunk the trawler. But she could just make it out in the night vision of camera feed #2.

And then she saw something else, just for a second, moving behind her on camera feed #1. She spun around, peering into the darkness then back at the phone screen, where a notification read: "Movement detected". She had seen two figures dressed in dark clothing disappearing between two net lofts.

Any tiredness was quickly swept away. She glanced down at the harbour basin. High tide was still a few hours away, so whoever she had seen on the livestream were definitely not fishing crew. Retrieving her can of pepper spray from her inside coat pocket, she started forward. The moon was obscured by clouds tonight and Blake's pen light was switched off, which meant there was a strong chance the intruders had not seen her. She moved quickly and quietly, ducking between the net lofts. She heard footsteps up ahead but could see nothing.

And then the footsteps fell silent. Blake froze, the can of pepper spray clutched in her hand. She held her breath, listening. Voices, low and whispering, floated in the air. She advanced, sliding her back along the wall of the net loft, her breaths coming thin and fast. She was debating whether or not to leap out and surprise the intruders when she heard the spark wheel of a cigarette lighter being struck. A few seconds later, the unmistakable aroma of marijuana swamped the air.

Reaching into her pocket with her free hand,

Blake took out the pen light. She switched it on, then swung around the corner of the building.

A young man in his late teens was pressed up against the wall, a joint hanging from his lips, while a young woman of about the same age stood in front of him, her hand inside his trousers and groping furiously. As the torch light fell upon them, they both looked up with startled expressions. The young woman immediately withdrew her hand and jumped back. The young man choked on the smoke he was inhaling, and the joint flew from his lips.

'Jesus, get a room!' Blake said.

The young man hastily zipped up his fly, while the young woman gaped at her.

Blake stared at them, half annoyed, half amused. 'What are you two doing here? Besides the obvious.'

The teenagers glanced guiltily at each other.

'Nothing,' the young man muttered.

'Doesn't look like nothing to me.' Blake eyed the joint on the ground. 'Do your parents know you've sneaked out on a school night?'

'I'm eighteen,' the young man said, daring to meet Blake's gaze. 'I don't go to school.'

'Me neither,' said the young woman, who was wise enough to keep her gaze fixed on the ground.

Blake arched an eyebrow. 'In that case, you should know I'm investigating a series of break-ins and acts of vandalism around the harbour. You wouldn't happen to know anything about that, would you?'

Now the young woman looked up, her eyes wide with panic. 'We only came down here for some privacy. We both live at home. We don't know anything about any break-ins. We're in love.'

'I'm sure you are. But there are nicer places to fool around than a fishy old harbour.' Blake turned her attention to the young man. 'And what about you? Have you heard anything about what's been happening down here?'

'No, why would I?'

Blake regarded them both, leaving them to squirm in the torchlight for a while longer. Finally, she shrugged. 'In that case, I suggest you lovebirds fly away home. Unless of course you want to be arrested for indecent exposure and possession of an illegal substance.'

They both shook their heads and turned a shade paler.

'Sorry,' the young woman said. She nudged her boyfriend, who begrudgingly muttered an apology.

They scuttled away, hurrying past Blake like naughty schoolchildren.

'Don't forget to use protection!' she called after them.

When they were gone, she rolled her eyes in the darkness. The joint was still alight on the ground, the end of it glowing like a tiny red sun. Blake stooped to pick it up. Maybe in her youth she would have been tempted to smoke the rest of it. But not now. Not when she had a case to solve. Instead, she stubbed it out against the wall then took a slow walk back through the harbour, shining the torchlight over the buildings, then across the boats and the incoming water, where it danced on the surface. No one else was here.

She returned to the car park and her lonely-looking vehicle. The adrenaline had already dissipated, and now she felt more exhausted than ever. Climbing into the driver's seat, she shut the door behind her and checked the camera feeds one last time. Satisfied, she started the engine and drove tiredly home.

5

Two days passed without incident. Business continued as usual at Porthenev Harbour. Blake kept careful watch over the camera feeds, waking each morning to "Movement detected" notifications from the app on her phone, only to find they had been triggered by gulls squabbling on the quayside or a stray cat sauntering past the harbourmaster's office. Both she and a few of the fishermen tentatively began to wonder if the saboteur had finally given up. Then the third day came.

Getting out of bed, Blake showered and dressed then dragged herself into the kitchen of the rented cottage she had called home for the past two months to make a pot of coffee. Mug in hand, she crossed the flagstone floor and sat down at the scuffed table by the window. Outside, the sky was thick with clouds. The small garden that belonged to the cottage had started to wake from its winter slumber, tiny shoots and leaves unfurling. Unlike her mother, Blake was not green-fingered, so she imagined it wouldn't be long before the garden became overrun by weeds.

Sipping her coffee, she opened her laptop, loaded the security camera programme, and began reviewing the previous night's footage. Again, there was little of interest. More gulls and a surprise appearance by a passing fox searching for food scraps. At 3:27 a.m., the first of the fishing crews arrived to take their boats out. Depending on the size of the crew some of the trawlers would be away for the next few days, while others would return either tonight or tomorrow. In any case, it appeared Porthenev Harbour had enjoyed another night free of trouble.

Blake drained her mug and refilled it. The caffeine was slowly energising her mind, but she needed more. She viewed the rest of the footage from the camera feeds at triple speed, watching people flit about the harbour, zipping in and out of the cold storage units and net lofts. Jasper Rowe arrived at 7:29 a.m., entering his office for another day of work. True to his word, the harbourmaster had emailed Blake's two requested lists on that first morning. The first had detailed a total of thirty-seven boats and trawlers that docked at Porthenev Harbour, and thirty-seven crews who used its facilities. Blake had skimmed through the names of the boats and corresponding crew members, the *Laura-Lynn* and Albert Roskilly leaping out at her from the screen.

The second list had tallied all the damage that had been done at the harbour, along with the names of everyone who had been directly affected. Out of all the boats only one had been attacked: Albert Roskilly's trawler, the *Laura-Lynn*.

As for the cold storage units, several of the fishermen's catches had been ruined by sabotage, including Albert Roskilly's. His nets had also been damaged in the attack on the lofts; she recalled Roskilly's crew on the quayside, working together to repair a large hole in a net. In fact, Roskilly's was the only crew on the list to have suffered damage in all three areas. But did that mean this was a personal attack? Blake was unsure. Other fishing crews had been affected by the sabotage, and there was the matter of the red "X" painted on the side of Tom Mathers' boat, which according to the list was the *Seraphine*.

Conrad Roskilly had told Blake the "X" had been painted with blood, but he struck her as someone who would exaggerate for attention, so it was possible the blood was actually red paint. Either way, it was clear the *Seraphine* had been marked as the next target. But with the crew camping out at the harbour and then setting off for sea the next day, the vessel had so far remained unharmed. According to Albert Roskilly, Mathers and his crew were due back yesterday. With different crews coming and going at the same times due to the changing tide, Blake hadn't noticed the boat come in. She wondered if it was because none of her cameras covered the tip of the north pier and the outer storm wall that formed a protective barrier between the harbour interior and the sea. But it wasn't a problem, she thought. As long as the main harbour area and the entrance through the car park was covered, she would catch the culprit in the act.

Continuing to review last night's footage, Blake made a mental note to return to the harbour after dark to replace the cameras' batteries. It was imperative no one except for Blake and Jasper Rowe knew about the cameras, in case an insider was responsible for the sabotage. She had even been reluctant for Jasper to know of their existence—in her experience no one was above suspicion, not even the client who hired you. At least Jasper was unaware of *all* the camera locations.

Her mobile phone began to vibrate on the table. Her mother was calling.

'Hi Mum, can't talk for long, I'm working.'

'Morning, bird.' Mary Hollow's voice was warm and melodic. 'I won't keep you long. I just wanted to know how my favourite daughter is doing. I haven't seen you in over a week.'

'Your *only* daughter is fine. Just busy.'

Blake's fingers hovered above the laptop screen as her gaze zoned in on camera feed #2. Several men dressed in waterproof trousers and jackets had entered the screen and were heading straight for the harbourmaster's office.

'How's the job going at Porthenev?' Mary asked. 'Your father's pleased you agreed to take it on. Said you were very confident down at the harbour, taking all those men on without a blink of an eye. Of course, he's concerned there are some among them who might not take kindly to a woman taking control of the situation and might cause trouble for you. But like I told him, we didn't raise no girl in pigtails. We raised a headstrong woman. My daughter can take care of herself.'

If Blake had been listening, she might have expressed surprise at her mother's change of attitude.

It hadn't been so long ago that Mary Hollow had been desperate for her only daughter to meet a handsome man to settle down with and give her grandchildren. Blake was almost forty, after all. But since Blake's brother Alfie had produced a son to carry on the family name, it seemed that Blake had been let off the hook. Or perhaps it was because Mary Hollow's daughter had cracked two big cases in as many years, both of which had been covered by the national press, and Mary had finally accepted that Blake was walking her own path through life, free of expectation and constraint.

Whichever it was, Blake hadn't heard a single word of her mother's praise. The men were inside Jasper Rowe's office now. She could see shapes beyond the window, but the grain of the camera and the dull morning would not let her see more. What was happening in there? The men's shoulders had been stiff and taut, their pace hurried.

'Hello? Are you still there, bird?' Mary said. 'Honestly, when are you getting that landline put in? This is what happens when you live in the middle of nowhere. No bloomin' phone signal.'

The office door was opening and the men were leaving. It was hard to make out their expressions, but Blake could tell none of them were smiling.

'Bird? Can you hear me? Hello, hello?'

Now, Jasper Rowe followed behind, slipping his arms into the sleeves of a coat before shutting the door behind him. He paused to glance up at the camera, unknowingly staring directly at Blake, then took off after the men.

Blake turned her attention to camera feed #4, saw

the men marching along the quayside before disappearing off-screen towards the end of the north pier.

Her mother sighed in her ear. 'Well, I guess I've lost you. If you can hear me, I'll try again later. Love you, bird.'

She hung up. Blake felt a twinge of guilt as she watched the camera feeds. Two minutes later, she watched Jasper Rowe hurry back to his office. A moment later, Blake's phone started to vibrate again.

'We need you here right now,' Jasper said as soon as she answered. There was fear in his voice.

'What's wrong?' Blake asked.

'Something's happened. Something terrible.'

'Okay, I'm on my way. But first tell me what it is.'

Jasper paused. When he spoke again, there was a tone to his voice that Blake couldn't decipher. Was it anger? Disappointment? 'Blake, you should know the boys are holding you responsible for what's happened. They're angry.'

She leaned back on the chair. 'Me? What did I do?'

'It's what you *didn't* do that's the problem. It's best you get down here as soon as you can and see for yourself. I just hope you haven't had your breakfast yet.'

'Fine,' she said. 'I'm leaving now.'

Jasper hung up, leaving Blake to stare at her phone screen. Slipping her laptop inside her bag, she poured the remains of her coffee into a travel mug, left the cottage through the front door, and hurried up the garden path. Her Corsa was parked on the tiny gravel drive, which lay just two metres from a narrow country road that snaked around Argal Reservoir and through the village of Mabe Burnthouse. As Blake started the journey towards Porthenev Harbour, nausea churned her stomach. She wondered what she was about to witness, and why the hell she was being blamed for it.

6

By the time Blake arrived at Porthenev Harbour, a crowd had gathered on the north pier, where a row of boats and trawlers were moored below on choppy water that had reached high tide two hours ago and was now slowly ebbing. As she drew closer, a mix of hostile and suspicious glares were cast in her direction. Blake found Jasper Rowe in the midst of a heated discussion with a group of men she hadn't seen before. He looked up as she approached, greeting her with a look that was equal parts relief and disappointment.

'Blake,' he said, with a curt nod. The men he had been talking with fell silent. They were standing on the very edge of the pier. A fishing trawler was docked below them, swaying restlessly. Blake could not see its name from this angle, but she could see the blood splattered over the windows of the wheelhouse.

'What happened?' she asked Jasper, who was a

shade paler than when she had last met him. Perhaps a little older looking, too.

He paused, as if choosing his words carefully. 'There's been another incident. This time on Tom Mathers' boat.'

Blake stared at the men, then back at Jasper. From the corner of her eye she saw Albert Roskilly and his crew watching closely.

'Do your cameras cover the entire harbour?' The man who asked the question was six feet tall, mid-forties, with a nest of dark hair and a scruffy beard that was in need of trimming. His dark eyes burned with anger. Yet there was something else there. To Blake, it looked like fear.

'They cover the main areas of the harbour,' she said, irritated that Jasper had told the men about the cameras. 'They'd certainly capture anyone trying to sneak in and out.'

'Well, they didn't,' the man said. 'Because some sick bastard's done a terrible thing on my boat that goes beyond a bit of vandalism.'

So, this was Tom Mathers, the man whose trawler had been marked for attack last Friday. Blake held his gaze, realising that he'd said something terrible had been done *on* his boat, not *to* it.

'Show me,' she said.

Mathers nodded at his crew, two men in their twenties and another in his mid-thirties. They shuffled to one side, revealing stone steps leading down to where the trawler was moored. Blake glanced at Jasper, then at Tom Mathers, who waved a hand towards the steps.

'Ladies first. I hope you've got a strong stomach.'

Blake brushed past him and began carefully descending the steps. She gripped the iron rail tightly, her gaze flicking from the swell of dark water to the blood-smeared windows of the *Seraphine*. Mathers followed behind. Blake reached the lower stone platform and pressed her back against the wall. Seawater lapped at her boots. She slid to the right, making room for Mathers, who effortlessly stepped off the platform and onto the stern of the trawler. He turned back and extended a hand to Blake.

'How are your sea legs?' he asked.

Blake reluctantly took his hand. 'Better off on land.'

She climbed onto the trawler and nodded her thanks. Immediately, she felt the swell of the tide beneath her, followed by the churn of her stomach. The stench of fish was overwhelming, forcing its way into her nose and throat. Seawater sloshed over the stern, soaking the cuffs of her black jeans.

'Watch your head for the net drum,' Mathers said, ducking beneath a large pulley system that hung above the stern and held the trawler's fishing net in a tightly rolled coil. Blake did as she was told, crouching unsteadily, following the man past a large winch and a bright yellow ladder that led up to the wheelhouse, then climbing over a knee-high barrier and entering a narrow doorway into a cramped interior.

Mathers' expression was grave. 'It's in here.'

He pushed open another door. The smell of blood rushed out.

'This is the berth,' he said grimly. 'Where the crew sleep.'

He stooped as he entered. Blake followed him inside.

The room, if it could be called that, was perhaps six feet long by five feet wide. Bunk beds lined two of the sides while a square table sat at the centre, taking up most of the floor space. There were no seats, the crew members having to sit on the lower bunk beds instead. A small door was set in the far wall, a sign for the toilet stuck on the front.

The blood was everywhere. Congealing on the tabletop. Drenching the bed sheets. Splattered across the door.

Blake stared at the carnage in horror. For a second, she couldn't speak.

'There's more of the same in the wheelhouse,' Mathers said.

Blake didn't hear him. Something had caught her attention. Something lying on the pillows of the bunk beds. Her eyes grew wide.

'Are those . . . ?'

Mathers slowly nodded. 'Like I said, the sick bastard.'

Blake stared at the severed heads resting on the pillows. Four pairs of lifeless eyes stared right back.

'Where are the bodies?' she whispered.

'I found them stuffed in the bloody fuel tank. That's the *Seraphine* grounded until we can get her fixed.' The man clenched his jaw as he surveyed the scene. 'What kind of madman cuts the heads off gulls? Never mind leave them in our beds. What did we do to anyone?'

Blake's mind raced. In her time as a private investigator, she had witnessed more acts of cruelty than she cared to remember. But nothing as bizarre as this. Nausea swelled in her gut as the trawler swayed and the coppery aroma of blood mingled with the stench of fish. The cabin closed in on her, already small but now feeling coffin-like.

'Let's go outside,' she said.

She retreated from the room with Mathers on her heels, until she was standing on the stern deck once more. The sky had grown greyer in the last few minutes, the sea more unsettled. Above them on the pier, the crowd of men stared down expectantly.

'So, what now?' Mathers asked her, scratching at his unkempt beard. His eyes were narrowed, full of their own storm clouds.

'This isn't bored teenagers.' Blake was desperate to get off the trawler and onto solid ground. 'This is something else entirely.'

The fisherman snorted. 'Something that should never have happened if your cameras had been working in the first place.'

The trawler rocked to the left as the sea grew irritable. Blake clung to the side railing and glanced up at the men on the pier. The cameras *had* been working. She had set them up to cover all the major areas of the harbour. So why hadn't they captured whoever had attacked Tom Mathers' boat?

She turned back to him. 'I'm going to ask you the same question I asked Albert Roskilly. Have you had any trouble lately? Any run-ins? Have you unwittingly caused someone to bear a grudge?'

'I'm either at sea or at home with my wife. Mostly at sea. Sometimes I'll go for a drink with the boys, but that's a rarity these days. I don't have time to cause trouble with anyone, and certainly not with anyone capable of going to the lengths of that.' He nodded at the cabin door. 'Some of the boys think it's a rival crew trying to cut down the competition.'

'But you don't?'

'If it had just been cutting up nets and busting the cold storage freezers, I would have agreed. Even Roskilly's trawler I could have bought. But cutting up birds and leaving them in our beds? I don't know how much you know about us fishermen and our ways, but we don't kill gulls. Ever. It's bad luck.'

Blake stared at him, an uneasy feeling clawing her gut. 'Don't touch anything for now. Leave it all exactly as you found it.'

'I can't do that. I need to get my boat back up and running. We've all got mouths to feed.'

'I know, but it's important. And don't let anyone else on board. There could be evidence.'

She left Mathers on the deck, shaking his head bitterly, and climbed off the *Seraphine* and onto land. The stone platform was wet and slippery beneath her boots. Icy water sprayed over her as she reached the steps and began climbing. On the pier, Jasper Rowe was still waiting with the other men. Albert Roskilly and his son Conrad stood close by. Ewan, the third member of his crew, hung back slightly from them, his frightened eyes watching Blake. The mood of the crowd was quietly hostile.

'Good job with your investigating,' Conrad called, his lips curled into a sneer.

Blake ignored him as she fixed her attention on Jasper.

'We need to talk,' she said. 'In private.'

In the harbourmaster's office, Jasper made coffee while Blake stood at the window and watched the unhappy men outside. She suddenly felt vulnerable, an unusual feeling that didn't sit right with her. But it was unusual to have a harbour full of angry fishermen all pointing the finger of blame in her direction, as if she had decapitated the gulls herself. She was deeply troubled by what she had witnessed, the bloody carnage of the sleeping quarters branded onto her mind.

'We fishing folk are a superstitious lot,' Jasper said, as if reading her thoughts. He handed her a mug of coffee as he joined her at the window. 'What's been done on the *Seraphine* will be seen as a bad omen.'

'You need to call the police, Jasper. This isn't about rivalry or bored teenagers. This is something personal. Someone has a grudge against the men of this harbour. I don't know why or what it's about, but whoever is behind this has just sent a very clear message.'

'What kind of a message?'

'That this isn't the end. That it's only going to escalate.'

'Escalate? How can you be so sure?'

'Because this kind of thing always does. Believe me, I've seen it before. This person is capable of violence, of torturing and dismembering animals. Who's to say his next target won't be one of your men?'

Outside, the crews dispersed into smaller groups, some of them returning to repairing nets, others towards their boats, their eyes bright with a desperate need to check they were not the next target.

The harbourmaster stared at Blake, his mouth opening then closing.

'Call the police, Jasper,' she said. 'This is beyond my remit. Don't let anyone else on board the *Seraphine*. It's a crime scene now. They'll want to get forensics down here.'

She sipped her coffee, which tasted like ash on her tongue.

Slowly, Jasper nodded, lines creasing the corners of his eyes. He set his mug down on his desk and stared at the phone.

'How did he do it? If your cameras cover the only way in and out of the harbour, how did he get in here without any of us noticing?'

It was a good question. One that Blake could not stop thinking about. She had a few theories, but she would need to review yesterday's footage again to be sure. Putting her mug down next to Jasper's, she crossed her arms over her stomach.

'I'm sorry,' she said. 'This shouldn't have happened on my watch. Tell the men I'll waive my fee. I'll hand all the camera footage to the police, then I'll be out of your way.'

Jasper had picked up the receiver and his finger was hovering over the buttons of the phone.

'Now hang on a minute,' he said. 'Let's wait to see what the constabulary has to say first. If they can't do anything we may still need you.'

'I think the men out there might have something to say about that.'

'They're just scared, that's all. Men like this, they

don't know how to handle fear so they turn to anger instead.'

Blake glanced through the window. At the far end of the north pier, Tom Mathers and his crew had joined Albert Roskilly and his men. They were huddled together in a tight scrum, deep in conversation. Even from this distance, Blake could see the tension turning their bodies rigid. Above them, the sky had turned to charcoal and was threatening rain. In the dark water below, boats rocked nervously.

As Jasper made the call, Blake kept her eyes fixed on the group. The trouble with men and anger was that often they could not control their emotions, especially when their livelihoods were threatened. And when men could not control themselves, what it really meant was they could not control their fists. People ended up getting hurt. Sometimes worse.

Jasper put the phone down and rejoined Blake at the window.

'They're sending someone out,' he told her. 'Should be here within the hour.'

Blake gave a silent nod. She would be glad to get away from here. Because there was more than just a storm brewing at Porthenev Harbour.

7

The Ship's Wheel was an ancient pub that had seen better days. The decor was oak and pine, with floorboards that were as lined and weathered as the hands of its fishermen patrons. Tabletops were scuffed and beer stained. Spiderwebs hung in corners, their occupants starved of insect meals. Coloured glass jars sat on shelves, waterfalls of old candle wax clinging to their sides. Like the man who worked behind it, the bar was thick and sturdy. It had stood for three hundred years, absorbing countless spilled drinks and drunken tales, some of woe, some sordid, some even murderous back in the pirate days. Whether it would withstand another three hundred years was debatable.

A fire crackled in the hearth, warming the pub. Lying on the threadbare rug before it, Wilson, the landlord's elderly black Labrador, watched the handful of drinkers through half closed eyes.

Sitting close by on a corner table, Martin Bennett

wrapped his fingers around a pint of cold beer and stared into space. Joining him were his fellow shipmates of the *Seraphine*, Shawn Brown and Brett Nicholls, who were both in their mid-twenties, at least ten years his junior. It had been a long, troubling day at Porthenev Harbour, filled with a buzz of police activity and growing anger among the fishing crews. Some spoke of retaliation and violence—even though they had no idea who to retaliate against—while others quietly worried who among them would be targeted next.

'I'm telling you,' Shawn said, wagging a finger at his fellow crew members, 'it's one of those bastards from down the way, trying to scare us.'

Brett smirked. 'Where exactly is "down the way"? You might need to be a bit more specific.'

'One of the other harbours.' Shawn leaned forward. 'Look, we all know fish stock is low and competition is fierce. It makes sense someone would want to keep their rivals stuck on land so they can catch all the fish.'

'I don't know, mate. Yeah, stock is still low, but it's been improving lately.'

'Still not enough to go around though, is it?'

'Anyway, I reckon you're looking too far afield. I reckon whoever's behind it might be closer to home than you think.'

Shawn stared uncertainly at Brett. 'What are you saying? That one of us did it?'

'Not us around this table. One of the other crews in Porthenev.'

'Bollocks. Why would they do it?'

Brett sipped his pint. 'Like you said, too much competition.'

'I don't buy it,' Shawn said, shaking his head. 'You mess up the cold storage units, you're only creating problems for yourself. No, that don't make sense to me. Everyone knows you don't shit in your own backyard.'

'Which is why no one would believe it if someone did. And maybe it's not even to do with the fish. Maybe someone's got a grudge about something else. Something personal.'

'Well, whatever it is, I don't like it.' Shawn swallowed half of his beer and stared at Martin, who, until now, had been lost in thought. 'You're quiet. Who do you think's behind it?'

Martin hesitated, avoiding his crewmates' gaze. He picked up his glass, noticed his hand was trembling, then quickly put it down again.

But Shawn had noticed too. His lips parted into a wide grin. 'You look like you seen a ghost, Bennett. What, a few dead birds scaring the shit out of you?'

He laughed. Brett smiled, but was sensible enough to not take it further.

'Fuck off,' Martin said through clenched teeth. He tried for his glass again, ignoring the tremor of his fingers, and brought it to his lips. He swallowed cold beer, gulping it down like it might drown the dread that was clawing his insides. 'I don't know who's behind it, but they've got it coming to them.'

Both Shawn and Brett growled in agreement, clinking glasses and swallowing more beer. In front of the fire, Wilson raised his head from the carpet, regarded the trio, then returned to his slumber.

'I wonder how long it will be before we can get back on the water,' said Brett. 'The police were still on board when I left. They had one of those guys in white suits taking blood samples. I heard one of them say to Tom they have to determine if the blood came from the birds.'

'Of course it came from the birds,' Shawn said. 'You can't chop off a gull's head without making a mess, can you?'

Brett had to agree.

Martin had removed his hands from the table and was now clasping them in his lap, trying to still the trembling. His mind was restless like the sea, churning up images and sounds that he had fought endlessly to sink down into the depths. But here they were once again, floating to the surface.

'Tom still down there?' he asked.

Brett nodded. 'Was when I left.'

Shawn emptied his glass, then leaned forward. 'Don't you think it's funny that it's the *Laura-Lynn* and our *Seraphine* that's been hit? Why not the other boats?'

He was staring at Martin, eyes completely focused.

Martin shrugged a shoulder and stared at the table. 'Maybe whoever it is has just got started. Maybe others are next.'

'Maybe, but why us before the others? That bloody "X" Conrad found. We were marked. We camped out and nothing happened. Then we went to sea, came back, and now we've got the police crawling over the boat. Whoever's responsible, why didn't they hit another boat while we were away?'

'Maybe that private investigator lady scared them off,' Brett offered.

Shawn smirked. 'You reckon? Far as I'm concerned, she's about as useful as tits on a bull. No, they waited for us to get back. Which means they were after us, not anyone else. Why?'

Quiet chatter from the other patrons filled the silence. In the fireplace, a log shifted, causing a flurry of sparks and crackles. Wilson opened one eye, then shut it again.

The images in Martin's head grew stronger, more graphic. He jigged his right knee up and down as his fingers entwined into knots. Suddenly, he wanted nothing more than to be at home with his wife and his twin boys, who were already six years old, and whose lives he felt he had hardly been a part of. Such was the life of a fisherman who had run out of luck a long time ago.

He pushed his seat back and got to his feet. 'I'm going home.'

'What do you mean you're going home?' Shawn said. 'What's going on with you?'

'Anyway, it's your round,' Brett said.

Pulling his wallet from his pocket, Martin removed a ten pound note and dumped it on the table.

'There's your round,' he said. 'I'm going home because I don't know when we'll next be at sea, and unlike you two I've got mouths to feed other than my own.'

Brett picked up the money from the table and tried to give it back. Martin shook his head.

'Don't get too pissed up,' he said. 'Tom will need

us tomorrow morning. We might be grounded but there's other work we can do.'

Another wave of images flashed in his mind, full of blood and screaming. His crewmates stared at him strangely, then glanced at each other.

'I'll see you,' Martin said.

He hurried towards the door, threw it open, and peered out at the darkness. Sucking in a breath, he exited the Ship's Wheel and let the darkness take him.

8

Back at her office in Falmouth, Blake sat with her shoulders hunched at her desk as she reviewed the camera feed footage from last night for the fourth time. Her eyes were dry and aching from staring at the computer screen for too long, and the rhomboid muscle between her shoulder blades felt uncomfortably tight. She leaned back for a moment, sat upright, and stretched out her arms. Joints popped. The forefinger and thumb of her right hand throbbed painfully, a result of the permanent nerve damage that had been inflicted by a serial killer.

Getting up from the desk, she paced over to the window and peered out at Falmouth Harbour. Darkness had fallen and she had barely noticed. Below and to the right, the Prince of Wales pier was illuminated by a row of Victorian style street lamps. Strings of bunting flapped in the evening breeze. The water beneath was black and agitated, lit up here and there by lights from moored vessels, and from quayside restaurants and bars.

Blake narrowed her eyes. *A boat*, she thought. The perpetrator at Porthenev Harbour had gained access by boat. No matter how many times she had reviewed each camera feed, paying particular attention to background shapes and shadows, she had seen nothing out of the ordinary. Which meant the perpetrator had not entered the harbour via the car park. Nor had they hidden within the harbour during the day so they might go about their unsavoury business once they were alone at night. Which left only one option.

They would have used a small boat, perhaps a dinghy with an outboard motor—although they would have used oars to row in so as not to attract attention. It being dark, they would have needed a light source. Unless they were familiar with the harbour's layout.

Her mind wandered back to the *Seraphine*'s sleeping quarters and the bloody carnage within. The perpetrator, whoever they might be, was dangerous and clever. But not *that* clever. Their decision to enter the harbour by boat told Blake several facts. Firstly, the perpetrator clearly had knowledge of the harbour layout and that there was only one way in or out by land. Perhaps at the beginning of their campaign they had gained access on foot, but with the escalation of their disturbing behaviour and the fishing crews on high alert, entering by boat under the cover of night reduced the risk of getting caught. Or perhaps they had always used a boat. It would explain how they had vanished into thin air on the night Conrad

Roskilly had witnessed a figure lurking next to the *Seraphine,* and discovered the bloody "X" painted on the trawler's side.

Secondly, the perpetrator knew exactly where the *Seraphine* was moored, and that it had returned from its latest fishing trip. Which meant he or she almost certainly knew the crew, or was, at the very least, aware of their comings and goings. For the perpetrator to know that meant it was extremely possible they frequented the harbour on a regular basis, either as a member of a fishing crew or one of the onsite harbour workers. And if *that* were true, they would know a private investigator had been hired and possibly even knew about the cameras.

'An inside job,' Blake muttered at her reflection in the window. Then added, 'Probably.'

Because you could never say definitively without concrete proof, of which she had none. Now that the police were involved it was unlikely she would get to see any, either.

Idiot, she thought. *The one place you didn't install a camera . . .*

At least she had only lost her pride. The distress that had been caused to the crew of the *Seraphine*, not to mention the rest of the fishing crews, was a loss she didn't want to think about.

As she peered down at the Prince of Wales pier, she cursed herself for making such a fatal error of judgement. Throughout her years as a P.I. back in Manchester she had never made such a mistake, because when it came to her cases, Blake Hollow simply did not *make* mistakes. So why had she made one now?

Turning away from the window, she snatched her mobile phone from the desk and made a call. The line connected almost immediately.

'What are you doing right now?' she asked, without so much as a cursory "hello".

'Watching shit TV and trying not to think about booze,' the voice on the other end said.

'Great. I'll be there in half an hour.'

'What? How do you know I'm not busy?'

'Because you answered the phone in less than a second. Come on, Kenver. You don't need to be a private investigator to work that out.'

'Fine. But bring food. I'm starving and too weak to cook.'

Blake hung up, put her laptop into her backpack and threw on her coat. Leaving the office, she had a sudden thought. Would Jasper Rowe tell her father about what had happened today? Blake could already picture her father's disappointment. She shrugged it off as she locked the door and took the stairs down to the street. Whatever he thought about Blake's error was none of her business. Besides, Ed Hollow hardly had the right to judge her, not when their relationship was still so fragile. Not when he had lied and cheated and had made what Blake considered to be the worst error of judgement in the history of the Hollow family.

No, if Ed Hollow had something to say about today, he could keep it to himself because Blake didn't care to hear it. So why then, as she entered the quiet high street and headed towards the car park, was anxiety making her stomach twist and churn?

9

Kenver Quick lived on the outskirts of Wheal Marow. He was tall and slim, with large, sad eyes and a shock of black hair that matched his skinny jeans and ripped t-shirt, while his body was heavily tattooed with Gothic images of ravens, snakes, and dead trees. Walking the streets of the decaying former mining town that both he and Blake had grown up in, Kenver was an arresting sight that often attracted the turning of heads and the occasional hurling of insults, such as "freak" or "fucking faggot".

His life plan had not included returning to this godforsaken town; when he had escaped to London at the age of eighteen, he had vowed never to return except for occasional family visits. Yet there he was, twenty-nine years old, soon to be thirty, living in a two-bedroom terraced Victorian cottage in Wheal Marow with no means of escape any time soon.

Blake knew why her cousin had returned to their

hometown. He had been living the high life a little too hard, and developed a burgeoning dependence on alcohol and recreational drugs. Fortunately, he had recognised what was happening before it was too late and elected to leave the city for a short while to get himself cleaned up. Except he had been in Wheal Marow for almost two years now. What Blake didn't know was why Kenver had embarked on a self-destructive path in the first place. Perhaps there was no reason other than brain chemistry. She had only asked him about it once, and he had made it bluntly clear that his reasons were no one's business except his own.

Letting herself into his home, Blake shrugged off her coat, walked through the living area and into the kitchenette, where she dumped a plastic bag filled with food containers on the counter.

'I brought Chinese food,' she said, taking plates out of a wall cupboard. 'It was that or pizza. When did the Indian takeaway shut down?'

Joining her in the kitchenette, Kenver took out chopsticks and cutlery from a drawer. 'I didn't realise it had. Seems like everything is shutting down these days. Pretty soon the only place left open in Wheal Marow will be the grave I'm slowly digging for myself.'

'That's cheery.' Blake shivered as she removed the lids of the food containers. 'It's cold in here. Has your Gothic heart finally decided to embrace the chill of winter?'

'Like that's ever going to happen. Anyway, who can afford to have the heating on all the time right now? Or didn't you notice we're in a cost of living crisis?'

'Well, it's usually like a sauna in here. And yes, I have. You try paying rent on a house *and* an office space.'

'I wish I had the privilege.'

With the food served, they took their plates into the living area and sat on the sofa.

'Chopsticks?' Kenver asked.

The nerve damage in Blake's right hand was still flaring painfully, so she opted for a fork. As she began to eat, she cast an eye around the room. It was reasonably tidy, which meant Kenver was still off the booze. It had been a few months since his previous relapse. Blake had been partly responsible for the slip. Asking for Kenver's help during last year's Trezise case had landed him in a bar, where temptation had got the better of him. He had gone off the rails for a while, but with some help from Blake he had managed to get the drinking back under control. Unfortunately, sobriety had come too late to save his data analyst job at the pharmaceutical company.

'How's the job hunt?' Blake asked tentatively.

Kenver shrugged his shoulders and crammed noodles into his mouth. 'It would be easier if I could get a reference from my last job, but seeing as how they fired me . . .'

'Which was grossly unfair if you ask me. You were technically unwell and trying to get better.'

'That makes me sound like I'm crazy. But if you hear of anyone needing a data analyst, hit me up.'

'I will. And it will get better. You'll see.'

'Now you sound like my mother.'

'And this is where I remind you, yet again, I'm only ten years older than you.' Blake picked at her food. Repeating images of decapitated birds and blood-spattered bed sheets were killing her appetite. She sucked in a heavy breath and blew it out through pursed lips.

'What's wrong with you?' Kenver said. 'You've had a face like a slapped ass since you got here.'

'Um, thanks?'

'Speaking of ass—'

'Wait, do I want to hear this?'

'—the other day I had a full on brawl online arguing that not all British people say "arse" and that here in the West Country and regions in the north, we've said 'ass' since time immemorial, and that's probably where the Americans got it from. But did anyone believe me? No, I don't think so because that's cancel culture for you.'

'That's how you're spending your time? Arguing with strangers about people's backsides?'

'It was a discussion about dialectal variation. Anyway, back to you and your face. What's wrong?'

'It's nothing. I made a mistake at work that caused some trouble. It's been a really shitty day.'

'Well, I'm glad it's not just me messing up. What did you do?'

Putting her plate on the coffee table, Blake told Kenver about the incident at Porthenev Harbour, and about how the fishing crews were holding her responsible due to her negligence.

Kenver listened intently, screwing his face into a grimace as Blake described the bloody scene discovered in the sleeping quarters of the *Seraphine*. When she had finished, he swallowed the food in his mouth and gave her a long, analytical look.

'Okay, first of all, what's going on with you? Because the Blake Hollow I know doesn't make mistakes. Secondly, while perhaps there was some negligence on your part, you weren't the psychopath who carved up a flock of birds and tucked them into the sailors' beds. Whoever it is, it sounds like they've watched *The Godfather* one too many times.'

'Kenver, what are you talking about?'

'You know, the scene where the guy wakes up to find a severed horse's head in bed with him. It's like that but in miniature.'

Blake rolled her eyes. This was not helping.

'Anyway,' Kenver continued, 'even if you had put a camera close to the *Seraphine*, you might have captured the psycho on film, but there was no one there to stop him from doing what he did. It doesn't necessarily mean you would have identified him either. If he's clever enough to come in by boat, maybe he's clever enough to cover his face.'

'But that would mean he'd have to know about the cameras, and I made sure no one knew about them except for Jasper Rowe, the harbourmaster.'

'Then maybe he's the bird killer.'

'No, he's close to retirement age. I don't think he'd have the strength to tear a hole in that other trawler. Besides, he's Dad's friend. That's how I got the job, because Jasper reached out to Dad to ask for my help.'

'Everyone makes mistakes. Even you. So, you just have to let this one slide.' Kenver put down his empty plate and picked up Blake's full one. 'Are you eating this?'

'It's all yours. I don't know where you put it.'

Kenver tucked in. 'I have a high metabolism. Anyway, what does dear old Uncle Ed have to say about today's shenanigans?'

'I haven't told him.'

'Someone will. Might as well be you.'

Blake slumped back on the sofa. Kenver was right. Someone would tell her father about what had happened on the *Seraphine*. But so what? It wasn't as if he had hired her to do the job. Not that it would stop him from being disappointed in her. She shook her head. Even after all these years, and after every terrible thing her father had done, the fear of letting him down was still very much a weight on her conscience.

'You know what?' Blake said. 'It doesn't matter if it's me who tells him, or someone else, his reaction will be the same. So let someone else do it.'

'Fair enough. Besides, Uncle Ed is hardly in a position to judge anyone considering recent events. He's lucky you're even talking to him.'

Blake couldn't disagree.

Kenver eyed her curiously. 'But there *is* something else bothering you besides today, isn't there? In fact, the last few times I've seen you, you haven't been yourself.'

'I haven't?'

'You've turned into a right Debbie Downer. Moping around and grumbling about life. What's going on? Is it because you killed someone last year?'

Blake stared at him, open-mouthed. 'What the

hell, Kenver? That was in self-defence and you know it! No charges were brought against me. Jesus!'

'Well, if it's not that, it must be the other thing.'

Blake was beginning to regret coming here tonight. 'What other thing?'

'The fact that you're not a hotshot P.I. anymore,' Kenver said. 'Not like you were back in Manchester. You've had to start over and it's been tough. And exhausting. Probably explains why you look so tired.'

'If you're trying to make me feel better, you're doing a really shitty job.'

'All I'm saying is I know how hard it is to start over, how much energy it takes. You just need to keep slogging away at it. One mistake today does not make you a bad P.I. It just makes you human like the rest of us.' He paused and stared at her earnestly. 'At least no one got killed, right? I mean, apart from a few innocent birds. So that's a win.'

Blake said nothing.

'Go home,' Kenver said. 'Get some sleep. Tomorrow's another day.'

Blake regarded her cousin through narrowed eyes. 'You know, I think I liked you better when you were drunk. At least then you were too inebriated to be spouting words of wisdom. When did you get so sage?'

'I always was, my dear. I always was.'

⁓

Leaving Wheal Marow behind, Blake drove through dark country roads, the headlights of her Corsa casting bright beams over hedgerows and cracked tarmac. She knew Kenver was right, that the struggle to re-establish her private investigator business since returning to Cornwall had been much harder than she had anticipated. She was tired and drained of enthusiasm, and it seemed unfair that she had not been able to rely on the solid reputation she had earned in Manchester. But that was just how life was sometimes. The only thing she could do was to keep trying.

'Screw you, Kenver,' she said, with a weary smile.

Despite his woeful lack of tact, she was happy to see him clean and sober. There had been a moment when Kenver had almost slipped past the point of no return. He would get a new job soon, Blake was sure of it. And she supposed he was right about something else. No one had died today, except for a few birds, which of course was awful. But the fishermen remained physically unharmed. She would take that as a win.

10

The salty air stung Martin Bennett's skin as he hurried up the hill towards home. The streets were quiet and empty, a lonely looking street lamp to his right losing a battle against the darkness. Porthenev truly was a ghost town off-season, but the isolation barely left a mark on Martin. The ghosts that haunted him persisted all year round.

When the incidents at the harbour had first begun, he'd had a brief moment of paranoia, which he had managed to talk himself out of. It was just kids, bored and frustrated, kicking off like he and his friends had done when they were younger. It was what you did as a teenager stuck in a small town. You acted up because there was nothing else to do. But then the *Laura-Lynn* had been attacked and a bloody mark had been left on the *Seraphine*. He had known in an instant that his initial paranoia had been fully justified.

Someone knew.

They knew and they were doing something about it.

He had tried to convince the others, but they had all agreed that it was nothing more than a coincidence and that he needed to calm down and stay quiet before people really did find out. He had tried and failed. Those few days at sea were filled with tension and a clawing fear of what he would find waiting for him when he returned to land, the nights plagued by terrible visions and nightmares.

The others weren't in denial now. He had seen it in their eyes earlier on the quayside when their gazes met then quickly shifted away. Fear. Cold and unforgiving. And chilling realisation that Martin had been right all along.

Someone knew.

The question now was: what could they do about it?

Reaching the top of the hill, Martin turned and stared down at Porthenev, at the harbour and the cold sea beyond. It was down there somewhere, lurking in the darkness. A secret chained and dumped overboard, left to sink into the depths of Davy Jones' locker, where the ghosts of drowned sailors would catch it in their hands and hold it close to their bony chests.

I should be down there with them, Martin thought. *We all should.*

He turned his back on the village and entered the modern housing development, where his family was waiting. If only they knew what their husband and father had done. How tormented he was.

Reaching the garden gate of his modest semi-detached home, Martin froze. All of the lights were off.

Reaching into his pocket, he removed his phone and checked the time. 8:28 p.m. At six years old the boys would already be in bed. But not his wife. Martin was late for the evening meal again, had forgotten to call Sharon and let her know. Before, when him being late was a rare occurrence, she would call him out of worry. But he had been coming home later and later, using work as an excuse, and Sharon had grown tired of calling. During their last argument she had told Martin that she could deal with him being away at sea for days at a time, but when he *was* home their time together as a family was precious, and he was pissing that time away. His boys were growing up with an absent father, she had told him. He barely knew them. That had hurt him more than anything else because he knew it was true.

But it didn't explain the lights.

He wondered if Sharon had gone to bed early in silent protest, then quickly discarded the thought. His wife was not the sulking type. She would tell him to his face if she was annoyed, and he respected her for it. Besides, hiding feelings was his own special talent.

Opening the gate, he walked down the garden path and paused outside the front door. The anxiety that had been plaguing him since the discovery of the mutilated birds was growing out of control.

Slipping his door key into the lock, he twisted it to the left and pushed the door open. Darkness greeted him under a blanket of silence. He entered his home, closed the door and locked it, then stood in the shadows. There were no sounds. But there was a smell, sharp and acrid, like chemicals.

Surely Sharon had heard about the bloody scene on board the *Seraphine* by now; news travelled fast in Porthenev. Even if she were annoyed with Martin, she would want to know the details of what had happened, if everyone was safe and well.

'Hello?' he called softly, not wanting to wake the boys. 'Sharon? Are you down here?'

He flicked the light switch to his left. The house remained in darkness. Activating the light on his phone, he located the fuse box, which was high up on the wall next to the front door. He took the foot stool that Sharon always sat on to remove her shoes, placed it under the fuse box and climbed up. His heart hammered in his chest. The main power switch had been turned off.

He flicked it back on. Bright light instantly flooded the hallway.

Climbing down from the foot stool, Martin waited a few seconds for his eyes to adjust then surveyed the hallway.

The fine hairs on the back of his neck began to prickle. A blue and yellow vase lay in pieces on the floor. Scattered among puddles of water were seven golden daffodils. His wife had picked them fresh from the garden that morning.

'Sharon?' he called loudly. 'Boys? Where are you?'

When they did not answer, he rushed forward, his stomach churning as he threw open the living room door and peered inside. The room was dark and undisturbed, the TV screen reflecting his silhouette and the brightly-lit hallway behind.

He tried the kitchen, switching on the overhead fluorescent lighting. One of the drawers had been pulled out and now lay on the floor, surrounded by cutlery. His eyes went to the butcher's block on the counter. He lunged towards it, grabbing the largest of the knives, and returned to the hall, where he climbed the stairs two steps at a time.

Reaching the landing, he slid to a halt. His and Sharon's bedroom lay to the right of the stairs, their sons' to the left. His gaze swung from door to door and back again, like the pendulum of a clock. Left or right? Right or left? Children or wife?

He chose the boys without a flicker of guilt. They were, after all, his flesh and blood.

He stepped towards their bedroom, the boys' names, Josh and Harry, screaming at him from brightly coloured name signs glued to the door. *His* boys. His *everything*.

He reached for the door handle. The chemical smell he had encountered downstairs was stronger here, burning his throat. Slowly, quietly, he opened the bedroom door. Light crept in, illuminating the foot of Harry's bed. Martin held his breath, felt the collision of his heart against his chest.

And there they were. His twin sons. Both face down with their heads turned to the side, mops of dark hair covering their features. Fast asleep in their beds.

Relief flooded through him like heroin through veins. Tears stung his eyes. He watched them for a few seconds, unable to turn away, then remembered Sharon, his wife, who had put up with so much crap from him over the years. Softly shutting the door, he headed back along the landing.

His fingers ached, his grip on the knife handle like iron. He did not enter the room straightaway. Something made him hesitate. Fear, perhaps? Or anticipation of another potential row? He pressed his ear to the wood grain and listened. He heard his blood rushing in his ears, the inhalations and exhalations of his unsteady breath. But nothing from inside the room.

With a trembling hand, Martin opened the door and crept inside.

He could see his wife's shape on the bed. For a moment he chided himself for leaping to such terrifying conclusions. It was the birds, that was all. They had triggered such fear in him and released terrible memories he had been trying to bury for ten long years. Sharon was annoyed with him, after all. She had taken herself to bed to spite him. For a second, he almost convinced himself it was true.

He switched on the bedroom light. His wife lay on her back, her head resting softly on the pillows. She was fully clothed. Her lifeless, bloodshot eyes stared up at the ceiling. Her mouth hung open, and her tongue, which had grown fat and black, hung from one corner. Her hands were curled into fists at her sides, and her bladder had released itself. Gently tucked behind her left ear was the head of a daffodil, its bright yellow petals and orange-red trumpet heralding the arrival of spring, the season of new life.

There was something tied around her neck. At

first he thought it was rope, but as he staggered closer he saw it was a length of fishing net.

The breath fled from Martin's lungs. His fingers released the knife and it fell to the carpet. He lunged towards the bed and collapsed to his knees. Pulling himself up, he took his wife by the shoulders and shook her violently.

'Sharon! For God's sake, wake up!'

It was a strange thing to say, he thought, because her eyes were already open. But he shouted it again, over and over, until his throat burned and his voice was ravaged.

And then realisation hit him, almost knocking him down again. Someone had done this to his wife. They had squeezed the air from her lungs. Ended her life with brutal violence while her children slept in the other room.

The boys.

The horror that gripped his body grew tenfold.

Had they really been asleep?

He was in a strange daze now, his sanity threatening to leave him. Forcing his body away from his wife, he bent down and reached for the knife. With the blade back in his grip, he raced back to his children.

They remained in the same position he had left them in, face down and perfectly still.

'Josh?' he whispered in a cracked voice. 'Harry? Time to wake up now.'

Were they breathing? He couldn't tell. All he knew was he had to get them out of this house.

The boys did not stir.

'Josh. Harry,' he said, louder this time. 'Come on, now. Please, open your eyes.'

He was about to go to them, to throw back the sheets and scoop them into his arms like babies, when a long shadow blocked out the hallway light. Martin turned.

A giant was coming towards him, stooping as he moved through the doorway, then straightening to his fullest extent. He had to be at least seven feet tall, His body rippled with powerful strength. There was something wrong with his face. It was misshapen, like a burst watermelon

Martin stared up at the aberration, scarcely able to believe what he was seeing. He tried to position himself in front of the boys' beds, a last stand to protect his children. But he was paralysed. Stricken by terror.

'They can't hear you,' the giant said, his voice as deep as the ocean. 'They're sleeping the long sleep.'

As his eyes adjusted to the figure before him, Martin saw the giant's face was not misshapen at all. He was wearing a mask, one depicting the face of a monstrous ogre.

'You killed my wife,' Martin managed to say. Tears squeezed from his eyes. He felt the weight of the knife in his hand.

The giant loomed over him. 'I took from you what you took from others. For I am Wrath.'

Instinct took over, primal and savage. Martin let out a bloodcurdling scream and sprang forwards, knife raised high above his head. The giant swung a huge arm. The end of a crowbar smashed into

Martin's temple. He went down fast and hard, landing in a tangle on the floor.

And even when the giant stood over their father and brought the crowbar down again, the boys did not stir.

11

By the time Detective Sergeant Will Turner and Detective Constable Rory Angove arrived at the crime scene, the house had been cordoned off with inner and outer barriers. The Crime Scene Investigation unit was already in attendance. A small crowd of neighbours was gathered in front of the outer barrier, while three uniformed police officers were standing sentry behind it. DS Turner, who was late forties with flecks of grey in his hair and a weariness in his eyes, could not yet see any press. But they would be here imminently.

Before moving to Cornwall six years ago, he had worked for a decade in the London Metropolitan's Criminal Investigation Department, where he had encountered what seemed like an endless conveyor belt of dangerous individuals and brutalised victims, which had eventually begun to wear him down. Applying for a transfer to Devon and Cornwall police had seemed like a gentler alternative to taking an early retirement. How wrong he had been to think that!

Reaching the inner cordon, Turner signed the crime scene register that a uniformed officer was managing. He handed the pen to DC Angove, who was in his late thirties but looked younger. A local lad born and raised, Angove had a calm energy that allowed him an easy rapport with both the criminals and victims they encountered from day to day. Turner had been like that once, but years of dredging through the sewers of life had left him sour.

'Who was first on scene?' he asked the uniformed officer who had signed them in.

'That would be PC Colin Bryant, Sarge,' the officer said. 'He's over there.'

Turner peered in the direction the officer was pointing, and saw a young police constable leaning against the side of the Crime Scene Investigation van. He couldn't have been more than twenty-five.

Turner leaned into DC Angove. 'Find out what you can from uniform, while I speak to our police constable over there.'

'Yes, Sarge.'

Behind the crowd of onlookers, a small silver van turned the corner and parked on the roadside. The first of the journalists had arrived.

Turner frowned. 'And make sure uniform keep the press at arm's length. Absolutely no Q&A until the boss decides to make a statement.'

He made his way over to the CSI van and PC Colin Bryant, who, upon seeing Turner, straightened up and checked his uniform.

'Morning Detective Sergeant Turner,' Bryant said. His eyes were dark and wide, with a slight glaze.

Turner gave him a curt nod. 'You were first on scene?'

'That's right. I live locally, so I got here as soon as the call came in.'

'Who made the call?'

'A neighbour.' Bryant pulled out his notepad and fumbled through the pages. 'Dorothy Brown, lives two doors down, said she woke at around 6 a.m. to hear a child crying in the street. When she looked outside, she saw one of her neighbour's sons wandering about. He was barefoot and in pyjamas. She went out to him, and he told her his mother and brother would not wake up. She went to knock on the front door, saw it was wide open, and took the boy inside. She found the mother dead in the master bedroom, and the boy's brother unresponsive in his bed. That's when she called.'

'Do we have names?'

'Yes, Sarge. The boy in the street is six-year-old Josh Bennett. The unresponsive brother, Harry Bennett, also six. Which makes them twins.'

'Great deduction, PC Bryant,' Turner said with a wry smile. 'We'll make a detective out of you yet.'

Bryant blushed and turned the page of his notebook. 'The victim's name is Sharon Bennett. Neighbours think she's in her early thirties. The children have been taken to Royal Cornwall Hospital for examination.'

'Any father on the scene?'

'Martin Bennett. One of the local fishermen. His

whereabouts are currently unconfirmed, but the neighbour believes he might still be at sea.'

'Has anyone checked down at the harbour?' Turner asked.

'Not to my knowledge. Would you like me to do that, Sarge?'

Turner regarded the young police constable, who was terribly pale and haunted-looking.

'Tell me something, Bryant. Was this your first body?'

'Yes, Sarge.'

'In that case, all I want from you right now is to go back to the station and write up your report.'

The young police officer expelled a deep breath. He nodded, went to leave, then turned back to Turner. 'Does it get better, Sarge? Dealing with the bodies?'

Turner tried to give him a sympathetic look. 'You'll grow more numb to it, if that counts.'

Bryant turned a shade paler as he headed to sign out of the crime scene.

Heaving his shoulders, Turner watched PC Bryant walk away then eyed the gathering crowd. It was still small and manageable, a benefit of it being off-season in a sparsely populated village. No other press had yet to arrive. The journalists that were here came from local newspapers, so were harmless enough, just as long as everyone on scene kept their mouths shut.

DC Angove had finished talking with one of the uniformed officers and was heading over. Turner met him halfway.

'So?' Turner said.

Angove quickly relayed the information he had learned about the victims, which was much of the same that PC Bryant had shared, but confirmed that Sharon Bennett was thirty-three years old, and that her sons had possibly been sedated while she had been murdered in the room next door.

'There are no indications of forced entry,' Angove told him, 'but possible signs of a struggle in the downstairs hallway, which suggests the victim encountered her killer before he dragged her upstairs.'

'Any word on the boys?' Turner was glad they had been unconscious and had not heard their mother fighting for her life.

'One of them, Harry Bennett, was still unresponsive when paramedics took them to Royal Cornwall. That's all I have.'

'Do we have anyone at the hospital right now?'

'A couple of uniforms. We're waiting on Children's Services to attend. No family members have been informed yet. As for Martin Bennett . . .'

'Whereabouts unknown.' Turner looked up at the house. 'Let's head inside.'

Returning to the CSI van, Turner and Angove were given protective white overalls, booties, gloves, and masks. As Turner dressed into them, he thought about the boys at the hospital. He was glad they had been spared by their mother's killer. Once you had seen the body of a murdered child, it haunted you until the day you died. In his long career he had encountered just one, not at London Met but right here in Cornwall. He shut his eyes and immediately pictured the child lying face down in the woods, one tiny hand sprawled out as if reaching for help that would come too late. That had been six years ago, but he could still see every detail.

They headed inside the house. It was a standard new build, with comfortable furnishings and family photographs hanging on the walls. If not for the CSI team working in every room, or the plastic evidence markers placed at different spots on the floor, he would not have expected anything out of the ordinary.

Careful to keep to the marked safe areas, Turner and Angove headed upstairs and stood on the landing. All of the doors were open. To their left, two crime scene investigators were busy doing a fingertip search of the twins' bedroom. One of them glanced up as the detectives approached.

'We're not done here yet,' she said.

Turner stopped in his tracks and glanced inside the room, where he saw shelves of toys and dinosaur print duvets on the beds. He nodded at the investigator then turned towards the master bedroom. Angove followed behind. Turner reached the doorway and saw the body on the bed. He grimaced and glanced at Angove, who wore a similar expression. Next to the bed, a male crime scene investigator was busy logging a piece of evidence. A length of what looked like fishing net.

'Murder weapon?' Turner asked.

The investigator sealed the net inside an evidence bag and began labelling the tag. 'It was embedded in the skin of her throat, so I imagine it was used to strangle her to death. But the pathologist will confirm.'

'Are you finished processing the victim?'

'Not yet.'

Nodding, Turner remained in the doorway and regarded Sharon Bennett. Her lifeless eyes stared at the opposite wall, her fat black tongue hanging from her lips like a large slug ready to feast on her corpse. One of her children had seen her like this, Turner thought. He turned to DC Angove.

'We need to locate Martin Bennett. I need to contact the coroner, then I'm heading up to the hospital to check on the boys. I'd like you to pay a visit to Porthenev Harbour to see if Bennett's there. If he isn't, someone will know if he's at sea and when he's due back. If he's not at sea, then we start contacting family members to find out if they know where he is, starting with his parents.'

DC Angove let out a breath and shook his head.

'It's always the husband,' he said.

'Almost always,' Turner corrected. 'Almost always.'

12

An hour later, DS Turner arrived at Royal Cornwall Hospital in Truro. The Bennett twins had been secured in a private room, with a uniformed police constable stationed outside. As Turner approached, the young officer stood up.

'Sarge.'

'What's the latest?' Turner asked.

'The doctor is with them now. Harry Bennett is awake. That's all I know.'

Turner nodded thoughtfully, relieved that the child had been revived. He leaned forward, peering through the small glass window of the door. The blinds were drawn in the room, and privacy curtains had been pulled around both beds. He straightened up and glanced at the police constable. His name was Jones, if Turner remembered correctly.

'Have Children Services turned up yet?' he asked.

'I believe so.'

'Are they inside?'

'Last time I saw them, they were headed for the coffee machine.'

The door to the room opened and a female doctor came out. She was in her early fifties, with brown skin, high cheekbones and dark, analytical eyes that studied the detective for a moment before she closed the door quietly behind her.

'Detective Sergeant Turner,' she said with a slight nod.

'Doctor Singh.'

Turner had come to know the doctor over the years via numerous hospital visits connected to violent crimes. Their first encounter had been six years ago when Turner was still a detective constable. A teenage boy, who had been missing for several years and presumed dead, had materialised seemingly out of nowhere and been admitted to the hospital. His reappearance had been the catalyst for a series of horrific events that still haunted Turner to this day. He wondered if Dr Singh was also haunted by the victims she came into contact with.

'Do you have a minute?' he asked. 'I wonder if you could give me an update on the Bennett boys.'

'When do I ever have a minute?' Singh said, with a sigh. 'Both boys are stable for now. We've managed to revive Harry Bennett. He's conscious but a little disoriented. Josh Bennett appears physically unharmed, but is suffering from shock. We've taken blood samples and conducted thorough physical examinations. No signs of assault, sexual or otherwise.' She paused. 'Have family members been informed? It would be good for the boys to see a familiar face. They're frightened and confused about what's happening.'

'Maternal grandparents haven't been informed yet. As soon as we're able, we'll have them brought here.'

'What about the paternal side of the family?'

'We have officers standing by to interview Martin Bennett's parents. For now, while he's still missing, the rest of his family will not be informed.' He paused, gathering his thoughts. 'Doctor Singh, how did those boys sleep through their mother's murder?'

'We're waiting for test results, but some sort of sedative was definitely used. I can't tell you exactly what right now.'

'And when do you think they'll be ready for questioning?'

The doctor gave him a hard stare. 'I'm aware this is a homicide case, Detective, and that you're eager to move forward. But the children are in a fragile state and are most definitely not ready to answer questions. Harry Bennett doesn't even know his mother is dead.' She shook her head solemnly. Turner instantly knew that she was indeed haunted, just as he was. 'The best I can do is have my people call your people if and when the children are ready. As I know you understand, their recovery is my priority. '

'Of course.'

Doctor Singh gave him a curt nod and walked away. Turner watched her disappear through a set of double doors, which slowly swung to a close. The police constable was still standing, his gaze fixed on the floor. Turner peered through the door glass once more, staring at the closed curtains that hid the young Bennett twins from view. His mobile phone buzzed in his pocket. Turner took it out and saw DC Angove was calling.

'What have you got for me, Rory?' he said, pressing the phone to his ear.

The sound of shrieking seabirds and whistling wind made it hard to hear Angove's words clearly.

'I'm down at the harbour, Sarge. Turns out that Bennett was last seen with some of his crewmates at the Ship's Wheel pub last night. They say he was in an agitated mood, and left to go home at around 8:30 p.m.'

'Do we know what was wrong with him?'

'I was just getting to that. It seems Porthenev Harbour has recently been the subject of a series of attacks, including the attempted sinking of one of the trawlers.'

'Bennett's?'

'No. But yesterday morning the trawler Bennett works on, the *Seraphine*, became the latest target.'

'Another attempted sinking?' Turner asked.

'Not exactly.'

DC Angove breathlessly told Turner about the discovery of the severed gull heads in the crew members' beds, and that uniformed officers and forensics had already been in attendance. Turner frowned. This case was becoming more complicated by the minute.

'There's something else,' Angove said, raising his voice over the background noise. 'Apparently, the fishing crew hired a private detective to investigate the goings-on at the harbour.'

'Oh, yes? And who exactly is the private detective?'

'You're not going to be happy.'

Turner felt the beginnings of a headache coming on. He already knew the answer to his own question.

'Blake Hollow,' he said.

DC Angove was right: Turner wasn't happy. He wasn't happy at all.

13

Rory Angove arrived at Blake's office in Falmouth at 6:03 p.m. It was dark outside. A strong breeze was stirring the surface of the inner harbour waters, making the yachts shift uncomfortably.

Blake was troubled. Rory had phoned an hour ago to say he needed to speak to her about her investigation at Porthenev Harbour. At first, she had been caught off guard.

'Porthenev? Why do you need to know about that?'

Rory had paused for the briefest of moments. Then he had said, 'There's been a homicide.'

Martin Bennett, a crew member of the *Seraphine*, was missing. His wife, Sharon Bennett, was dead. Murdered while her children slept in the adjacent room. The crime was already public knowledge; it was hard to contain something like murder in a small town, especially in a community as close-knit as Porthenev.

Now, Blake made coffee, cheap and instant, while Rory glanced around the office space with inquisitive eyes. He was still dressed in the navy blue suit he wore while on duty as Detective Constable.

'Nice place,' Rory said, accepting a mug of coffee. 'I especially like the decorative crack that runs along the ceiling.'

Blake ignored him. 'Tell me what happened.'

'I've already told you what I'm allowed to. Sharon Bennett was found dead in her bed in the early hours of this morning, a victim of homicide. Martin Bennett is still missing.'

'Did they have kids?'

'Twin boys. They're safe, at the hospital.' He paused. 'We think the killer drugged them.'

'Christ. How was Sharon Bennett killed?'

'None of your business.'

'There's nothing else you can tell me?'

'Not right now.' He checked his watch, which amused Blake. Rory was one of the few people she knew who still wore one. 'A press conference is taking place about now, but apart from a public appeal requesting information about Martin's whereabouts, they'll be told as much as I've told you. And before you ask, it's not because we're holding anything back. That's all we have until either Bennett is found, or the post-mortem examination is completed, or forensics gets back to us. Whichever comes first.'

'Well, it certainly won't be forensics,' Blake said. 'And of course you're holding something back. You always do in a murder case. But I'll be good and won't pry.'

Rory sipped his coffee and almost spat it back out. 'How many spoonfuls did you put in this?'

'Three.'

He set the mug down on Blake's desk. 'Tell me what you know about Martin Bennett. Did you speak to him during the course of your investigation?'

'No, I didn't. The crew of the *Seraphine* was at sea until the day before yesterday. When they discovered the mutilated birds I talked to the captain, Tom Mathers, who took me on board and showed me the carnage.'

'Was Bennett there?'

'Not on the boat, but maybe up on the pier. There were a lot of men in the harbour who were very angry with me, which made it hard to focus on individual faces.'

'Angry at you? Why?'

Her cheeks flushing slightly, Blake told Rory about her failure to set up complete camera coverage of the harbour.

'That doesn't sound like you,' Rory said.

Blake shrugged. 'Everyone makes mistakes. Even you, Detective Constable.'

Scratching the stubble that was beginning to sprout on his chin, Rory asked Blake to go over the case with him once more, from the beginning.

As she talked, starting with her first meeting with the harbourmaster, Jasper Rowe, Blake began to wonder about all the events that had occurred. The vandalism, the break-ins, the sabotage, the attempted sinking of the *Laura-Lynn*, the gross mutilation of the gulls displayed onboard the *Seraphine*. And as each image flashed in her mind like images from a projector, she remembered the words she had said to Jasper Rowe yesterday morning. *Someone has a grudge against the men of this harbour. I don't know why or what it's about, but whoever is behind this has just sent a very clear message.* Jasper had asked what kind of message, and Blake had told him that this wasn't the end, that the situation was only going to escalate.

Homicide was most definitely an escalation. But why target Martin Bennett's wife?

Rory was staring at her.

'I've lost you,' he said. 'Where did you go?'

Blake crossed the room and peered through the window. Below, the soft glow of the harbour lights provided little comfort. She turned back to Rory, who was standing in the centre of the room with his arms folded across his stomach.

'It doesn't make sense that Martin Bennett is a suspect,' she said.

'Why not?'

'If we assume both cases are connected, then it would mean Bennett is behind the sabotage at the harbour. Why would he attack his own workplace? Why stuff a bunch of dead birds in the engine of the *Seraphine* when that trawler provides his family with food on the table? And what the hell does everything that happened at the harbour have to do with murdering his wife?'

Rory shrugged. 'Obviously we don't know that yet.'

'How certain are you that he's guilty?'

'We aren't. It's guesswork at this early stage. But it's always the husband, isn't it?'

'Most of the time, but not always.'

She didn't think it was the husband now. Unless the incidents at the harbour and the murder of Sharon Bennett were not connected. But that would mean the timing was a mere coincidence, and although Blake believed coincidences could happen, this one was too much of a leap to entertain.

'Listen, it's been a long day,' Rory said. 'Before I head home, I need some information from you. A list of everyone involved in your investigation, including possible suspects, plus a list of all the incidents that have occurred so far, and any other information you think might be useful. I also need the footage from your cameras.'

Shit. The cameras. With all that had transpired over the last twenty-four hours, she had completely forgotten they were still installed at the harbour. Well, she was not going to get them right now. She would wait until tomorrow evening when the harbour was quieter and there were less angry men around who were dying to confront her. Blake moved over to her desk and ran her fingers over the computer keyboard. A few seconds later, the printer whirred to life and began churning out paper. Picking up the printouts she handed them to Rory.

'I'll need to do an online file transfer to send you the camera footage.'

'Get it to me first thing tomorrow?'

Blake said that she would.

'And call me if you think of anything else related to the case.'

'Yes, Detective Constable.'

He opened the door to Blake's office then glanced back over his shoulder. 'One more thing. I have a message for you from Turner.'

Blake rolled her eyes.

'He says for you to stay as far as humanly possible away from this case,' Rory said. 'And he really means it this time.'

'Well, you can tell my favourite detective sergeant not to get his knickers in a twist. I'm off the Porthenev Harbour case. He doesn't need to worry about me.'

Rory smiled tiredly, waved goodbye, and shut the door behind him. Blake returned to the window, concern washing over her. A woman had been murdered. Not any woman, but the wife of one of the crewmates of the *Seraphine*, which, just a few days ago, had been marked with an ominous "X". And, just yesterday, had been covered with blood and animal parts. This was no coincidence.

She peered out at the night, wondering where Martin Bennett was right now, if he was even still alive. She did not believe he was responsible for his wife's murder or the sabotage at the harbour. She had no evidence to back up her theory, only an uneasy feeling in her gut that fluttered its wings like a panicked bird, desperate to escape. Something was very wrong in the village of Porthenev. But for now, it was no longer her business.

14

Mason Kitto stood at the foot of the stairs in the narrow hallway, listening to the sounds of the TV floating through the half open living room door. He had already dressed in his waterproof trousers and jacket upstairs. Now, he quietly slipped his feet into a pair of black rubber boots. Moving as silently as possible for a person of his size, he reached for his keys that hung from a hook next to the front door. As he took them between his thick fingers, two of the keys clinked together. He held his breath. A slurred voice rang out from the living room.

'Mason? You're not going out, are you?'

Mason heaved his round shoulders. He was twenty-seven years old and still hadn't moved out of the family home. Which meant his mother still treated him like a child.

'I know you're there,' she called. 'Come in here, I want to talk to you.'

Swearing under his breath, Mason lumbered into

the living room, where forty-eight-year-old Delores Kitto sat on a shabby sofa watching a reality TV show in which a group of fame-hungry nobodies were humiliating themselves in a series of physical trials. He studied his mother for a moment, noting her heavy-lidded eyes and glazed expression. He wondered how much Valium she had taken this evening.

'You're not going fishing at this time, are you?' she said without removing her gaze from the television set. Her words were slow and ran into each other. 'You've got work in the morning.'

A heavy sigh escaped Mason's lips. 'I'm just going for an hour or two. I've got a thumping headache. The sea air will clear it.'

'Have you taken a painkiller?'

'They don't work for me.'

'It's because you're so big. You shouldn't be going out tonight. Not with a murderer on the loose. You heard what happened down at Porthenev. What if they break in while you're gone?'

'Porthenev is five miles away,' Mason said. 'Why would they come here?'

His mother said nothing. Mason thought she was so out of it that if a killer did break into the house she wouldn't even notice if they slit her open from her gullet to her pubic bone.

'I'll lock the door when I go. I won't be long,' he said.

'Please stay with me. I'm scared.'

Mason looked at her. If she was afraid, she was doing a bloody good job of not showing it. This was just one of her usual tricks. Emotional blackmail to stop him from going out. But even if he wanted to stay home the sea was calling to him. And he was hungry for it. Practically starving. Such was the power the water had over him.

'I won't be long,' he repeated.

His mother sucked in her lips as she continued to watch the TV. 'Fine, do what you want. Just don't be out too long. You've had one too many late nights lately, and you can't afford to lose another job. We need the money.'

Mason shifted his weight and let out another heavy sigh. Perhaps if his mother got off her lazy backside their money troubles wouldn't be as bad.

'Give your mum a kiss then.'

He sloped towards her, huffing and puffing, deliberately blocking his mother's view of the TV. He peered down at her as she continued to stare through his bulk at the television screen, as if he were invisible. She looked so small huddled in the corner of the sofa, like time and misery had been gradually devouring her life force. She had been that way ever since his father had died, which still surprised Mason because his father had been a vicious bastard who had regarded Delores Kitto like shit on his shoe.

Bending down, Mason planted a kiss on his mother's cheek.

'Don't forget to lock the door,' she said.

'I won't.'

Mason shambled out of the room and into the hall. Opening the front door, he stepped out into the night. He deliberately left the door unlocked then hurried along the garden path. Excitement thrummed in his veins. He could hear the ocean singing to him like a siren. His heart sang back to it.

∽

The seawater was icy cold as Mason waded through the shallows, pushing the two-man dinghy out to sea. Once it was buoyant, he climbed in, slotted a pair of oars into the oarlocks, and began to row away from the beach. As the shore shrank away, he peered up at the night sky. It was smothered by clouds, with no stars to help navigate his way. Mason was not worried. He had made this journey hundreds of times.

The water was deeper now, so he drew in the oars and carefully moved to the stern, where he tilted the outboard motor into position, connected the fuel line to the fuel tank and the kill cord to his lower leg. He tugged the pull cord with one powerful hand. The engine sputtered to life. Taking a seat on the starboard side, Mason gripped the engine's tiller and guided the dinghy through the darkness.

For a while, tiny lights from towns and villages glinted along the coastline, but after a mile or so they all vanished. In the rear distance, the beam from Godrevy Lighthouse, which stood on a small island of rock in St Ives Bay and had been made famous by Virginia Wolfe, sliced through the blackness. But it was of no use to Mason out here.

He was silent as the dinghy moved through the water, the only sound the *putt putt putt* of the outboard engine. The sea had calmed, the waves gentle beneath him, as if it were helping Mason on his way. Keeping close to the coastline, which had grown higher and rockier, he fixed his gaze on the water. After two more minutes, he pulled the kill switch and the engine cut out. He was close now.

A waterproof sports bag lay between his feet. Unzipping it, he removed a torch and switched it on. A powerful beam of light splashed across the ocean surface. There were rocks lurking beneath the water, patiently waiting to grind boats into dust. Mason knew where most of them lay, but he still had to be careful. He slotted the torch into a holder he had attached to the dinghy's bow, then returned the oars to the oarlocks. He began to row, slowly and carefully, stopping every few metres to check his position. It was as if he could sense the rocks beneath him; another gift from the ocean, he presumed.

Soon, after careful navigation, he drew the oars in a little, retrieved the torch and pointed it to his right. His heart pounded with excitement. The mouth of the sea cave was like a narrow black wound in the side of the cliff. Almost invisible to the unaware, Mason had known of the sea cave since childhood. His father had introduced it to him, had made him never forget it.

Picking up the oars once more, he guided the dinghy towards the mouth of the cave. The torchlight bounced off slimy walls. Water lapped at rocky edges. Drawing in the oars, Mason got to his feet and moored the dinghy to an iron stake that had been rammed into a naturally formed jetty many years ago. Grabbing his bag and the torch, he climbed out and headed into the cave. He had to duck in several places, but a few metres along a thin tunnel, he came upon a chamber where he could stand to his full, intimidating height with room to spare.

His fingers itched as he set the bag on a workbench in the corner, then switched off the torch and plunged himself into pure darkness. From the bag he took a battery powered LED lantern and placed it on the ground. Orange light illuminated the chamber, making shadows dance on the walls. As Mason's fingers found two more objects in the bag, he smothered a squeal of delight.

He straightened up again and his eyes found Martin Bennett. The fisherman was hanging upside down, his hands tied behind his back with a length of rope, and his bound ankles fixed to an iron hook that sprouted from the cave ceiling. A gag was tied around his mouth. He was half conscious, eyes rolling back in their sockets.

Mason slipped on the mask. The fisherman's eyes suddenly snapped open and saw the face of a grotesque monster staring at him. He began to struggle like a moth trying to free itself from its cocoon.

'Fee-Fi-Fo-Fum,' Mason boomed. 'I smell the blood of an Englishman.'

In his hand was a filleting knife with a six inch blade that was thin and viciously curved. He stepped towards Bennett, whose cries and pleas were muffled by the gag. Slowly, Mason unbuttoned the man's shirt, revealing the flesh beneath.

Now the tip of the blade was running along Bennett's skin from his groin to his throat, gently slicing through the outer layer, leaving a thin red line.

Mason leaned closer, his breath hot and heavy

against the inside of the mask. He pulled back, moved to the corner of the chamber, and picked up a rusty bucket. Returning to the centre of the room, he placed the bucket beneath Martin Bennett's head. Then stood in silence, listening to the man's muffled cries. He tightened his grip on the filleting knife, its curved blade glinting in the lantern light.

He felt himself retreating inside his body, seeking refuge in the shadows, making room for the Other. And as he disappeared, the Other came. And when he spoke, his voice was pure darkness.

'You brought this on yourself,' Wrath said. 'You should never hurt a child.'

As Bennett struggled on the hook, thrashing in one final, pitiless attempt to free himself, Wrath plunged the blade deep into the man's body and twisted it, snapping the man's sternum. With a flick of his wrist, he began to cut upwards. Beneath Martin's spasming body, the bucket started to fill.

15

Blake drove into the concrete farmyard and switched off the engine. She grabbed her travel mug from the cup holder and drained the last of her coffee. She had slept poorly, tossing and turning as she replayed the day's events over and over in her head, until her brain could take no more. Now, it was a little after ten a.m. It had rained heavily overnight, drenching the countryside and leaving the narrow, winding roads slick with mud that splattered Blake's car and had her participating in a solo cross-country rally.

Shutting the driver's door, Blake glanced around the dirty farmyard, noting the metallic red Renault Megane she had parked next to. A cowshed stood to the right, a lurid stench of animal waste wafting through its open doors. Other stone outhouses with corrugated roofs flanked the yard, all of them quiet and unremarkable. Blake had already passed the farmhouse before reaching the yard, a quaint country cottage that was in need of restoration, but she didn't think the person she was looking for would be inside. Turning full circle, she gave her car another cursory glance and decided she would need to visit the car wash once she was done at the farm. Maybe the local garage too. Rusty patches speckled the Corsa's bodywork here and there, and over the past couple of days a strange knocking had been coming from the engine. Blake wondered how long it would be before her faithful old car finally keeled over and died.

Checking the other outhouses and finding them empty Blake called out, but it seemed no one was around. She had not dressed for the farm, had still not purchased a pair of Wellington boots despite being back in rural Cornwall for almost eighteen months. Now, as she crossed the farmyard, picking her way through puddles of rainwater towards a muddy track that led to the fields beyond, she felt a wave of regret. Perhaps not buying the boots was a sign she had yet to fully commit to a permanent return. Or perhaps she really was a city dweller at heart.

A few minutes later, her shoes and the hems of her jeans were soaked through. A field filled with sheep lay before her. At its centre, two figures stood talking beneath an oak tree. The figure on the right, a young farmhand in his late teens who was dressed in dirty blue overalls and green Wellington boots, glanced up as Blake opened the wide field gate. The other, a blonde haired woman in her late thirties dressed in a wax jacket and dark jeans tucked into black Wellington boots, was busy scribbling into a notebook. She did not notice Blake approach. It was the start of the lambing season in Cornwall, and several young lambs huddled close to their mothers.

'Can I help you?' the young farmhand asked, a puzzled look on his face. Surprise visitors were clearly not a common occurrence this deep in the countryside.

Blake smiled. 'Cute lambs. How could anyone eat them?'

The woman glanced up and a dark look spread across her face like wildfire.

'What are you doing here?' she said, unable to hide the irritation in her voice.

'Sorry to barge in while you're working,' Blake replied. 'I need to talk to you.'

Judy Moon and Blake had known each other since school. They had grown up together in Wheal Marow and formed part of a tight circle of close friends. When one of those friends disappeared one night, it had sent shock waves through the town. Blake and Judy had never been the same. Blake had left Cornwall behind as soon as she could, vowing never to come back. Judy had returned home after studying journalism at university. She had stayed ever since. Over the years their friendship had drifted. Now that Blake was back, they had grown close again. But that didn't stop Judy from getting annoyed.

'Sorry, I didn't mean to criticise your business,' Blake said, turning to the young farmhand, who was still perplexed by the sudden intrusion. 'But look at those little faces. They're so cute!'

The farmhand blushed and turned to Judy for help.

'Thanks, I think I have all I need here,' Judy told him. 'Do you mind if I stick around for a little while and take some pictures? My *colleague* here must have left her camera in her car.'

The man muttered that would be fine, shot Blake an awkward sideways glance, and headed back towards the farmyard.

When they were alone, Judy glowered at Blake. 'How many times have I told you not to turn up unannounced when I'm working? It makes me look unprofessional.'

'Sorry. I wouldn't have but it's important.'

'How did you find me anyway?'

'I'm a private investigator,' Blake said with a shrug. 'Finding people is literally my job. Besides, it only took a couple of minutes to break your colleague, Rod. I don't think he likes me very much.'

Shaking her head, Judy tossed her notebook and pen into her shoulder bag. 'Maybe if you didn't harass him every time you saw him, he'd have a different opinion.'

'Maybe. But what would I do for fun?'

'I don't know. Have you tried the gift of kindness?' Taking out her phone, Judy began snapping pictures of the sheep and their lambs. 'Are you going to tell me why you're interrupting my very important work here. The lambing season is no joke, you know. It always gets the paper a nice bump in sales.'

'People do love little lambs,' Blake said. 'Especially with roast potatoes. Did you hear about what happened down at Porthenev?'

'The missing fisherman and his murdered wife? Yes, I did. Nasty business.'

'I assume *The Cornish Press* is covering the story?'

'We are. But it's Rod's gig. See, you should have stayed back at the office instead of getting your fancy boots covered in mud.'

'Rod won't tell me anything. You know that.'

'I return to my earlier point. Why are you so interested in what happened anyway?'

Finished with taking photographs, Judy slipped her phone inside her bag then indicated to Blake it was time to leave. Together, they worked their way through the sheep and headed towards the field gate. As they walked, Blake told Judy about the disturbing events at Porthenev Harbour that she had been hired to investigate, and about her subsequent failure to apprehend the culprit.

'Decapitated seagulls?' Judy grimaced. 'Whoever did that can't be in their right mind.'

'And now Martin Bennett is missing and his wife is dead. He was one of the crew members of the *Seraphine*, where they found the gulls. The police have pegged him as the chief suspect, but I'm not so sure.'

Judy's eyes were bright and alert. Her journalistic curiosity had been piqued.

'Why not?'

'It's just a gut feeling. Why cause all that trouble down at the harbour then go and murder your wife? One act doesn't connect to the other.'

'Unless Bennett is completely unstable. Then his actions wouldn't have to make sense.'

'But why lose it now? If that's the case, wouldn't there be a trigger?'

'I suppose.' Judy chewed on her lower lip as they walked. 'Do the Bennetts have children?'

'Young twin boys. Police found them unconscious in their beds, next door to their mother's body. They suspect they'd been drugged.'

'Jesus. How do you know that? Are you sleeping with Rory again?'

Blake jabbed Judy in the arm. They had reached the farmyard, where the young farmhand was nowhere to be seen and a group of hens had found their way in and were busy scratching and pecking at the ground.

'Don't be offensive,' Blake said. 'We stopped all that business months ago. '

'He still likes you, I reckon.'

'Well, I reckon I'm very happy living the single life, thank you very much.'

'Okay fine, but you still talked Rory into giving you case details, didn't you? You're going to get him fired one of these days.'

'I didn't force Rory to do anything. He's a grown man. Besides, it was a mutual sharing of information.'

Blake felt a small twinge of guilt in her chest. Did she really use Rory like Judy was insinuating? Maybe, she thought. Maybe not.

As they reached their cars, Judy regarded Blake through narrowed eyes. 'Did you really drive out here just to find out if I was working the murder story? You know I write the farming news.'

Blake shrugged and scuffed the ground with a mud-caked boot. She wasn't really sure why she had come here. She was no longer working the Porthenev case, and she knew Judy wouldn't be covering the story. Judy had told Blake before that she was happy to write the farming news, even if it did get boring sometimes. She didn't want to write about grisly murders or the drugging of children, not if it meant being haunted by images that she would inevitably take back home to her young family.

Why had Blake come here? It was because even though she was off the case, she still had a hunger to uncover the truth. The police were not going to tell her anything more, not even Rory. Although Judy was not covering the story for *The Cornish Press*, she might be able to find out details that Blake wouldn't have access to. She met Judy's searching gaze then glanced away. Did she use Judy too? Blake had leaned on her friend for information in the past, but wasn't that just the nature of their jobs? To uncover information? To share and exchange with each other? Had Blake shared anything with Judy over the past eighteen months? Standing in the farmyard, she couldn't think of a single example.

She glanced back at Judy and offered a shrug. 'I was just wondering, if you hear anything on that police scanner of yours, you could let me know?'

'I've told you before, it's not my police scanner. It just happens to be in *The Cornish Press* office.'

'You do know listening in on police scanners is illegal in this country?'

'I'm well aware of the law.' Judy sighed. 'And yes, if I learn anything of interest, I'll think about letting you know. Just as long as you don't reveal where you got the information. And vice versa. If you find out anything, you tell me so I can pass it onto Rod.'

Blake screwed up her face.

'You know we could have done this over a phone call,' Judy said.

'I know. But then you wouldn't get to see my lovely face.'

Blake blew her a kiss. Judy rolled her eyes then climbed into the driver's seat of her car.

'Come over for supper one evening next week,' she called.

'Even better, get your husband to babysit so we can go and get drunk.'

'On a school night?'

Now it was Blake's turn to roll her eyes. 'Okay, loser. Supper it is.'

16

A sombre hush settled over Porthenev Harbour like a thick fog rolling in from the ocean. Fishermen and harbour workers went about their business, barely making eye contact with each other. The little conversation to be had was muttered and monosyllabic. After a night of heavy rain, the sun had returned, bringing with it a chilly breeze that stirred the grey-green water below and jostled the boats from side to side. The crew of the *Laura-Lynn* huddled around another large fishing net on the quayside, their nimble hands busy repairing its many holes. With the trawler still out of action and the previous day's events weighing heavy on their minds, fixing the other crews' damaged nets was a welcome distraction. Except it wasn't quite working.

Albert Roskilly glanced at his son, who looked as if he hadn't slept for a week and was fumbling with the net, making mistake after mistake with his repair work. Next to him, young Ewan kept his eyes on his hands, his pallor that of a crate of dead fish. He looked afraid. But the truth was Ewan always looked afraid. It was because of Conrad, who kept the boy in a constant state of terror, goading and humiliating him, sometimes even going so far as to physically threaten him.

Albert had tried to raise his son to be a good man, but sometimes he had been forced to discipline him due to his unruly and wayward behaviour. Albert had been disciplined by his own father, a swift crack to the back of the head here, a fist to the stomach there. It had been good for him, for Albert had grown into a strong man with strong values. But no matter how much he had tried, he knew deep in his heart that he had somehow failed Conrad. Because Conrad was not a good man. He was selfish and cruel. Yet Albert still loved him, no matter what. He loved him because he was his son, and a father must love his son, even when they were a disappointment.

'For fuck's sake,' Conrad hissed under his breath, his fingers slipping once more. Next to him, Ewan tensed his shoulders. Conrad glared at him. 'What the fuck are you looking at, shit stabber? Mind your own fucking business.'

Ewan flinched, whispered an apology.

Usually, Albert would intervene, warning Conrad to reel in his bad attitude like he was reeling in a prize catch. But Albert was distracted, his thoughts a confused kaleidoscope of bad memories and worries about the present situation. Had Martin Bennett really murdered his wife? And where the hell was he right now? His absence was like a black hole that would surely devour everything in its path. It was only a matter of time, Albert thought, before the ghosts of the past came for them all. Unless everything that was happening right now was just one big coincidence.

He glanced across the harbour and out to sea. Images crept from the shadows. He quickly forced them back. He returned his attention to the quayside. His heart thumped noisily in his chest. One of the other fishermen was walking towards him at a hurried pace, his face lined and pale.

Conrad looked up, saw the man, then glanced fearfully at Albert, who gave a subtle shake of his head.

Terry Lawrence was in his late thirties, but the dark rings beneath his eyes and the deep lines burrowed into his forehead made him look much older. He was a tall man, lean and stringy, with receding hair and eyes as grey as the ocean. He hadn't shaved in days, which was unlike him; Terry was a man who was always clean-shaven, no matter if at sea or on land. He came to a halt in front of them and looked at Albert, then at Conrad, then back to Albert, ignoring Ewan completely.

'Albert,' Terry said, pausing to nervously lick his lips. 'We need to talk.'

'We're busy here, Terry.' Albert gestured to the net. 'No time for chatting.'

'Well, you need to make time. It's important. You know why.'

Conrad was staring at his father again, his teeth clenched together like a vice.

'We'll talk later, once this net's done with,' Albert said, a warning tone in his voice.

Terry took a step closer. 'There may not *be* any later. We talk now.'

Albert's heart was pounding harder. For ten years he had attempted to convince himself that this terrible business was over, that they could all move on with their lives. But he knew, deep down in his rotten core, he knew that one day it would all come floating back to the surface, a bloated corpse of a secret dredged up from the dark below.

'Ewan,' he said. 'You keep working on this net. We'll be back in a minute.'

Ewan made brief eye contact, gave the barest of nods, and returned his focus to his hands.

Releasing his grip on the net, Albert glared at Terry, who held his gaze, then indicated to his son to follow. Conrad slapped the back of Ewan's head with an open hand, causing the young man to let out a startled cry, then followed his father. The three men walked in silence along the quayside, Albert in front, Terry and Conrad just behind. Albert stopped, checked no one was watching, then ducked in between two of the net lofts. Halfway along the narrow alleyway, he slid to a halt and wheeled around to face Terry.

'What the hell do you think you're doing?' he snapped.

'I'm scared, Albert,' Terry said. 'Aren't you?'

'About what?'

'Everything that's happening right now. The boats. The gulls. Martin disappearing and his wife getting fucking murdered!'

'Keep your voice down.' Albert spoke slowly. 'I'm

not scared because none of that has anything to do with us.'

'Don't be stupid. It has everything to do with us and what we did. It's obvious. Someone knows, Albert. Someone knows what we did and they're coming for us.'

'Dad?' Conrad glanced at his father. To Albert, he looked like a child again, small and frightened, like how he used to be when it came to turning out the light at bedtime.

Albert returned his focus to Terry. 'No one knows anything. We made sure of that, didn't we? And we all made a promise, that none of us would ever tell a soul. So what's happening now can't have anything to do with us, can it?'

He paused, glaring at Terry, his heart pounding in strange, erratic rhythms. He did not believe the words that were coming out of his own mouth, but he had to try because Terry was clearly at breaking point. Judging by the growing fear on Conrad's face, Albert's son wasn't far behind.

'Maybe he's right, Dad,' Conrad said. 'It makes sense, doesn't it? First our trawler, then the *Seraphine*. Now Martin and his wife. Why weren't any of the other boats hit? It can't all be a coincidence.'

'Did something happen on your boat, Terry?' Albert asked.

Terry shook his head. 'No, but—'

'There you go then. Seems to me that Martin finally snapped, did some damage to our boats, killed his wife, and has probably gone off to kill himself. He was always weak. If any one of us was going to break, it was him. There's nothing to worry about here.

We'll go about our business as usual, until this all blows over.'

He stared at Terry, then at Conrad, challenging them to disagree. Inside, panic had taken hold. They had been so careful these past ten years. They had cleared up their mess and left no trace. The police had been satisfied an accident had occurred. Nothing more, nothing less. So why were Terry and Conrad looking as if they didn't believe him? Why didn't he believe himself?

Perhaps someone did tell. Perhaps one of them wasn't able to hold it in any longer and had vomited it out like poison. Albert's right eye began to twitch.

'We've all kept our promise here, haven't we?' he said, his gaze fixed on Terry, who quickly glanced away. 'Haven't we?'

'Of course, Dad,' Conrad said.

Terry was silent.

At the end of the alleyway, two men sauntered by, one casting a curious glance in their direction before disappearing from view.

'Because we all remember what we said would happen if someone told the truth, don't we? That we'd slit them open and spill their guts and use it for fish bait.'

'Yes, Dad. Of course, Dad.' Conrad nodded emphatically, again reminding Albert of the frightened little boy he had once been.

'You remember that, don't you, Terry?'

Terry leaned back a little. 'I'm not stupid, Albert.'

'Because if this really has to do with what happened, it's interesting that your boat wasn't hit.'

'I've kept my mouth shut this whole time. If you

want to accuse someone, maybe have a word with your son here. He's looking pretty shifty to me.'

Conrad clenched his fists and stepped towards Terry. 'What the fuck are you saying? I'm no snitch.'

'Maybe. Maybe not. But I've seen you running your mouth enough times when you've been pissed up in the pub. Who's to say you didn't let it slip one night? Maybe you told the wrong person.'

Albert shifted on his feet as he stared uncertainly at his son. It was true Conrad liked to drink, and it was true he would get into arguments and fistfights when he'd had too many beers. On more than one occasion, Albert had been forced to talk the landlord of the Ship's Wheel out of barring Conrad for life. Was Terry right? Had Albert's son drunkenly told the wrong person one night?

Veins were pulsing at the centre of Conrad's forehead.

'Fuck you, Terry,' he hissed. 'I'll put your face through this wall if you don't watch your tongue.'

The older fisherman stiffened and puffed out his chest. 'I'd like to see you try.'

'That's enough from the pair of you,' Albert said sharply. He turned to his son. 'Are you sure you haven't told anyone?'

'Of course not!' Conrad's face flushed a deep red. 'Jesus Christ, Dad. You're really going to believe him over me?'

'Well, he's not wrong about you running your mouth when you've been drinking. Even when you're sober you've got a habit of talking too much. The situations I've had to get you out of . . .'

'I don't believe this! My own father thinks I'm

stupid enough to get us all sent down. I'm not the idiot you think I am, Dad. Anyway, what about you? Who's stupid idea was it to bring a private detective to the harbour when we've all got secrets to hide?'

'That was before the *Seraphine* and before Martin and his wife. We were just trying to make the harbour safe again.'

'Conrad's got a point there,' Terry said. 'Bringing someone in like that was just asking for trouble, which was why I was against the idea in the first place. But no one ever listens to me, do they? You're not even listening to me now when the shit's hitting the fan.'

'The shit's not hitting the fan,' Albert said. His head was beginning to hurt.

Conrad glared at him with wide eyes and flared nostrils. 'You know what I think, Dad? If you were dumb enough to hire a private detective, maybe you were dumb enough to tell Mum, and she's told someone else, and now we're all fucked.'

Albert leaned in towards his son, black clouds rolling over his eyes. 'Watch who you're talking to, boy. Or do I need to remind you that you're the reason we got into this mess in the first place?'

Conrad flinched as if he had been slapped.

'What do we do?' Terry said in a low voice. 'What if Martin is just the first?'

Squeezing his eyes shut, Albert sucked in a breath, held it, then let it out. 'We don't do anything. We don't know if Martin is alive or dead. Maybe he really did snap and kill Sharon. We don't have any proof this is connected to us, so until we do, it's business as usual.'

'I don't accept that,' Terry said. 'What? We just sit around, twiddling our thumbs, until another one of us vanishes from the face of the earth, or worse? I don't think so. I'm going to sort this out right now.'

'And how exactly are you going to do that?'

'It's obvious who's behind it all, isn't it? So I'm going to have a word with him. Tell him if he doesn't stop what he's doing he'll be the one with a dead wife as well as a dead—'

Albert wrapped a powerful hand around Terry's throat and shoved him backwards, slamming his head against the wall. He squeezed, digging fingers into the man's flesh, choking the breath from him. Terry's eyes bulged in their sockets. He grasped at Albert's hand but could not free himself. Conrad stood in frozen silence.

'I'll tell you what you're going to do,' Albert said. 'You're going to shut the fuck up and do nothing. Or so help me God, I'll kill you myself.'

He squeezed tighter. Terry's jugular throbbed wildly beneath his fingertips.

'You got it, Terry? Do you understand me?'

Tears welled at the corner of Terry's eyes. He managed to nod. Albert released his grip and stepped back. Terry slumped against the wall, gasping for air.

'Not a word,' Albert said, pointing a finger at him. He turned away and began heading towards the quayside with Conrad hurrying behind.

Terry pushed himself up and swiped at the tears staining his face.

'You're wrong, Albert, and you know it!' he croaked. 'We're all as good as dead.'

Albert's heartbeat was regaining a more regular

rhythm. The pounding in his head dropped to a whisper. He filled his lungs with a gulp of salty air and expelled it. Conrad walked quietly beside him, his complexion still red but slowly fading.

Ewan watched them curiously as they approached. Avoiding the boy's gaze, Albert picked up a portion of the net and returned to his repairs.

'Don't fucking stare at me,' Conrad growled as he cuffed Ewan on the ear.

Ewan did not retaliate or even reply. The three of them continued to work in silence. Below in the harbour the ocean churned relentlessly.

17

Mary and Ed Hollows' two-storey home stood within half an acre of land a few miles west of the town of Wheal Marow. It was the home Blake had grown up in, along with her younger brother Alfie, and the home she couldn't wait to leave as soon as the opportunity arose. It wasn't that she had a difficult or loveless upbringing, far from it. But life had irreparably changed the day her best friend Demelza vanished at the age of eighteen. Suddenly the family home had felt cramped and claustrophobic, as if the walls were slowly closing in on Blake. She had not known why back then, but she did now. It was because of her father. Because of what he and Demelza had done together.

It was six-thirty in the evening. Blake sat in her parents' dining room at the left side of the table, while Ed and Mary sat at the ends. Mary had prepared a dinner of lamb stew, with freshly baked bread to mop up the gravy. The rich flavour of the lamb made Blake feel nauseous as she tried her best to swallow it down so as not to offend her mother, the irony not lost on her after her morning visit to the sheep farm.

Her father ate in silence, rarely looking up from his plate, while her mother chatted happily as she picked at her meal, telling Blake about the latest gossip she had heard while shopping in Wheal Marow earlier that day. Blake pretended to listen and smiled at all the right places, but her mind was distracted by all that had transpired in the past few days. The events at Porthenev Harbour still troubled her. As did the fact her father had yet to mention a single word about it since Blake had arrived an hour ago. Why hadn't he? Jasper would have told him about the grim discovery on board the *Seraphine*. And if he hadn't someone else would have passed it on. As for the murder of Sharon Bennett, it was all over the news. Everyone knew about her death.

'Goodness,' Mary said. 'Here I am rabbiting on and I haven't even asked you how the house is coming along. You had time to give it a lick of paint yet?'

Blake pushed a chunk of lamb to the edge of her plate and speared a slice of potato instead. 'Not yet. I've been too busy.'

'Well, perhaps if you invited me and your father over one of these days we could help out. You've been there for two months now, and we still haven't seen what you've done to the place.'

'Like I said, I've been busy. So you'd have a hard job of playing spot the difference.'

'Oh, bird,' Mary said. 'Are you telling me you

haven't done a thing since you moved in? That cottage was barely fit for purpose in the first place. It's a wonder it hasn't fallen down and killed you while you slept.'

Blake sucked in a breath and slowly let it out. She knew her mother meant well, which was why she was attempting to keep her irritation to herself.

'It's honestly not that bad, Mum. There aren't any leaks, and the wood burner does a good job keeping the place warm. What more do I need?'

She glanced at her father, who continued to eat with his eyes glued to his plate.

'Well, a lock on the front door that works for starters,' Mary said. 'Your father said that lock needed replacing when you first moved in. Tell me you've at least done that.'

Reaching for her glass of water, Blake avoided her mother's gaze and nodded. It was a lie of course, but she knew Mary would have a heart attack if she found out the truth.

'That's something at least, I suppose,' her mother said. 'Although I still say it's your landlord's responsibility to fix that place up. Isn't that right, Ed?'

For the first time, Ed looked up and briefly glanced in Blake's direction, then at his wife.

'Yes, it is,' he said, then returned to eating.

'You're both right,' Blake said. 'But if I waited for my landlord to get things done, I'd still be complaining about it from my grave.'

Mary shook her head. 'Seems to me landlords get away with murder these days. How about I come over tomorrow and see what needs to be done? I can finally hang the curtains I made for your kitchen window the week you moved in, so every Tom, Dick, and Harry can't go peeping in at you.'

'I don't think Tom, Dick *or* Harry would go that far out of their way just to masturbate over my frankly shocking culinary skills.'

'For heaven's sake, Blake! Is there any need to talk like that while we're eating?'

'Sorry. Fine, come over in the afternoon. You need me to pick you up?'

'No, I'll drive over.' Mary paused, a ripple of concern creasing her brow. 'I just don't know why you chose to live in the middle of nowhere and not in town. A woman on your own like that. What if somebody tries to break in?'

'You don't live in town.'

'Yes, but I have your father to protect me. You've got nothing but an allegedly repaired locked door.'

Blake arched an eyebrow. She decided not to tell her mother about the illegally obtained Taser that lived inside her bedside drawer, and which was probably better protection than Ed Hollow, who was close to retirement age and slept like the dead at night.

'We've had this conversation, Mum. I'm a mile away from Falmouth. I have a car and a phone, and I know how to take care of myself. There's nothing for you to worry about.'

Mary remained unconvinced. 'Living all the way out there, it's almost like you want to invite trouble in. Isn't it, love?'

Ed looked up and was quiet for a moment. Then he said, 'Blake is old enough and wise enough to make her own decisions. And it seems to me she's got herself out of trouble on more than one occasion just fine.'

He gave Blake a curt nod and for once held her gaze. She supposed she should have felt grateful. Perhaps in another lifetime where her father hadn't spent almost two decades lying to her face, she would have thanked him. But there at the table she merely looked away.

Mary muttered under her breath, then cleared her throat and stabbed a chunk of lamb with her fork. The ensuing silence grew thick and heavy. It was moments like this, a slight difference of opinion between Blake's parents, that the past seemed to suddenly reappear and show its unwelcome face. Blake was sure her mother had not yet fully forgiven her father for his infidelity and deceit, but she also knew forty years of marriage had been impossible for Mary to throw away. And although their relationship would never be the same again, Blake's parents seemed happier together than apart.

'It's a terrible business down at Porthenev, isn't it?' Mary said, when the quiet started to overwhelm. 'That poor woman. Everyone's saying it was her husband who did it. Is that what you think too?'

Blake shifted on her chair, which suddenly felt hard and uncomfortable beneath her. Her father watched her in silence.

'I don't know,' she said. 'I suppose we'll have to see what the police investigation uncovers.'

'So you're not looking into it anymore?'

'I was never investigating anyone's murder, Mum.'

'What's Jasper saying about it, love? Does he think that fella killed his wife?'

Ed shrugged a shoulder. 'I haven't talked to Jasper in a couple of days.'

Blake could feel his eyes on her, but she would not look at him. Was he waiting for her to admit her blunder at Porthenev Harbour? To apologise for making him look like an idiot in front of his friend? She glowered. Why did she have to say anything to her father? Yes, Jasper was a friend of his, but Ed Hollow wasn't paying her bill. It didn't matter to him whether or not she had cracked the case. And it wasn't *his* reputation on the line.

She forced more lamb into her mouth and chewed. She would say nothing for now. She was not responsible for the death of Sharon Bennett. A violent psychopath was.

And yet if one of her cameras had caught the culprit on board the *Seraphine* there was a chance he would have been identified and apprehended. Then perhaps Sharon Bennett would still be alive and her children would not grow up bereft and traumatised. Suddenly, the meat she was chewing tasted rotten. Blake swallowed it down with a grimace and reached for more water.

'It's a nasty business either way,' Mary said with a shake of her head. 'I hope they find the husband soon. I hate to think there's a killer on the loose around these parts again.' She paused, glancing worriedly at Blake. 'Why don't you stay the night, bird? I can make up your old bed, then we can drive over to your place in the morning.'

Blake's typical knee-jerk reaction was to say no

thank you, she was perfectly fine and safe in her own home. But guilt was starting to spread through her veins like wildfire. Was she responsible for Sharon Bennett's death? Could it have been avoided if Blake had done her job properly?

She looked at her mother and suddenly felt like a child, lost and afraid and in need of comfort. She wanted to stay, for her mother to tuck her in and kiss her gently on the forehead and softly say, 'Goodnight, sleep tight, don't let the bed bugs bite,' before leaving the bedroom door ajar just wide enough to let in a sliver of the landing light. But Blake was no longer a child, and she couldn't stay because she had somewhere to be.

'Next time,' she said quietly. 'And I won't be sleeping in that deathtrap of a bed either, not when there's a brand new double bed in Alfie's old room.'

Mary rolled her eyes. 'We'd get a new one for your room, but you've got your own place now, haven't you? And Alfie and Violet live three hundred miles away, and with the baby that makes three, so they needed a bigger bed. It's not favouritism before you say anything of the sort. Me and your father, we love our children equally.'

Blake flashed her a wicked grin. 'Christ, Mum. I was only pulling your leg. No need to have a nervous breakdown.'

She flashed a quick glance at her father, who was smiling at his flustered wife. Blake looked away again, a flash of irritation wiping the grin from her mouth. She stood and leaned over to kiss her mother on the cheek.

'Thanks for dinner.'

'You're going right now?' Mary said. 'At least finish your food.'

'I have to be somewhere. A work thing.'

'At this hour?'

'Yes, at this hour.'

Blake refrained from saying more. Instead, she managed a weak smile at her father, who muttered a goodbye, then headed for the front door.

18

The roads were dark and quiet as Blake left her parents' home and drove towards Porthenev Harbour, her mind confused by conflicting emotions. She really was glad that her mother appeared to be happy again after months of pain and anguish, but she was still struggling to forgive her father. She wanted to, she truly did. He had demonstrated regret for his devastating actions taken all those years ago, and he was clearly trying to make amends. Yet resentment still bubbled under the surface of Blake's skin, and she hated the way she still sought his approval. As she turned onto the A3047, the car's headlights illuminating the skeletal trees that flanked the road, she supposed that when you spent your entire lifetime believing your father didn't love you, it was hard to shake it off when you found out they had loved you all along.

Ten minutes later, Blake pulled into the car park of Porthenev Harbour and switched off the engine.

With high tide not due until the early hours of the morning, she would be free to collect her cameras without incident. Yet the emptiness of the car park left her feeling more on edge. Whoever had killed Sharon Bennett and committed the atrocities on board the *Seraphine*, be it Martin Bennett or someone else, was still free to come and go as they pleased. And Blake was about to head into the harbour alone in pitch blackness. She opened the car door, paused, then leaned over to flip the lid of the glove compartment and take out her can of pepper spray. Pocketing it, she walked around to the back of the car, where she removed a black bag and a telescopic ladder from the boot.

A pool of weak light spilled from the single streetlamp in the corner of the car park, flickering on and off every few seconds. Over in the main harbour, darkness devoured everything. Unzipping her bag, Blake took out a pen light and switched it on. A bright, thin beam sliced through the shadows. Its reach was not far but the beam gave Blake courage. She glanced once over her shoulder, locked her car, then headed towards the quayside.

The night swarmed around her, the penlight fighting hopelessly against it. The lights of the harbourmaster's office were off, and the two external lamps that hung over the quayside had still not been fixed. The only sounds were the wash of the tide as it slipped back and forth like fingers delving into the shadows and the occasional clink of metal as the ocean breeze toyed with the workings of the docked dinghies and trawlers. Setting her bag on the ground, Blake gripped the pen light between her teeth and extended the telescopic ladder. Resting the ladder against the tower of one of the ice plants that stood next to the cold storage unit, she climbed up and reached for the tiny camera she had placed there just a few days ago.

She froze, the fine hairs on the back of her neck tingling. Twisting slowly around, she removed the pen light from her mouth and pointed it at the quayside below, moving its beam from left to right.

She had heard a sound, like the shuffling of feet or a boot scuffing the ground.

Blake held her breath as she swung the pen light to the left again. No one was there. She waited a second, then twisted around to face the ice plant, replaced the pen light between her teeth, and removed the camera with a sharp tug. Climbing back down, she stood for a moment, staring at the tiny camera resting in the palm of her hand. A wave of guilt crashed over her, which she attempted to shrug off. She crouched down, placed the camera inside a case and returned it to her bag.

It wasn't long before she had removed all three cameras from the harbour. That left one final camera, which was still attached to the steel litter bin in the far corner of the car park. With all the comings and goings of the fisherman and harbour crew, all of the camera batteries would have expired at least a day ago. They would still be worth checking though, Blake thought, in case there was more footage she had not seen. After all, revelations could always be discovered hiding among even the most mundane of actions.

She was turning to leave when she thought she

heard another sound coming from the direction of the north pier. The beam of the pen light did not reach that far, so she gently set the ladder down along with her bag and crept forwards.

She froze again, sweeping the penlight over the pier and down into the outer harbour, where the *Seraphine* hid in shadows on the water. All was still.

'Just go back to your car, idiot,' she muttered to herself. But she knew she couldn't, not yet.

Sliding one foot forwards, then the other, she slowly made her way along the north pier. A frosty gust of wind blew up from the water and stung her face. She gasped, breathing in salty sea air that tasted bitter on her tongue. Blake slid to a standstill and pointed the pen light directly at the water beneath, where the *Seraphine* shifted up and down. The blood had been cleaned from the windows of the wheelhouse, leaving the glass slightly smeared. She moved the light across the trawler, from the port to the stern. There was no one on deck, and she wasn't foolish enough to climb down and check if someone was lurking inside.

Instead, she turned to face the opposite edge of the pier and shone the light upon the sea below, which stretched out all the way to the horizon under the cover of darkness. It would have been easy for someone to row in and board the *Seraphine* without being noticed. Especially when her cameras hadn't covered the end of the north pier.

'Stupid.' Blake shook her head.

She cast one last glance at the *Seraphine* then turned on her heels. Her mind had been playing tricks on her, that was all. Nothing more, nothing less. Returning to the quayside, she swept up her bag and the ladder, and hurried back towards the car park. Even though it was just Blake's overactive imagination toying with her, the nervous tension that gripped her body was still trying to convince her otherwise. With a racing heart, she scurried over to the far corner of the car park to remove the final camera. The magnetic strip was firmly attached to the side of the steel bin. It took Blake three attempts to pull the camera free. Hurrying back to her car, she threw her equipment into the boot, then cautiously shone the pen light through the back windows. One could never be too careful with a killer on the loose.

Satisfied she would be travelling home alone, Blake climbed into the driver's seat and started the engine.

Forty minutes later, Blake parked on the gravel drive, climbed out of the car, and tiredly opened the front door of her cottage. She switched on the hall lights, then paused to poke a finger at the broken door lock. She resolved to call a locksmith tomorrow, once her mother had come and gone. Tonight, like every night since she had lived here, the top bolt would have to suffice. She slid it across, then dragged her aching feet into the kitchen, where she dumped her belongings on the table, poured herself a glass of red wine, then shuffled into the bathroom and turned on the bath taps.

A sudden tiredness overcame her, draping itself across her shoulders. It had been a difficult few days. Blake longed for sleep but wondered if she would be allowed it. She stared at the dark rings circling her eyes in the bathroom mirror and frowned. When was the last time she had slept soundly without the threat of nightmares? She honestly couldn't remember. She stared at the water filling the bath, changed her mind and pulled out the plug. The remaining camera footage still needed to be checked, but that task could wait until morning. Until then, she intended to climb into bed, shut her eyes, and wait for peaceful sleep to come.

∽

Sleep did come eventually, but it was far from peaceful. As Blake tossed and turned, tangling herself in her bed sheets, she dreamed she was on board the *Seraphine.* In her hand was a hunting knife with a cruel and serrated edge. She was standing over the crew members as they slept in their beds. She bent down and, one by one, slit their throats from ear to ear. Fountains of blood spilled forth from the wounds, soaking the sheets and raining on the floor. She cut deeper, slicing through muscle, cartilage, and bone, until their heads were severed from their bodies. And as she cradled each one in her arms, gently rocking it from side to side while singing a soft lullaby, a shadowy figure watched her from the doorway. It grinned as it stepped out of the darkness. At first she thought it was Martin Bennett. But when Blake looked again, she saw it was her father. And in his hands, which he held up to Blake, was the body of a headless bird.

19

Will Turner's stomach churned as the jet black police boat cut through the waves. The sky above was clear blue, the water below the colour of charcoal. A gusty ocean breeze whipped the detective sergeant's face. He gripped the edges of the central seat more tightly, which he was forced to straddle as if hitching a ride on the back of a motorbike. Having spent much of his life in London, he had little experience of being on the sea, much less of speeding along in the inflatable rigid boats used by the Devon and Cornwall Police marine unit, which formed part of the Force Support Group. Standing next to him, Detective Constable Rory Angove was at ease on the water. Angove gave Turner a quick glance.

'You're looking a little green around the gills, Sarge,' he said.

'I wasn't born with sea legs,' Turner replied. 'I'm happier with the ground very much beneath my feet. How about you?'

Angove smiled. 'I grew up around boats. When I was a boy, my dad used to take me sailing.'

The marine unit officer piloting the boat sat in front of Turner, dressed in black over trousers and a jacket, and a black police-issued baseball cap. They all wore inflatable life rings around their necks. The pilot turned his head slightly and raised his voice over the roar of the engine.

'We're approaching the scene, Sir.'

Turner slightly tilted to the right, trying to get a clear view. He saw the towering cliffs of the coastline up ahead, and a flock of gulls hovering just above. The boat sliced through a large incoming wave and slammed back down, the impact almost bringing Turner's breakfast back up. Angove's smile had already faded, replaced by a familiar furrowing of his brow that Turner knew was a sign that his detective constable was mentally preparing for the crime scene.

The phone call had come at 7:42 a.m. A dog walker had been taking an early morning stroll along the North Cliffs, situated between Portreath and Godrevy on the West coast of Cornwall, when she had happened to glance down and see a body lying spreadeagled on North Cliff Beach, known locally as Dead Man's Cove.

After a short struggle to find the exact location of the walker, uniformed officers arrived on scene at 8:14 a.m. One of the officers had immediately radioed in and, in a shocked voice, described the scene as a bloodbath. Access to Dead Man's Cove by foot was all but impossible, and so the marine unit was called out. Two boats were already on scene, one having transported a trio of Crime Scene Investigators, who arrived at the cove at 9:12 a.m.

Now, as the police boat drew closer to shore, Turner saw the white suits of the CSI team, still small in the distance but growing larger by the second. He checked his watch: 10:27 a.m. He had a bad feeling in his gut, which was more than just seasickness.

They were fifty metres from Dead Man's Cove, which was small and narrow, with a pebble beach not suitable for sunbathing or even dog walking. Large rocks sat here and there, fallen from the crumbling cliff face that towered above. Even if the cove was easily accessible by foot, it was a dangerous, unwelcoming spot. Now it was also a crime scene.

Turner gasped as the boat slowed and he saw for the first time the bloody carnage. Next to him, Angove drew in a shocked breath and said, 'Jesus Christ!'

Up front, the pilot muttered even stronger words. They reached the shore. The pilot beached the boat, which was light enough to push back into the water when they were ready to leave. Turner and Angove climbed out. Turner's legs were unsteady beneath him, and it took him several seconds to feel grounded. His stomach threatened to empty itself as he stared open-mouthed at the scene before him. He had witnessed the grisly aftermath of several murders in his time with the London Met, but nothing quite as grotesque as what lay on the beach of Dead Man's Cove. He shot a quick look in Angove's direction. The detective constable was deathly pale. Above their heads, the gulls swooped and cried.

The three Crime Scene Investigators were hard

at work. A couple of plastic evidence markers had already been placed on the ground. Two of the investigators continued with their search, while a third was busy taking photographs. She looked up as the detectives approached and held up a warning hand.

'No further, gentlemen. And please suit up.'

The investigator nodded to a spot close to the shoreline, where the team had set up a temporary camp for their equipment. Turner and Angove made their way over, with the investigator following close behind. Turner recognised her immediately. He had met Amanda Le Bretton, who was a senior Crime Scene Investigator, several times during his time with Devon and Cornwall Police. He found her to be an extremely competent and exemplary team player who was ruthless when it came to ensuring a contamination-free crime scene. She greeted Turner and Angove as they quickly dressed into white protective suits, gloves, and booties.

'I hope you haven't eaten,' she said. 'It's a particularly grim scene.'

'What can you tell us so far?' asked Turner.

'Well, you can see for yourself it certainly wasn't a clean kill. And we're very much against the clock. We've been told high tide is due at 11:49 a.m., which means we don't have long to work the scene. We're doing the usual, photographing, fingertip searches. We found a couple of bloody boot prints so far, but that's about it.'

'And the victim?'

'We can only photograph him for now. What we really need to do is get the body out of here as soon as possible before the tide washes away any evidence, DNA or otherwise.'

'Along with the body, no doubt,' Turner said.

Le Bretton smiled. 'Oh, he won't be going anywhere. He's been crucified to a rather large boulder with some rusty iron stakes. Which is why we need this.'

The Marine Unit officer who had transported Turner and Angove to the cove was approaching with a large metal suitcase.

He handed it to Le Bretton, who thanked him, then sent him back to wait at the shoreline.

'What's in there?' Angove asked. He was sweating despite the ocean breeze.

'A stone cutter. We'll try to free those hands without removing the stakes.'

'And if you can't?'

'Well, I suppose we'll just have to cut his hands off.'

Angove widened his eyes. Turner couldn't tell if Le Bretton was joking. To do the kind of job she did sometimes needed a very dark sense of humour.

'How close can we get to the body?' he asked.

'Closer than this. Just stay on the walkways.'

Turner glanced at the plastic panels that formed the walkways. They were a common sight at crime scenes, laid down and traversed upon to prevent contamination.

'Time is ticking,' Le Bretton said, and returned to the scene to continue photographing.

Turner and Angove headed carefully along one of the walkways until they were standing just two metres away from the body. The first thing to attack their senses was the overpowering stench of blood and other bodily fluids.

Angove swore under his breath, turning away for a moment before forcing himself to look back. Turner tried to swallow but his throat was too dry.

It was a truly horrific sight to behold. The man had been stripped naked and was lying on his back with his arms outstretched in a Christ-like position. Two rusty metal stakes had been hammered through his palms and driven into the rock beneath. He had been eviscerated, sliced open from groin to sternum, the layers of flesh pulled back to reveal the bloody cavity within. His chest had been violently torn open, exposing chunks of breastplate and a gaping hole where his heart had once sat, pumping life through his veins. Except the heart had been taken, along with the man's eyes. Turner briefly wondered if birds had devoured them. Then his gaze fell upon the dead man's neck. At first, he thought a noose of rope had been wrapped around it and pulled tightly. But it was not rope. It was a section of the man's own intestines.

He shot a glance at his detective constable, who was now the colour of milk left out too long in the sun.

'If you're going to throw up,' Turner said quietly, 'please do it away from the crime scene.'

Angove spun on his heels and hurried back along the walkway towards the shoreline, where he doubled over and promptly vomited on the pebbles.

Turner felt his own stomach heave but managed to keep his reflexes under control. He returned to the body and furrowed his brow. Whoever killed this man was completely deranged, fuelled by fury and an insatiable hunger to commit atrocious violence. This man had not just been murdered. His body had been desecrated, cut open, stripped back, until it was nothing more than a pulpy mass of flesh and blood, barely human anymore. Perhaps that had been the point, to strip him of his humanity.

He stared at the man's eyeless face, at his gaping mouth fixed in a silent scream. Was it Martin Bennett? It was hard to tell under all the blood. But Dead Man's Cove—what a joke that was—lay just a few miles along the same stretch of coastline as Porthenev. There were tattoos covering the victim's arms, a plethora of nautical motifs and red roses that had faded over time. If this really was Martin Bennett, they could be used to confirm positive identification by a family member without subjecting them to the horror that was the rest of his body. And if it really was Martin Bennett lying there it meant Turner was no longer investigating a murder-suicide as he had first suspected.

Amanda Le Bretton and a second member of her team approached the body and began examining the rock face, discussing where they should make their incisions to free the victim's hands while keeping the stakes intact. Over by the shore, Angove had finished emptying the contents of his stomach and had sensibly decided to stay back. Now the body was being covered in plastic sheeting while Le Bretton marked the rock face with chalk lines. Turner checked his watch, then the advancing tide.

Le Bretton called for everyone to stand back. 'That includes you, Detective Sergeant.'

Retracing his steps along the walkway, Turner joined Angove and placed a hand on his shoulder.

'Feeling better?' he asked.

Angove blushed and nodded. He had kicked sand over his vomit, but there was a spot on the left lapel of his jacket.

'It's nothing to be ashamed of. We've all done it,' Turner said, his furtive gaze fixed on Le Bretton and her team. One of the investigators activated the stone cutter and drove the blade into the rock. An ear-splitting screech filled Turner's ears, making him wince. Dust and small chips flew through the air, some landing on the canvas covering the body.

'Do you think it's Bennett?' Angove asked.

'We won't know until we have a positive ID, but I'm thinking along those lines.'

'What kind of maniac did that to him?'

Turner didn't answer. The stone cutter continued to slice through the rock. A minute later, the victim's left arm came free. Le Bretton carefully lifted the limb while another investigator pulled back the protective sheet, then gently rested it underneath, the stake and a small chunk of rock still intact. The sheet was pulled over him once more, and the stone cutter was set to work on the other hand.

'Did you see that?' Turner was staring, his mouth slightly ajar.

Angove shook his head. 'See what?'

'They were able to move his arm freely, which means rigor mortis has either completed or is on its way out.'

'Maybe it hasn't set in yet.'

'It's 10:53 a.m. The body was discovered at 7:42.

I was up at seven this morning for a run. The sun wasn't quite up yet but there was just enough light to see.' The crime scene investigator was still cutting through the rock face, attempting to free the second hand. Turner watched, his eyes flitting back and forth as his mind worked. 'We don't know where the killer came from, but we have to factor in journey time to get here, then time to cut the body up and nail it to the rocks, then to get away without being seen before sunrise. Rigor mortis starts to set in the face at around two hours after death, and in the limbs over the next few hours, with full body rigor mortis setting in between six and eight hours after death. It stays for another twelve hours before starting to dissipate. The whole process is complete within thirty-six hours after death.'

'Are you sure you shouldn't have become a pathologist?' Angove said.

'That arm was loose when they moved it just a second ago. It's highly unlikely the body had been here thirty-six hours before being discovered. I imagine people walk their dogs up on the cliff all the time. Which means the victim was killed off site.'

Angove furrowed his brow. 'But that doesn't make sense. There's blood everywhere.'

'So the mutilation was done after death. I don't know. We'll have to wait for the results of the post-mortem.'

'The killer murders his victim, puts him on a boat, sails out to Dead Man's Cove, where he cuts the body open, takes pieces from it, crucifies it, then sails away again before daylight.' Angove scratched his chin. 'Why the hell would he go to all that trouble?

And if that is Martin Bennett lying there—and the timing works out if your theory is correct—why kill his wife too?'

'That's the golden question,' Turner said.

The second hand was free. Le Bretton called for a time check. One of the investigators announced they had less than an hour. Le Bretton beckoned Turner over, who signalled for Angove to stay put, then made his way along the plastic walkway.

'We have to move the body now,' Le Bretton told him. 'We'll try to keep it intact as much as possible, but you can see the mess we're dealing with. Hopefully we won't have any spillages.'

'You're taking him out by boat?' Turner said.

'There's no safe landing space for a helicopter, and the way the cliff leans over the cove means we can't airlift the body out either. Besides, we can't have a helicopter flying over the scene, unless you want to forget about us finding any remaining evidence in the very little time we have left. So we get the body out now, then two of us will stay here until the last possible minute. You never know, we might get lucky.'

A body bag was being carried over. Turner had already decided he would not be staying to watch. He thanked Le Bretton, told her he would see her at the next crime scene, then returned to the shoreline, which was growing closer with every passing minute. He nodded at Angove that it was time to leave, then cast one final glance at the dead man lying under the plastic sheeting. Whoever had killed the victim had done so with extreme violence. The rage and force it would take to inflict such injuries frightened Turner.

He had seen enough death to last three lifetimes over, certainly more than anyone should be exposed to without losing a piece of themselves. As they headed back towards the police boats, he silently hoped he wasn't dealing with another serial killer on the loose in Cornwall.

20

Standing at the kitchen counter, Blake stared at the screen of her laptop while waiting for the kettle to boil. Her mother had arrived half an hour ago and was now stretching precariously on top of a three legged stool as she hung the pair of curtains she had made for her daughter.

'Careful, Mum,' Blake said, peering up from the screen.

'You mind your own business. I've hung more curtains in my lifetime than you've had hot dinners. I know what I'm doing.'

'Even so, that stool has seen better days and so has your leg. Or have you forgotten it wasn't that long ago you broke it?'

Mary tutted and shook her head. 'I'm not senile, Blake. Anyway, that was over a year ago.' She smiled. 'There we go. All done.'

Blake reached out a hand, which Mary took as she stepped off the stool and onto the floor. Together, they peered up at the curtains, which were red and white gingham with matching sashes.

'Very nice,' Blake said. The curtains were not to her taste, but she supposed they enhanced the cottage's rustic aesthetic. 'Thank you.'

'You're very welcome, bird. At least they'll give you some privacy.'

'From what exactly?'

Blake peered out of the window at the overgrown garden and the sloping fields beyond. There was a reservoir nearby which was hidden from view. She made a mental note to take a walk down there once the weather grew warmer.

Mary followed her gaze. 'Be honest with me. Why did you choose to live somewhere so remote? It makes me worry.'

'I don't know. I like my peace and quiet, plus I don't have to worry about nosy neighbours.'

'At least get a dog for company. It could keep watch at night.'

'I'm not around enough to keep a dog. It wouldn't be fair.'

'A cat then.'

The kettle began to whistle on the stove. Blake turned off the gas and poured hot water into two mugs.

'Cats are psychopaths. Anyway, we've had this conversation. I'm fine. There's nothing to worry about.'

She reminded herself to call a locksmith to fix the front door, then busied herself with making tea for her mother and strong coffee for herself before returning her attention to the laptop screen.

'No teapot yet?' Mary stared dubiously at the contents of her mug. She took a sip as she hovered behind Blake. 'What have you got there?'

'The last of the camera footage from Porthenev Harbour. There's probably nothing on it, but I need to check it all the same.'

'It's a terrible business what happened down there. I honestly don't know how you do the job you do. I wouldn't have the stomach for it.'

Blake was quiet, her eyes flitting over the footage from camera #1, which had been positioned over the harbourmaster's door and covered the central section of the quayside. She was reviewing the footage at double speed. As expected there was little of interest, just the comings and goings of the fishermen and harbour workers. Even at double speed, she could see tension emanating from each person, the news of Sharon Bennett's murder undoubtedly troubling their minds.

Mary took another sip of tea, wrinkled her nose, and set the mug down on the counter.

'I'll just give your living room a quick dust and polish,' she said.

'You don't need to do that,' Blake replied without looking up.

'Are *you* going to do it?'

'Eventually.'

Mary shot her a look that said, *who did I raise?* Then she located a can of polish and a couple of dust cloths from a cupboard under the sink and left the kitchen.

Alone, Blake leaned closer to the laptop screen as the footage from camera #1 came to an abrupt end.

Switching to camera #2, she continued her review. Ten minutes later, the footage from all three cameras covering the main harbour area had been checked and deemed uneventful. Each camera had run out of battery during the hours of Thursday morning, with the last time marker being 11:37 a.m. That left the footage from the car park.

To Blake's surprise camera #4 still had a little battery life left. She supposed it made sense though; the car park would have seen the least amount of action, just the arrivals and departures of the fishing crews. Loading the footage she began to review it, once again at double speed. Cars zipped in and out of the car park. People entered and exited the harbour. Night turned to day, day to night. And then, in the eerie green of the camera's night vision, Blake saw her Corsa drive into the car park and then herself climb out. This was the camera footage from last night. Recalling the feeling of being watched, she returned the speed to normal.

She watched herself collect the bag and telescopic ladder from the car boot, pause to look over her shoulder, then disappear through the harbour entrance. The camera footage jumped to twelve minutes later, and showed her emerging from the shadows with the bag slung over her shoulder and the ladder carried in her hand. Dropping the equipment by her car, on-screen Blake walked towards the camera, growing larger with each second, until she filled the screen. She looked spooked, frightened even. She sank down to her knees, then the palm of her hand filled the screen and the picture blurred as she attempted to prise the camera from the litter bin.

As on-screen Blake freed the camera, the entrance to the harbour swung into view for the briefest of moments. Standing at the kitchen counter, Blake froze. She hit the pause button and quickly rewound the footage by a few seconds. She pressed the play button and watched it again, this time at half speed.

She gasped. 'What the hell?'

She replayed the footage once more, this time slowing the speed so it played at one frame per second. As the harbour entrance juddered into view, she hit the pause button and stared with wide eyes at the laptop screen.

Someone was standing at the mouth of the harbour, watching Blake from behind. A chill ran up the length of her spine, making the fine hairs on the back of her neck stand to attention. She really *had* heard someone moving in the shadows last night. Here was the proof.

She ran her fingers over the keyboard, zooming in on the figure frozen at the centre of the screen. The picture quality was dark and grainy but she was sure the person standing there looked just like—

'All done,' Mary said in a sing-song voice as she entered the kitchen. 'When was the last time you polished, girl? There was a layer of dust in there as thick as a slice of bread. I've opened a window to let some air in. Don't forget to close it if you go out.'

She returned the dust cloths and can of polish to the cupboard under the sink, then joined Blake at the kitchen counter. Blake quickly snapped the laptop shut.

'You all right, bird?' Mary brushed loose strands

of hair from Blake's face. 'You look like you've seen a ghost.'

Blake batted her mother's hand away. 'I'm fine. Just tired.'

'Well, if there's nothing else, I'm all done here. I should get back and start on tea for tonight. You're welcome to join us again.'

Blake stared into the distance, her jaw clenched and her thoughts tripping over themselves.

Mary frowned. 'Are you sure you're all right?'

'I'm fine. Thanks for your help today, and for the curtains.'

'Any time, bird.'

Mary leaned in for a kiss on the cheek. Blake's phone buzzed on top of the counter. She snatched it up to see that Judy had sent a text message. She quickly unlocked the screen and read the message.

Police have uncovered a body near North Cliffs. No ID yet, but possibly Martin Bennett.

Blake stared at the words. She read them again.

'Shit.'

'Mind your language in front of your mother,' Mary said. 'What's wrong?'

'It's nothing. Just work stuff.'

Locking her phone, Blake kissed her mother, thanked her again, and walked her to the front door, which she quickly opened before Mary could inspect the lock.

'Drive safely, Mum. Text me when you get home.'

Her mother tooted the car horn as she pulled away. When Blake was alone, she raced back to the kitchen and read Judy's text message again. There was no point in phoning her; it was Saturday, which was family day for Judy, and even though she had texted Blake, family strictly meant no work-related calls. Besides, the message had likely relayed all the information Judy had been given. Flipping open her laptop, Blake stared at the figure frozen on the screen, which was washed in the green monochrome of the camera's night vision mode.

Blake couldn't talk to Judy about what she had discovered, but she could talk to someone else. Trying not to jump to conclusions, she snatched up her phone, selected a name from her contacts list, and tapped the call button.

21

The young calf wailed and thrashed about in the narrow pen, its eyes rolling back and forth as it sought a means of escape. The air was thick with blood and death, and tasted of blind terror. Mason Kitto towered over the pen, watching the calf as it bucked and cried. He crouched down, until his massive form was almost folded over the side of the pen. With one powerful hand gripping the bars, he reached out the other and lightly stroked the back of the calf's neck.

'Quiet now,' he whispered. 'You're scaring yourself for no reason.'

His fingers moved from the calf's neck up to the area between his ears, where he began to gently massage its scalp.

'Come on, calm down. There's no need to cause a scene.'

The calf seemed to react to his hushed tone and

soft touch, its body growing less animated, its cries less panicked.

Mason continued to massage the calf's skull, then moved his fingers along its spine from neck to tail.

'That's it,' he said, with a slight smile. 'Nice and calm. Nice and quiet.'

The calf's cries softened until they were no more than a barely audible whine. Its stiff limbs loosened, and when Mason placed a large palm against its flank, he felt its frightened trembling grow less violent.

'Good boy,' he cooed. 'That's a clever little calf.'

'Hey, Doctor Dolittle. Are you trying to fuck it or fry it? It's almost lunchtime.'

Mason looked up and saw one of the other workers, George, staring at him impatiently, his long apron smeared with blood and gore. Standing next to him, George's partner-in-crime, Mickey, giggled childishly.

Heaving his shoulders, Mason returned his gaze to the calf, gave it one last gentle stroke, then reached for the large, electrified tongs. He placed them over the calf's head and watched as a surge of electricity shot through the animal's brain. Instantly stunned, the calf went down fast and hard.

Hanging up the tongs, Mason reached inside the pen, grabbed the unconscious calf by its legs, and hauled it into the air. He attached the hind legs to a pulley system hanging above, reached over to press a button on a panel, then watched the calf's rag doll body move along until it came to George, who quickly slit its throat with a sharp blade. A fountain of blood gushed from the wound, raining on the ground below and splattering George's already soiled apron.

Next to him, Mickey giggled again and glanced in Mason's direction. 'Doctor fucking Dolittle.'

'That's lunch,' George called.

The last of the calf's blood dripped from its body, and the carcass was dragged along the pulley system, ready for the next stage of processing.

∼

The staff canteen at the abattoir was large and pristine, with not a drop of blood in sight. Men of various ages, for there were no women working at this establishment, sat around tables and talked loudly as they ate their sandwiches. Mason had removed his work overalls and scrubbed his hands thoroughly. As he entered the canteen, a few heads were raised and faces pointed in his direction, like they always did when he entered any room. He was such a large, imposing figure that someone had once joked even the blind could see him. But as quickly as his co-workers had glanced up to see what was blocking the light, they turned away again and returned to their chatter.

Mason crossed the room, his gaze fixed on the floor and his ears pricked as he headed towards an empty table in the corner.

As he passed George and Mickey, who were sitting with a small group of young men at least twenty years their junior, Mickey began to sing a few bars of *Talk to the Animals*, one of the more popular songs from the 1967 film *Doctor Dolittle*. The others sniggered, although Mason presumed they had never watched *Doctor Dolittle* or knew the song Mickey was singing. Mason had watched it though. He had watched it so many times as a boy that his father had grown so sick of him singing the songs around the house, he had beaten Mason until he had blacked out.

Taking a seat at the corner table, Mason placed his lunch box on the surface and shot a glance at Mickey and George.

'What sandwiches has Mummy made for her special boy today?' George called. The others laughed. 'How old are you now, Dolittle? Twenty-four? Twenty-five? Isn't it about time you grew the hell up and moved out on your own like a real man?'

Mason dropped his gaze back to the tabletop. Beneath the table his hands slowly tightened into fists.

'Maybe his mummy doesn't want him to move out,' Mickey said. 'Maybe she loves him *so* much she can't bear to see him leave. Do you love your mummy, Mason?'

'Oh, he loves her all right. I bet they have a special relationship, don't you, Dolittle? A *very* special relationship.'

One of the young men from the group opened two fingers, raised them to his lips and proceeded to dart his tongue in and out of the gap, sparking a cacophony of guffaws from his friends.

The other workers in the room continued their chatter, none of them wanting or caring enough to intervene. Mason dug his nails into his palms, breaking the skin.

'What's the matter, Mason?' Mickey said in a childlike voice. 'Are you going to run all the way home and tell your mummy the nasty men are being mean to you?'

Another round of laughter.

Mason glowered at them. He didn't have the wit or the timing for a snappy retort. But he did have the strength to grip Mickey and George by their throats and crush their windpipes with his bare hands. He could rip those windpipes out with a snap of his wrists and hold them up for the men to see as they bled out on the floor. And he could do it without the dignity of stunning them with electrified tongs, so they would feel every tear of their flesh, every jolt of exquisite pain, and smell their shit and piss as they evacuated their bowels, and hear their final rattling breath as it fled from their bodies. Mason could do that. He could make it happen, and there was no one in this room who was strong enough to stop him.

'Knock it off, you two,' a voice growled. 'You're acting like bloody children, not middle-aged men.'

Mason looked up to see Wesley Thomas striding past him. He was a stocky man in his late forties, of average height, with thick brown hair, a full beard, and dark eyes teeming with ghosts. He gave an almost imperceptible nod to Mason as he walked by. Mason felt a warmth ignite in his chest and spread out to his limbs.

'Lighten up, Wes,' George said with a shrug of his shoulders. 'We're only having a laugh.'

But the laughter stopped there, and so did the

jokes. George and Mickey turned back to their table and ate their lunches, their small group of young followers doing the same.

Wesley stood for a moment and stared at the room. Mason saw tiredness in his eyes and black shadows beneath them. He sensed the man's pain and anguish, felt it in his heart as if it were his own. Wesley had always been kind to him. He had defended Mason when people like Mickey and George tried to bring him down. Wesley was a good man, kind and caring, yet so filled with sorrow. Staring at him, Mason wished that Wesley was his father, because then he could throw his arms around him and hold him tight, and tell him to cheer up because the world wasn't so bad. Even though Mason knew that would be a lie. The world was a terrible place, vicious and bloodthirsty, filled with violent denizens who preyed on the innocent like vampires. Denizens like Mickey and George. Like Martin Bennett and the others.

He stared at Wesley, willing him to come over, to sit with him and share their lunch hour together. But Wesley didn't even look in his direction. Instead, he sat down with a group of older men, at an angle which left Mason with a view of the back of his head.

It doesn't matter, Mason thought. He knows who you are. That you matter.

Opening his lunch box, he removed his sandwich and carefully peeled back the foil. He checked no one was looking, then lifted the top layer of bread. Inside was a slab of raw meat and muscle that was still slick with congealed blood. He examined it with the sharp eye of a pathologist performing a post-mortem procedure. Then Mason smiled, closed the sandwich, and lifted it to his open mouth.

22

Jasper Rowe lived in a semi-detached cottage halfway between Porthenev Harbour and the summit of the hill that the town stood upon. The cottage was two hundred years old, built from Cornish stone, had a slate roof, and plant boxes on the external windowsills of the lower floor from which blooms of golden daffodils flowered. Blake had left her Corsa in the harbour car park and walked back up. Even though it was Saturday evening, the most sociable evening of the week, the streets were eerily quiet. There was an elderly male dog walker, who nodded warily in Blake's direction as she passed him by, and a middle-aged woman exiting the village shop and off-licence, from which locals could buy the basic necessities, as well as newspapers and alcohol.

Arriving at Jasper's home, Blake pressed the doorbell and peered at the flowers in the window boxes. The first signs of spring, she thought, and almost smirked at the irony. Spring was meant to hail the birth of new life. Yet here in Porthenev there was only death.

The front door opened, and Jasper greeted Blake with a strained smile. He was dressed in a pair of casual trousers, brown slippers, and a thick grey jumper that Blake suspected had been knitted by his wife. He ushered her inside, shut the door, and led her into a small and cramped kitchen that had all the mod cons.

'I've made a pot of coffee,' Jasper said, ushering Blake towards the kitchen table and pulling back a chair so she could sit. 'I know we Cornish are meant to be big tea drinkers, but personally I've never been able to stand the stuff.'

Blake smiled. 'Controversial.'

'My wife certainly thinks so. She's not here by the way. She's gone to her sister's for the evening.'

'I'm sorry to barge in on your weekend.'

'It's no problem. Me and my sister-in-law don't always see eye to eye.' Jasper brought the coffee pot over to the table and filled two mugs. Taking a seat opposite Blake, he stared at her with troubled eyes. 'I suppose you've heard about what happened to Martin Bennett's wife, Sharon.'

Blake said that she had.

'Terrible business. Just terrible. No one deserves to die like that.'

'Did you know her well?'

'Not well enough to call her a friend, but she seemed very decent. A good mother and supportive wife. I'm sure she was much more than that, too.' He paused, tapped a finger on the tabletop. 'People are saying Martin did it.'

'What do you think?' Blake asked.

'Honestly, I find it difficult to believe. But how well do we really know anybody? Martin has always been a grumpy sod, bad tempered and quick to fire off that mouth of his, but he works hard. I did hear through the grapevine that he and his wife have been struggling to make ends meet, especially with two young boys to feed. But most of us are struggling right now, aren't we? Well, except for the rich and those fat cats in government. Anyway, where Martin Bennett's concerned, I want to believe he didn't do that to his wife. But someone did. And if it wasn't him, where the hell is he now?'

Blake stiffened, thinking about the text message she had received from Judy. For now, she kept that particular news to herself.

Across the table, Jasper took a sip of coffee and leaned back on his chair. 'Is that why you wanted to see me? To talk about Martin and Sharon Bennett? Because I don't know anything more than what I already told you.'

'Sharon Bennett's murder has nothing to do with me. It's official police business,' Blake said, reaching for her bag. She removed her tablet, tapped the screen, and slid it across the table towards Jasper. 'I'd like you to tell me who you see in this picture.'

Puzzled, Jasper reached for his reading glasses, which hung around his neck on a thin black cord, and propped them on the edge of his nose. He picked up the tablet and stared for a long time at the image that Blake had captured from last night's camera footage. Deep lines spread across his forehead.

'This is from the cameras you set up at the

harbour?' he said.

'I came back late last night to collect them, then reviewed the remaining footage. This is what I found.'

Jasper stared at the image again and let out a heavy sigh. He slid the tablet back to Blake. 'Well, I can't say for sure because it's dark and the picture quality isn't very good, but to me . . . Well, it looks a lot like young Ewan Jenkin.'

Blake slowly nodded. She had thought exactly the same.

'But why would Ewan be skulking around the harbour after dark?'

Rather than answer his question, Blake asked him one of her own. 'What do you know about Ewan Jenkin?'

'I know he's a good boy,' Jasper said, removing his glasses. He paused to scratch his beard. 'But he's very timid, like a mouse. Not cut out for a fisherman's life. Still, he tries I suppose. To tell you the truth, I don't think he ever wanted to work on the boats, but that father of his didn't give him a choice.'

'What do you mean?' Blake asked.

'I mean Lance Jenkin is a nasty piece of work. Nothing more than a drunk and a layabout. He used to work on the trawlers himself. In fact, he was pals with Albert Roskilly years ago, back when they were just lads. They used to crew together. Then Lance got into a car accident. Well, I say "accident" but if the rumours are true, he was drunk behind the wheel. He wrapped the car around a tree and that was the end of his life on the boat.

'Anyway, about six months ago, Lance talked

Albert into giving Ewan a job on the *Laura-Lynn*. Apparently the money he gets from the government isn't enough to feed his drinking habit and pay the bills, so poor Ewan has been pushed into a life he doesn't want.'

'Why doesn't he just leave? Tell his dad to get stuffed and move out of the family home?'

'Because like I said, Lance Jenkin is a nasty piece of work. Likes to knock his wife and children around when he's been drinking. I don't think Ewan wants to leave his mum and little brother in the middle of all that, despite sporting a black eye more than once for his troubles. Besides, you've met him. He wouldn't say boo to a goose, never mind stand up to his father. I tell you, if I was thirty years younger, I'd give Lance Jenkin a beating myself.'

Blake thought about the few times she had encountered Ewan. Each time the teenager had struggled to lift his gaze from the ground. She supposed it was safer not to look anyone in the eye when you lived under the roof of a monster.

'You're right,' she said. 'I've seen Conrad Roskilly giving Ewan a hard time, and not once did he try to defend himself.'

Jasper's eyes darkened. 'If I had my way, I wouldn't let Conrad Roskilly within six feet of this harbour. There's something wrong with that man. And you're right, he treats Ewan something awful. Oh, Albert tries to step in when he can, but he can't control that son of his. Mark my words, one of these days Conrad is going to put someone in the hospital, if not worse.' He cocked his head slightly. 'What's this all about, Blake? Surely you don't think Ewan had anything to do with what happened to Sharon Bennett?'

Wrapping her fingers around her mug, Blake brought it to her lips and took a slow sip of coffee. Did she share her theory with Jasper? What if she was wrong and got the boy into unnecessary trouble? But what if she was right? If Ewan's father was as violent as Jasper had described, would she be throwing the boy to the wolves?

'No, I don't think that,' she said. 'I was just wondering why he was down at the harbour at night, that's all. But from what you've told me, it sounds like he was probably trying to get away from his father.'

Jasper narrowed his eyes then scratched his beard once more. 'Well, if you want to check in on him, I can tell you where he lives. But don't tell him it was me who told you.'

'You have my word.'

Standing, Jasper moved over to the kitchen counter, where he located a notepad and pen. He wrote down Ewan's address, tore off the sheet and handed it to Blake.

'You know,' he said, 'Sharon's murder and Martin's disappearance have cast a dark cloud over what's happened here at the harbour. The boys are convinced Martin is responsible for the damage, though I can't see any reason why he would ruin his chances of going to sea when there's money problems at home. Even if he didn't have money worries, why would he go wrecking boats and people's livelihoods? Mind you, why would he kill his own wife? None of it makes any sense.' He stared at Blake, as if willing her to provide him with the answers he so desperately needed. 'The point I'm trying to make is the boys don't want to pay for any more of your time, so you don't need to keep investigating.'

He looked almost mournful, sorry to be the one to tell Blake the news. But Blake smiled, reached over and gently patted Jasper's hand.

'It's fine,' she said. 'Like I said, this is police business now, not mine.'

She stood up to leave, thanked Jasper for his time and for the coffee. He walked her to the front door, where she suddenly stopped still.

'One more question, just out of curiosity,' she said. 'You told me Ewan's father and Albert Roskilly used to crew together. What about Albert and Tom Mathers?'

'Tom Mathers?' Jasper repeated. 'Why do you ask?'

'Because both of their boats were targeted. I thought there might be a connection between them.'

Jasper opened the front door, letting the cold air in. 'As far as I'm aware they've never worked together. I don't even think they're friendly. Not in a bad way, just that their paths haven't crossed much.'

As Blake said goodbye, she felt a wave of crushing disappointment. It wasn't that the fishermen no longer required her services—she had been expecting that—but that she had run out of leads. Unresolved cases frustrated her more than anything else. They were rare enough that when they reared their ugly head, Blake didn't quite know how to process her feelings. Perhaps Ewan Jenkin might provide her with another lead, even if the case was no longer hers.

23

Ewan Jenkin lived with his family in a three-bedroom house on a rundown housing estate on the outskirts of town, just out of reach of visiting tourists in summer. There were hundreds of housing estates all over Cornwall, where hard-working families lived their lives but still struggled to get by. You would never see their faces advertised in holiday brochures or on posters at the tourist information centres. Blake could understand why—poverty didn't fit with the sunny images of sandy beaches and stunning landscapes that brought millions flocking to the county each year—but she still thought this sanitised, holiday-friendly presentation of Cornwall was a far cry from reality.

Having fetched her car from the harbour, Blake now sat behind the driver's wheel, parked twenty metres down the street from Ewan's home. It was dark, coming up to ten-thirty p.m. She had not eaten dinner and she had forgotten to refill her glove compartment with energy boosting snacks. Her empty stomach grumbled as she watched the windows of the house. The downstairs lights were off. Only a single light emanated from one of the upstairs windows.

She suspected a housing estate like this kept a close community, who all looked out for each other. A strange car parked on the roadside would undoubtedly draw suspicion, especially when it had driven up and down a couple of times before coming to a standstill. Especially when the driver still remained inside. Blake was sure her battered Corsa did not give off undercover police detective vibes, yet she had still been on the receiving end of a few wary glances from passers-by, one even slowing down to look back over his shoulder. It was understandable, considering a local woman had been murdered and the chief suspect was currently at large. More like dead, Blake thought, as she returned her gaze to the house.

She had been sitting here for about two hours and had seen no sign of Ewan Jenkin. She didn't even know if the teenager was home. It was Saturday night, after all. Most young people of his age would be at the pub trying to score underage drinks or partying at a friend's house. But Blake suspected Ewan didn't have many friends, if any at all, and that he would not be allowed to socialise with them when Lance Jenkin's glass needed to be refilled.

The minutes rolled by. Blake's stomach growled loudly and her eyelids started to droop. At 10:43 p.m. she considered getting out of the car and knocking on the front door. But it was too late to receive guests, and she didn't want to cause more trouble for Ewan than he was already in, not when he had a violent drunk for a father. She was about to give up and drive home, maybe find a fast food place that was still open on the way, when the front door of the house suddenly opened and Ewan Jenkin stepped out. She watched him quietly shut the door behind him, lock it, and creep up the garden path, where he paused to glance up at the illuminated bedroom window. Then he exited through the garden gate and scurried along the road, passing under the electric bloom of a streetlamp. He was heading in Blake's direction on the opposite side of the street.

Blake reached for the door handle. She paused. Did she get out and follow him on foot, even though she already knew where he was going? Or did she leap out and surprise him, confront him where he stood? At best, caught unawares, he would be stunned into a confession. At worst, he would make a run for it and she would probably lose him.

On the opposite side of the road, Ewan zipped past her car.

Blake moved quickly, throwing open the door and darting across the road to block Ewan's path. The teenager emitted a startled cry as she flew in front of him. He stumbled backwards, tripped over his own feet and landed hard on his backside. He immediately began to retreat on his elbows, oblivious to who was in front of him, his survival instinct activated and taking control. It was only when Blake called out and identified herself that he slowed to a halt.

'I'm sorry, I didn't mean to scare you like that,' she said as she stepped towards him. She held out a hand to help him up. Ewan stared at it but remained frozen on the ground.

Blake continued. 'I need to talk to you. It's important. Otherwise, I wouldn't be out here lurking in the dark like a psychopath.'

She stretched out her fingers, waggled them about. Ewan reluctantly reached up to grab her hand. She helped him to his feet. His reaction had been startling, but unsurprising considering his father had used his fists on the boy more than once.

'What—what do you want?' he said in a breathless whisper.

'I want to ask you some questions. About what you were doing in the harbour last night.'

He gaped at her, his mouth opening and closing. 'I . . . I wasn't there last night.'

'Come on Ewan, you and I both know that's a lie.'

Now his gaze was moving beyond her, to the empty road. His fingers twitched at his sides. Then balled into fists.

'I wouldn't run if I were you,' Blake said. 'That will make it all too easy for me to go to the police and tell them exactly what you've done.'

His eyes shifted to meet hers. Even in the relative darkness she could see the terror that filled them.

'I haven't done anything,' he said. 'I haven't, I swear.'

'You can keep saying that, or we can get in my car and talk about the truth. Or we can stand right here in the middle of the street and do it. If neither of those options are acceptable, I can call my friend Detective Constable Angove and ask him to come down here so the three of us can talk together.'

Ewan shook his head violently. His gaze shot to Blake's car then back at his house, where the upstairs light was still on, then beyond Blake in the direction of the town. His shoulders sagged.

'The car,' he muttered.

Blake smiled. 'See, I knew you would make the right choice.'

They crossed the road and Blake opened the passenger door. Once Ewan was inside and she was sure he wasn't about to make a run for it, she went around to the driver's side and climbed in. They sat in silence for a moment. Then Blake reached for the overhead light.

'I don't want to talk here,' Ewan said in a trembling voice. 'My dad's in the pub and he'll be walking back soon. If he sees me with you . . .'

'Won't your dad notice you're gone anyway?'

'No, he'll be drunk and fall asleep on the sofa, just like he always does. But if he catches me out here talking to you in the street, it won't just be me who gets a beating.'

Blake lowered her hand. She knew Ewan wasn't talking about her. Inserting the key into the ignition, she started the engine.

'Where do you want to go? The harbour?'

In the shadows of the passenger seat, Ewan shook his head. 'I know a place, it's not far. Maybe a five-minute drive.'

Blake pulled away from the roadside and performed a U-turn.

'Good. Seat belt on and let's make this quick,' she said. 'I'm not in the mood for getting charged with child abduction.'

24

They drove in silence along the dark road, heading out of town and along the coastline. They saw no other cars or people, no signs of life. After a few minutes Ewan directed Blake down a track on the left and into a small gravel parking area. Blake switched off the engine and peered through the windscreen at the vast space beyond. There were no clouds, only countless stars shimmering over the expanse of a fathomless ocean, and a half moon whose silver light poured over the water like spilled paint.

'I can see why you like it up here,' she said. Ewan remained silent.

Blake reached up and flicked the overhead light on, filling the interior of the car with a soft orange bloom. Ewan squinted slightly as his vision adjusted. He looks so lost, Blake thought, reminding her of a frightened child she had once encountered in a supermarket, who had wandered off and become separated from his mother. She felt a great pity for Ewan. What a raw deal he had been given in life. Nevertheless, she still needed answers.

'Are we just going to sit here and admire the view, or are you going to tell me why you were following me at the harbour last night.'

'I already told you, I wasn't there.' Ewan's voice was low and sulky. 'I was home all night.'

'It's late and I'm too tired for games,' Blake said, reaching for her bag and removing her tablet. 'If you weren't there last night, explain to me how you showed up on my camera footage.'

She dumped the tablet on his lap. Ewan shot her the briefest of glances then picked up the tablet and stared at the image on its screen. His fingers began to tremble.

'That's not me,' he whispered.

'Oh, really? Well, Jasper Rowe and I think otherwise.'

At the mention of the harbourmaster's name, Ewan froze, his already washed out complexion growing more pallid.

'I'll ask you again. Why were you following me at the harbour last night?'

He stole another glance at the image, then turned to face the passenger door window.

'I wasn't following you,' he said. 'I go there at night sometimes to get away from Dad, when he's been drinking a lot. It's quiet down there. Peaceful. I like listening to the sea. But I wasn't following you, I swear. I heard someone coming, so I hid. When I realised it was you, I wondered what *you* were doing there. So, I watched you for a little bit, that's all. I didn't mean to scare you.'

'Your dad drinks a lot, doesn't he?' Blake said softly.

Ewan nodded but did not turn around.

'And he lashes out? Hurts you and your family?'

'It's because of the accident. He can't work anymore and it gets him down. Makes him angry.'

'But that doesn't give him the right to hurt you. Or your mother or little brother.'

Now Ewan turned to face her, mouth agape, eyes searching. 'How do you know I have a little brother?'

'I know a lot of things,' Blake said. 'I know you never wanted to become a fisherman, that your dad pushed you into it regardless of your feelings. I know you want nothing more than to leave, but you stay for the sake of your mum and brother because they depend on you, and the money you bring in. And I know that you're angry, at your dad, at the choices that have been made for you, choices you would never have made if your father wasn't around.'

Ewan stared wildly at her, a maelstrom of emotions colliding in his eyes. There was anger and bewilderment at her intrusion into his private affairs, rage at his father and the unfairness of the world, then pure, unadulterated shame.

She didn't feel good about it, but Blake knew she had to press on. 'Is that why you destroyed the fishing nets at the harbour? Why you sabotaged the cold storage units and put a hole in the side of the *Laura-Lynn*? So you wouldn't have to go to sea anymore? Surely you know those are temporary fixes. You'll have a few weeks off until the boat gets repaired, then you'll be back out there again and hating every minute of it. Unless of course you *wanted* to get found out so Albert Roskilly would fire you. But then you'd have to face your dad, and we both know what would happen to you then. To your mother and little brother.'

In the passenger seat, Ewan trembled violently. He shook his head, over and over. 'You don't know what you're talking about. You have no idea.'

But Blake could see the guilt in his eyes.

'Ewan, listen . . .'

'No! I said I didn't do it. You can't prove anything, so it's my word against yours. The men at the harbour don't even like you. They said you did a shit job, so they're not going to believe anything you tell them.'

Blake felt rage and terror pulsing from him in waves. She leaned back against her seat and stared through the windscreen. What did she do? Did she scare a confession out of him by threatening him with the police? Or did she continue with a more gentle approach and eventually win him over? She stared at his tensed shoulders and clenched jaw. Soft words were not going to break him.

'Ewan, listen to me. You're not grasping the seriousness of this situation. People's livelihoods are at risk because of what you did. People you've worked with, that you see every day, are going to go hungry this month. But worse than that, the police believe that whoever tried to sink the *Laura-Lynn*, whoever killed those birds and left them on board the *Seraphine*, is the same person who murdered Sharon Bennett. I *know* it was you who sabotaged the net lofts and cold storage. If I go to the police with this information, they're going to put two and two together and—'

Ewan jumped out of the car and slammed the door behind him. He stormed away, melting into the darkness as he headed towards the cliff edge.

Blake switched on the headlights, threw open the driver's door, and followed after him. She slid to a halt. Ewan was standing at the very edge, peering down at the dark ocean below. Wind whipped his hair and pulled at his clothes.

'Come away from there,' Blake said.

He glanced briefly over his shoulder and she saw that he was crying. Above him the stars glittered like encrusted diamonds. Below and to the west, tiny lights illuminated the houses of Porthenev. A coastal fog was slowly rolling in towards the harbour, smoky tendrils reaching over the water.

'Ewan, please,' Blake said. She took a step closer.

'I didn't try to sink the *Laura-Lynn*,' the boy sobbed. 'I didn't kill those seagulls or Martin's wife. I lost my temper one night, that's all. I was angry because I didn't want to be here anymore. I didn't want to work on that stupid boat, and I thought if I smashed things up, if I made it look like someone was threatening everyone, they'd all be too scared to go to sea, including Albert.

'When that didn't work, I thought about doing something to the *Laura-Lynn*, but when we came in one morning and it was sinking in the harbour, I saw someone had done it for me.' He turned around again, his eyes imploring Blake. 'I'm telling the truth. I swear on my little brother's life.'

Blake believed him, she did. But she still didn't fully understand.

'You must have known your antics wouldn't have worked,' she said. 'That destroying the fishermen's catches would be the one thing that would send them back to sea.'

'Not without their nets.'

'But you're still stuck at the harbour, fixing the damage you did. You're still working in the one place you don't want to be for a lot less money.'

Ewan stared down at his feet, the tips of which were hovering over the cliff edge. 'Yes, I am. But I'm not at sea, and that's all that matters.'

'Why? What's so different between being at sea or being stuck at the harbour? You're still with the same people.' But Blake knew the answer before the words had finished leaving her mouth. 'It's because of Conrad, isn't it? Because Albert does a really shitty job of controlling his son. I've seen the way Conrad is with you. He's a violent prick and a bully. You don't deserve the way he treats you, which I imagine is even worse when it's just the three of you out there.'

The boy had grown very still, his gaze having shifted from his feet to the stars.

'It must be frightening to be trapped on a boat with him for days at a time, miles from land.' Blake took another step forward. 'Having your father beating you at home is bad enough, but having Conrad do the same to you at sea—I can understand why you'd do anything to stop that from happening. But destroying people's livelihoods, scaring them, don't you see you're behaving just like Conrad, whether you mean to or not?'

Slowly, Ewan turned towards her, his face twisted with anger. 'I'm nothing like Conrad! You don't know him. You don't understand how dangerous he is or what he's capable of. You don't know what he—'

Ewan clamped his teeth together, glowered at Blake, then turned back to face the ocean.

'What do you mean? What is Conrad capable of? What did he do?'

He was sobbing now, his entire body racked with tremors. Blake felt panic rising inside her. She took another quiet step towards the cliff edge.

'I know life is really hard for you right now,' she said. 'It must seem like there's no good way out for you. But there is. There are charities, domestic violence agencies that can help you and your family get away from your dad. With their help you could leave all of this behind, forget the harbour and Conrad Roskilly. You could do something you really want to do with your life without the threat of a beating. I can help you, Ewan. I can point you and your mum in the right direction. As for the vandalism, let me talk to Jasper and make things right. It doesn't have to be a police matter. Insurance should cover most of the damage. You'll still have to make amends somehow, even if it's just an apology. But you don't have to think about that right now. Just come to me. Step away from the edge and let me help you.'

'You can't help me,' Ewan said. 'Mum will never leave him, and I can't leave without her.'

'Maybe she'd follow you if you could show her the way.'

'No. Getting people involved will just make things worse.'

Blake was close to him now, but not close enough to take him by the arm. 'Or maybe getting people involved will make all the bad things go away.'

'There's no point!' Ewan cried. 'I'm trapped here no matter which way I look at it. No one can help me. Not even you.'

'Let me try.'

'No. I don't want to do this anymore.'

Ewan shut his eyes and, with a desperate howl, let gravity take him.

Blake flew forwards, grabbed a fistful of his hoodie, and yanked him back towards her. They both toppled, hitting the ground and rolling once. They came to a standstill, a tangled mess of limbs and racing hearts. Then Ewan tried to fight her, thrashing wildly as he struggled to free himself from her grip. But Blake would not let him go. She held on tightly, as if she were fighting for her own life, until he suddenly relented and collapsed in her arms, sobbing like an infant.

∼

They drove back to Porthenev in silence, Ewan too devastated to speak, Blake unsure of what to say. Turning onto Ewan's street, she pulled over just down from his house but kept the engine running. There was a light on in Ewan's living room. Daddy had come home.

Blake peered at the teenager sitting in her passenger's seat. He looked small and fragile, like a broken thing beyond repair.

'Are you going to be all right?' she asked.

Ewan's gaze was fixed on the living room window. 'Yes. I'll be fine.'

His voice sounded robotic, his words like a lie.

'I'll talk to Jasper first thing in the morning. I know it's going to be difficult for you, but Jasper is a good man, and just from talking with him earlier today I know he cares about you. He'll listen. We'll try to find a way to make this work, and I promise I'll handle it as discreetly as possible so your father doesn't find out.'

'It doesn't matter. He'll find out anyway.'

'Not on my watch.' Blake offered him a smile, but his eyes were still glued to the yellow light filtering through the living room window.

She didn't want to leave him here, not with his father drunk and probably still awake. But what was the alternative? Take him to a police station and demand they arrest his abusive father? Ewan would never agree to it. Besides, the police would want to know why Blake was with him that night, which would inevitably lead her to reveal his involvement in the sabotage at the harbour. She knew she would have to tell them eventually, sooner rather than later, because it would be important for their investigation. But she needed to find a way to tell them without getting Ewan into further trouble. Perhaps Rory could help with that. Either way, going to the police right at this moment was not a viable option.

Blake drummed her fingers against the steering wheel. What else? She supposed she could let Ewan sleep on her sofa for the night so he would avoid a confrontation with his father. But then he would have to explain to his family where he had been all night, which would probably lead to a beating anyway. Besides, she could only imagine how letting a teenager stay overnight at her home would look to an outsider.

No, she had to leave him here. There was no other choice that didn't lead to more trouble.

She glanced at him again, feeling a twinge of guilt.

'Everything is going to be fine,' she assured him. 'We'll work it out, I promise you.'

Ewan was silent for a long time. Eventually he nodded and said, 'Thank you.'

Before Blake could say another word, he opened the door and climbed out. She watched him cross the road and walk up to his house, saw him pause at the garden gate and briefly glance back over his shoulder. Then he was gone, hurrying along the garden path and through the front door.

Blake waited for a minute. The house remained unchanged, the living room light still glowing like a beacon. She pulled away from the roadside, turned the car around, and drove away, heading for home. She felt wretched, tormented by doubt. Was leaving Ewan here with his father the right thing to do? It didn't feel like it. But even though she felt terrible, she knew there was an even bigger problem looming on the horizon.

If Ewan hadn't attacked the *Laura-Lynn* and the *Seraphine*, it meant someone else had. Someone who had wanted their crew members to be stuck on land for a very different reason. Blake was now more certain than ever that whoever had damaged the boats was the same person who had murdered Sharon

Bennett and now, in all likelihood, Martin Bennett. The question was why? As Porthenev dwindled in her rear-view mirror, a theory began to form in the back of her mind. If her theory was correct, more people were going to die in extremely violent ways.

25

Terry Lawrence stopped dead in the street, his breath lodging in his throat. He had recognised the blue Corsa pulling over on the roadside instantly. It was the private investigator's car. He remembered it because he had burned everything about the woman into his mind the morning she had first set foot in the harbour. He did not trust her. Worse still, he was afraid of her. Afraid of what she might find out. When Jasper Rowe had suggested hiring the PI to investigate the sabotage at the harbour, all Terry had thought at the time was that it was a monumental mistake. But the rest of the men had agreed because they were worried about their livelihoods—including, unbelievably, Albert Roskilly. Terry had thought Albert had finally lost his mind. And now the private investigator was parked on his street, not fifteen metres from where he stood, the taillights of her car glaring at him like two demonic eyes.

Paralysed, Terry watched as the passenger door

opened and none other than Ewan Jenkin stepped out. Terry felt a sudden urge to cry, until a frustrated, high-pitched growl sounded from below. He glanced down at his wife's Pomeranian dog, Sprinkles. He hated the dog and its stupid name, had always said it resembled a sewer rat dressed in a fur coat. Sprinkles peered up at him, desperate to get moving. But Terry was going nowhere.

Why the hell was Ewan Jenkin with the private investigator? What had they been talking about? A sliver of ice slipped between Terry's shoulder blades. Ewan crewed with Albert Roskilly. He was a quiet boy, so quiet Terry often wondered if something was wrong with him in the brain department. He had barely heard Ewan say more than three words in the six months he had been working for Albert. Surely he couldn't know anything about their little secret. That was impossible. But maybe the private investigator did. Maybe she was trying to use the boy, persuade him to ask questions and find out what he could.

Terry swallowed hard. Next to his feet, Sparkles stamped her paws. Up ahead, Ewan shut the passenger door and headed towards his home. The private investigator waited a minute, then she pulled away from the curb and began to perform a U-turn. Panicking, Terry ducked down, hiding his lanky frame behind his neighbour's parked car. Sparkles squealed as he dragged her towards him and hauled her up into his arms.

As the Corsa drove past him, Terry risked a quick glance over the bonnet of his neighbour's car and saw a brief flash of the private investigator's profile. Then she was gone, turning left at the end of the road and driving out of Porthenev.

Terry placed the dog on the ground and got to his feet. Nausea churned his stomach. He glanced towards Ewan's house and quietly hoped the boy would get a beating from his drunken prick of a father. He deserved it for talking to that private investigator.

'He can't know anything,' he whispered.

Could he? What if one of the others had told him their secret. No, they wouldn't. None of them were that stupid, not even Conrad.

Terry gave a sharp tug on the lead and got walking again. Reaching the end of the road, he took a right and descended the hill. Below him, a coastal fog had crawled from the water and onto land, where it quickly devoured the harbour. Terry walked towards it, his paranoia growing with every step. Sprinkles' tiny claws click-clacked on the pavement.

I told them, didn't I? Terry thought. Hiring a private investigator was utter madness. But did anyone listen to me? No, they bloody didn't. Now we're all in the shit!

He walked on in silence, making his way down the hill, passing terraced cottages whose occupants were already in bed. Terry envied them. He hadn't slept properly since Martin Bennett had disappeared and his wife had been murdered. He didn't care what the others said, Terry knew they were connected to what was happening at the harbour, and he knew what was happening at the harbour was connected to what they had done all those years ago. He had warned Albert, and that caveman of a son of his, but they were too arrogant to listen. The Roskillys thought they were going to get away with it. But not Terry. He had always known that one day they would all suffer a reckoning. Well, now it was upon them whether the Roskillys wanted to believe it or not. Just this evening, Terry had heard from one of his neighbours that the police had found a body at Dead Man's Cove. People were already saying it was Martin Bennett. Speculation or not, Terry knew it was true.

One down, three to go. Which one of them would be next?

He reached the bottom of the hill and the fog enveloped him, wrapping tendrils around his frame like a spider cocooning a fly. Sparkles whimpered and pulled back against the lead.

'Shut it, you ugly runt,' Terry hissed. He dragged the dog along until she submitted and started walking again without fuss.

The harbour car park was empty, or so it seemed; the fog was so thick it was hard to be certain. Keeping to the edge, Terry felt his way to the harbour entrance. A moment of clarity hit him. What the hell was he doing? A killer was on the loose, who had Terry's name on some sort of hit list, yet here Terry was walking through the streets like a moving target with his stupid wife's stupid dog. Anyone with half a brain cell would assume he had gone stark raving mad. But walking helped to clear his troubled mind, to put his thoughts in order. But more than that, Terry wanted to check on his boat.

It was just a one-man show for him these days. None of the other crews would hire him. Word had got around that he was too jumpy, that when he crewed with others he made mistakes at sea and cost them money. Terry thought that was pretty insulting seeing as how he had been to sea more times than most of these youngsters. He was also sure Albert Roskilly had started that rumour to keep Terry separated from the others, so he wouldn't be tempted to talk.

He entered the harbour. The fog grew heavier, making vision impossible beyond more than a metre. Digging in his jacket pocket, he pulled out a torch and flicked the power switch. Its bright beam cast the fog in eerie light, but did little to help him find his way. Not that Terry needed help; he knew every inch of the harbour. He could navigate it with his eyes shut. It was just that the torch beam made him feel safer. It was a lighthouse to his ship.

Sparkles was complaining again, whining and pulling on the lead. Ignoring her, Terry shuffled forwards. He was not usually afraid of fog like this, but tonight was different. Tonight, the fog could be hiding all sorts of evils.

He could hear seawater splashing on his right, as it lapped at hulls of docked boats and the bases of the harbour walls. He stepped towards the sounds, until he was close to the edge. He walked another metre then dropped to his knees. Looping the handle of Sparkles' lead around his wrist, Terry gripped the edge of the quayside with one hand and directed the torch beam down at the water with the other. He could just make out his boat below, a two-man rowboat with an outboard engine, which was a far cry from the larger fishing trawlers he had once taken to sea. Now, fishing for him consisted of days and nights sticking close to the shore, of slim pickings and moths in his wallet. What a failure he had become while Albert Roskilly had thrived. Until last week, of course. Now Albert Roskilly was going nowhere with that bloody great hole in the side of his precious boat. Good, Terry thought. Albert Roskilly had been too smug for too long.

He continued to stare at his boat, which was still unharmed. Seeing it undamaged gave him slight relief. Made him feel it wasn't yet his turn. A question formed on his lips. Why had his boat remained untouched while the others had been rendered unseaworthy? First the Laura-Lynn then the Seraphine, not that Tom Mathers had ever been involved in their guilty little secret, just one of his crew. So why not Terry's rowboat?

It's because I wasn't as involved as the others. Because I refused to have anything to do with it.

That hadn't stopped Albert from incriminating him. He had told Terry that his mere presence made him just as guilty as the rest of them, and so Terry was made to swear on his life that he would never tell a soul what the others had done. And he had kept his word. All these years. Maybe that was why his boat was still untouched. Because Terry had been a mere bystander at the wrong place and time. Or maybe Albert was actually right, that recent events were nothing more than a tragic and bizarre coincidence.

Terry stood and brushed the dirt from his knees. Don't be a fucking idiot, he thought. What was happening now was retribution. There was no other explanation. Martin didn't snap and kill his wife. He didn't sabotage the boats to keep everyone on land. But someone did, and Terry knew exactly who it was.

Albert had warned Terry to stay quiet, to not do anything rash. But Terry didn't want to wait around, too terrified to sleep, almost pissing himself every time he heard a strange sound, until at last it was his turn to die.

'Screw you, Albert Roskilly,' he muttered. 'Screw your dick of a son, too.'

Tomorrow, Terry was going to put things right. He was going to get in his car and make a short journey to confront someone he had been desperately trying to avoid these past ten years. He was going to tell him to stop, threaten to kill him if he had to. And if he wouldn't stop, well, Terry would have no other choice to make that threat a reality. Even if it meant going to pri—

From out of the fog came a long, low whistle made of two notes, the first rising, the second dropping like a stone.

Terry froze. His skin prickled. What the hell was that?

He spun on his heels, unsure which direction the sound had come from. The fog appeared to pulse and thicken, the light from his torch bouncing off it at unnatural angles.

The whistle came again, repeating the same two notes. Next to Terry's feet, Sparkles started to growl. Terry spun around again. This time he thought the whistle had come from his left. He shone the light in that direction, but the fog was impenetrable. He began to tremble. Why was someone whistling at night in the harbour? Every Cornish fisherman knew that to whistle at night was to bring bad luck in on the tide. Sparkles began to bark, a shrill and frightened yapping that hurt Terry's ears.

'Quiet!' he hissed. But Sparkles would not be silenced.

The whistle came again, this time closer and to Terry's right. He swung the torch like a baton. Sparkles lunged on her lead, snarling and barking. Terry swooped down and snatched the dog up, wrapping a hand around her snout. Sparkles squirmed and struggled, her bark turning into a stressed whine. The torch slipped from Terry's grip and hit the quayside. The bulb shattered and the light went out. The fog closed in.

Terry squeezed his eyes shut and listened for the sea. Blood rushed in his ears, roaring loudly. He tried to shut it out, heard the lap of seawater directly behind him. Which meant the harbour exit was on his left. His hands still clamped over the dog's snout, he turned ninety degrees and ploughed forwards. As he hurried in the direction of the car park, he was vaguely aware of his laboured breathing and the small, panicked noises coming from his throat. He was going to have a heart attack. That was how he was going to die. Ten years of stress and anxiety, regret and fear, were finally catching up with him, doing God's work. Not that Terry had ever believed in God, or hadn't until ten years ago, when he had changed his mind, just in case.

A sharp pain jolted through his finger. He yelped loudly as Sparkles bit down harder. He threw the wretched dog, heard her land on her feet with a yelp.

She could find her own fucking way home, hopefully turn in the wrong direction and fall into the sea.

Terry was running now. He could see the entrance to the car park just up ahead. The fog swirled and writhed, trying to get a grip on him. From up ahead, Terry thought he heard a sound. His feet became cement blocks and he almost tripped over them. Righting himself, he stood paralysed with his eyes bulging and his mouth open in a silent scream. He listened. Waited. Whatever sound he thought he had heard did not come again.

But another sound did. A whistle, long and low, just two notes, the first rising, the second dropping like a stone. Right behind him. Close enough to feel the whistler's breath on the back of his neck.

With a cry, Terry spun around. He looked up. Kept on looking up. Standing in the thick of the fog was a giant. Terry laughed in disbelief. Then pissed himself.

'I am Wrath,' the giant said, as he wrapped powerful hands around Terry's throat and lifted him from the ground. 'Hear me roar.'

But all Terry heard as the world turned dark around him was the sound of the ocean and the desperate, horrendous cries of a young boy echoing across the waves from ten long years ago.

26

Albert Roskilly stood in front of the shelf of Sunday newspapers at the local corner shop, listening to the conversation that was transpiring at the counter. A frown carved deep grooves into his forehead, and his heartbeat raced a little. Taking a newspaper from the shelf, he folded it neatly in half and carried it through the cramped aisles to the counter, where the elderly shopkeeper Frida Jones was talking with Albert's next door neighbour Ben Taylor, who wasn't so young himself. As Albert approached, they both looked in his direction.

'Morning Albert, how's Jan?' Frida asked in a thick Cornish accent. She was pure Porthenev, born and bred.

'Jan's just fine,' Albert replied. His gaze flicked between the two.

'Did you hear about Terry Lawrence?' Ben Taylor said, raising his bushy silver eyebrows.

The air seemed to retract from the room. Albert

tried to suck in a deep breath but only managed a thin wheeze.

'What about Terry Lawrence?'

'There's a police car outside his house. He's missing.'

'What do you mean he's missing?'

Behind the counter, Frida visibly shuddered. 'It's true. Last night, he took the dog for a walk before bedtime and didn't come back home. The dog did, mind you. Terry's wife found it yapping in the street. She waited a minute, then went out looking for him. But Terry was nowhere to be found.'

Albert was silent, a sliver of ice lodged in his gullet. He cleared his throat.

'Do the police know what happened to him?' He was aware his voice had a nervous edge to it.

Ben shrugged his bony shoulders. 'We all know what's happened to him, Albert. Terrible things have been occurring in this town. First poor Sharon Bennett is murdered in her bed, then Martin Bennett goes missing—although I think we all know who that body they found at Dead Man's Cove belongs to, don't we? So, I expect it's safe to assume Terry Lawrence has met a similar fate.'

Frida made the sign of the cross and gripped the small silver crucifix hanging around her neck. 'I tell you, I've lived in this village my entire life, all seventy-six years of it, and not once have I ever felt afraid to go to sleep at night. Until now.'

Albert dug into his pocket for loose change, counted out the correct sum for the newspaper, and placed the coins on the counter. 'Maybe we should wait until we hear what the police have to say before jumping to conclusions.'

'If you say so,' Ben said, doubtfully. 'But I for one have started putting the bolts across my front door at night. Porthenev is no longer a safe place to live.'

Albert stared at him dumbly, unable to disagree. Instead, he told Ben and Frida to take care of themselves, then headed for the exit. With each step forwards, the ground seemed to grow soft and spongy, making it hard to walk. Leaving the shop, he stood in the street for a moment and tried to catch his breath. The world spun around him.

First Martin, now Terry, he thought. Had Terry been right all along? Was the past finally catching up with them? But why now? Why now, after ten years of nerve-racking silence?

Albert took off up the hill, the muscles in his legs and arms firing like pistons, his right hand clutching the newspaper as if it were a baton and he was competing in a relay race. Halfway up the hill, he crossed the road and swung left, turning on to Bocox Road, where he slid to a halt in front of a small stone cottage. He rapped his knuckles on the door and waited. When there was no answer, he tucked the newspaper under his armpit, removed a bunch of keys from his pocket, and unlocked the door.

It was dark in the narrow hallway, the air dry and musty. Albert placed his newspaper on a side table then peered through the open living room door on his right. Empty beer bottles and junk food wrappers littered the coffee table in front of the battered sofa. He continued onwards, ascending the staircase and moving silently along the landing until he reached the door at the far end. He paused for a second and listened. Then Albert threw the door open and stormed inside.

Stale air thick with alcohol invaded his nostrils. The curtains were drawn, with just a little light seeping in through the centre parting. Conrad lay face down on the bed, naked except for his underwear, the sheets kicked off and pooling on the floor.

Albert felt rage coursing through his veins. He stomped across the floor, snatched up a glass of water from the bedside table, and dumped it over his son's head. Conrad's reaction was instantaneous. He sprang up, twisting in midair, and emitted a sharp, shocked gasp. Water rained down from his hair, spilling over his back and chest. Leaping to his feet, he spun around to face his father, then furiously rubbed his eyes as water dripped into them.

'Who did you tell?' Albert bellowed.

Conrad was still reeling from his rude awakening, confusion overwhelming him as he heaved air into his lungs.

Albert stepped forward and struck his son hard in the face. Conrad stumbled backwards and slammed into the bedroom wall.

'I said who did you fucking tell?'

Conrad recoiled, pressing himself against the coldness of the wall. 'What are you talking about?'

Albert slapped him again, harder this time, and saw a perfect red imprint of his open hand swelling on his son's face.

'Terry Lawrence disappeared last night,' he said through clenched teeth. 'The police are at his place right now. You know what this means, don't you?'

Conrad pressed a hand to his smarting cheek. He stared at his father with wild, frightened eyes and shook his head.

'It means Terry was right when he came to us the other morning. Someone knows what we did and they're coming for us. I didn't tell anyone. I've kept my word for ten years. Which means you didn't. So who the hell did you tell?'

'I—I didn't. I promise you, Dad. I swear on Mum's life I'm telling you the truth.'

The rage inside Albert erupted. He saw his hand shoot out and wrap tightly around Conrad's neck. He saw himself slam the back of his son's head against the wall, saw his teeth smash together and his eyes squeeze shut.

'You keep your mother's name out of your dirty fucking mouth,' he said. 'Terry was right about all of it. And he was right about you. You've run your mouth one too many times. This is your fault. I covered up your mess because you're my son, and it's a father's duty to protect his children, no matter how much of a disappointment they are. But I should have let you hang, boy. You haven't learned a damn thing. Nothing!'

Albert's fingers tightened around his son's throat.

'I have!' Conrad cried in a strangled voice. 'I have learned!'

Albert leaned in until their noses were almost touching. He could smell last night's alcohol on Conrad's breath. 'No, you haven't. History is already repeating itself with Ewan. That boy hasn't lifted a finger to you. He's done nothing wrong and yet you go out of your way to make his life a living hell. Why do you do it, Conrad? It's like you enjoy hurting people! Did I not raise you right? Did I not teach you to respect your fellow man, to treat others in the same way you expect them to treat you?' Albert faltered, wretchedness and failure weighing him down. 'Well, that's what you're getting now. Someone is coming for us and we're going to pay for what we did. They're coming for us and it's your fault.'

Tears welled in Conrad's eyes, then broke free, mixing with the water that still wet his face.

'I didn't tell anyone,' he croaked. 'I swear.'

Albert glared at him for a while longer. Then, with a slow shake of his head, he released his grip on his son's throat and backed away.

Conrad slid down the wall, clutching at his bruised throat as he gasped for air.

Turning his back on his son, Albert's face crumpled into despair. What did he do? Conrad did not deserve his protection, yet Albert felt the undeniable urge as a father to provide it. The trouble they were in was undoubtedly Conrad's fault. But it was Albert that had come up with the plan. It was Albert who had made everyone swear to secrecy on pain of death. Did that not make him just as guilty as his son? The two were inextricably linked together, by genes and guilt. Albert could not leave his son to die, even if he wanted to. Besides, Jan would never forgive him. So the question was not should he protect his son? The question was *how* should he protect his son?

Stay or go? Fight or flight?

Conrad sobbed pitifully behind him. The sound made Albert queasy. Crying was not for men, not even in life-threatening situations like this. Crying was yet another sign of his son's weakness. Without Albert's protection Conrad would die.

Stay or go? Fight or flight?

For Albert the answer was easy. He felt as if he had been running for the past ten years, even though he had never left Porthenev except to go to sea. He was tired. Exhausted by ten years of broken sleep and terrible nightmares, of waking up so paralysed by guilt that sometimes it took him minutes to get his arms and legs moving. No, for Albert running was not an option. But for Conrad . . .

'You should go,' Albert said, with his back still turned. 'Hide out for a while until this is all over.'

Conrad was still slumped on the floor, his spine pressed against the cold wall, his face and neck red and swollen.

'Go where?' he sobbed.

'To the cabin.' Removing a bunch of keys from his trouser pocket, he removed one and placed it on top of a chest of drawers. 'You stay there and you stay out of sight until you hear from me.'

'What about you, Dad?'

Albert fixed his eyes on the open doorway. 'Just pack a bag and get going.'

'Dad?' Conrad's voice was small and broken, like a frightened child's. 'I didn't tell anyone, I promise you.'

Albert left the room without looking back. He felt burning shame. For laying hands on his son. For raising a pathetic specimen of a man. He went downstairs, picked up his newspaper from the side table in the hallway, then stopped still by the front door. He took a moment to compose himself, brushing down his clothes and running fingers through his hair. Then he left Conrad's home and continued the uphill journey towards his own.

As he walked, terrible memories filled his head. He suddenly staggered, the weight of the guilt he had been carrying for ten years knocking him off balance. Righting himself, he cleared his throat and quickly looked around to see if anyone had noticed. But he was alone on the hill. Ten years ago, he had felt his actions had been right and just, necessary even; he had a family to protect and a crew to care for. But now, with Martin dead and Terry missing, Albert wondered if it had all been a terrible mistake. The past always had a way of searching you out, no matter how deeply you buried it. His life was hanging in the balance. Conrad's too. And while he would fight tooth and claw to protect his son, Albert was unsure if he had the right to fight so desperately for his own life. Did he really deserve to go on after what he had made the others do? Ten years already felt like stolen time.

How could he stop this? There was an answer he had been dancing around, one that had been whispering to him from the shadows. *Fight back. You know who's behind it all. Find them and end it, even if it means taking a life.*

Taking his phone from his coat pocket, he scrolled through the contacts list with a trembling thumb. Finding the number he was looking for, he hesitated. He had not spoken to him in almost ten years, had only kept his number in case a moment like this finally arose. He stared at the phone screen, guilt stabbing him repeatedly in the chest. Then he moved his thumb away and returned the phone to his pocket.

What right did Albert have to tell him to stop? He had destroyed the man's life. Taken away the one thing that would have given him closure. Albert had done it to save Conrad. And even if Conrad had never shown a shred of remorse, or gratitude, even if he hadn't changed his ways and was as violent and cruel now as he had been back then, Albert did not regret his decision. But that did not mean he had the right to stop what was coming for them both. He would try to protect Conrad by sending him to the cabin, but Albert knew his son was broken in some dark, terrible way. That history really was repeating itself with poor Ewan Jenkin, and it was only a matter of time before Conrad went too far again.

Albert had reached his home. He looked up at its facade and let out a weary sigh. He was exhausted. There had been no joy in carrying such a guilty burden. Let him come, he thought. Then I'll decide whether I want to keep living.

Jan was in the kitchen, cooking eggs and bacon for Albert's breakfast. She smiled at him over her shoulder, making the guilt burn brighter in his chest.

'There you are,' his wife said. 'Stopped to chat again, did you?'

Albert hovered in the kitchen doorway, staring at the back of his wife's head. 'I bumped into Ben Taylor at the corner shop. You know how he likes to go on.'

'That I do. Well, sit yourself down at the table. Breakfast won't be long.'

Albert remained in the doorway. Jan glanced over at him and frowned.

'Everything all right, love?'

He nodded stiffly, forced a smile, and sat down at the kitchen table.

'Everything's fine, Jan. Everything's going to be just fine.'

27

When Blake finally woke up on Sunday morning, she was surprised to discover it was 10:42 a.m. She rarely slept in late these days, even though insomnia plagued her most nights. Last night had been particularly turbulent, with her mind refusing to rest and continually recycling the same troubled thoughts about Ewan Jenkin. He had tried to take his own life right in front of her. Blake tried to imagine leaping to her death from the edge of the cliff, pictured her body smashing onto the rocks below in a spray of blood and bone. She shuddered, climbed out of bed, and went to the kitchen to make a pot of coffee.

When it was ready, she filled a mug and took it over to the table, where she sat down and took slow sips while staring at the curtains her mother had hung just yesterday. She hoped Ewan was all right, and wondered if she should drop by his house to make sure. But by doing so would surely invite trouble from his father. Blake rested her chin in her hands with her elbows propped on the tabletop. She knew she should probably tell someone what Ewan had tried to do. But who? His father was a monster who would see Ewan's actions as weak and pathetic, deserving of another beating. As for Ewan's mother, Blake imagined she lived in constant fear, scared of saying or doing the wrong thing that would trigger her husband to lash out. But if Blake told Ewan's mother what he had tried to do, about the raw desperation he had displayed, would she find the strength and courage to finally take her children and leave her husband for good?

Domestic violence was a terrifying beast. Victims were often too afraid and psychologically beaten down to escape their abusers without help. Perhaps Blake could be that help. But she was a stranger to the Jenkin family, someone they didn't know well enough to trust. Perhaps then she could involve the police. But what if Ewan and his mother denied the abuse for fear of violent repercussions, their self-esteem all but destroyed?

Sitting at the kitchen table, Blake felt helpless and frustrated. Perhaps she could talk to Rory to find out how the police could intervene in such a case, or to her mother or Judy, who might have suggestions beyond Blake's own knowledge.

Ewan's home life had not been the only problem keeping Blake from sleep last night. There was also what he had said about Conrad Roskilly. 'You don't know him. You don't understand how dangerous he is or what he's capable of.'

What had Ewan meant? Blake didn't think he had

been referring to Conrad's everyday bullying and all-round thuggery; she had witnessed that with her own eyes and understood it clearly. This was something else entirely, as if Ewan knew a terrible secret that he was too frightened to disclose.

And what about the decapitated gulls left in the crew members' beds on board the *Seraphine*? Or the almost successful attempt to sink the *Laura-Lynn*? What about the murder of Sharon Bennett? What about the body found at Dead Man's Cove that was in all likelihood Martin Bennett? Ewan wasn't responsible for any of these acts. But someone was.

Was it Conrad Roskilly? Was that what Ewan had been referring to? Conrad certainly had the malice in him to commit such heinous crimes. But did he have the motive?

Blake drained her cup and refilled it with thick black coffee. She heaved her shoulders. It was late Sunday morning. She should have been relaxing, perhaps driving over to Wheal Marow to visit her parents or check in with her cousin Kenver. Yet here she was, slowly driving herself insane with an unresolved case that was no longer hers. But the fact it was no longer her case didn't matter. She had an itch to scratch. A need for answers. For closure. She was emotionally invested now, whether she wanted to be or not. Blake drummed her fingers on the table as her gaze settled on her backpack, which was hanging over the opposite chair.

Detective Sergeant Turner would not be happy if he discovered she was conducting her own investigation alongside his, but the alternative was to walk away from Porthenev with the vain hope she might one day forget the terrible events of the past few days and her own failure that felt like a catalyst to it all.

Blake put down her cup. She grabbed her bag, and removed her laptop. She really did hate unresolved cases.

If Turner wanted to arrest her for interfering in police business, then so be it. He would thank her eventually, once she had found something to help with his investigation.

Putting another pot of coffee on the stove, Blake retrieved the two lists Jasper Rowe had given her at the beginning of the week, opened a web browser, and got to work.

An hour later, she sat back on her chair and stared at the laptop screen with wide eyes. What she had found sent a shiver travelling through her body from head to toe.

28

As Conrad Roskilly stood in the fading light and stared up at the house, his hands slowly balled into fists. His left cheek was still swollen from where his father had struck him. There were finger-shaped bruises on his neck. The humiliation he felt was all-encompassing. But it was quickly turning into rage. How dare Albert Roskilly treat his only son like that? His own flesh and blood! And for what? Conrad had not told anyone their secret. Except maybe one person. But he had blurted it out in the heat of the moment, as a warning of what he was capable of. A display of power.

So, no, everything terrible that was happening right now was not Conrad's fault. But he knew exactly whose fault it was.

Opening the garden gate, he strode up the path and knocked on the front door. He waited, tried to temper the anger pumping through his veins until it was time to set it free. From somewhere inside the house he heard a slurred male voice yelling for someone to get the door. Seconds later, the door opened a few centimetres and the pale, frightened face of a woman in her early forties peered out. She looked up at Conrad through large, round eyes. He noticed a bruise on her left cheekbone, which was turning from black to yellow.

As he stared, the woman's expression turned to one of recognition, and her eyes took on a hardened sheen.

Conrad relaxed his clenched hands and flashed his most charming smile. 'Hello Mrs Jenkin, how are you? I was wondering if Ewan was home.'

Mrs Jenkin's gaze moved slowly from Conrad's swollen cheek down to the bruises on his neck. Still, she did not speak, as if she somehow knew a wolf was standing on her doorstep, badly disguised as a friendly face.

Clearing his throat, Conrad tried again. 'Dad asked me to pass a message on to Ewan, about work. Is he here?'

Mrs Jenkins opened her mouth to say something. Then the same male voice Conrad had heard just a minute ago boomed out from within.

'Who is it?'

Again, Mrs Jenkin tried to speak, but this time it was Conrad who silenced her.

'Good evening, Mr Jenkin,' he called. 'It's Conrad Roskilly, Albert's son.'

Mrs Jenkin glared at him. Then her entire being wilted like a dying flower as a figure loomed behind her in the hallway, bringing with it a stench of alcohol that thickened the air. Powerful fingers clamped over the edge of the door and pulled it wide open. Ewan's mother grew even smaller.

Lance Jenkin was a short and stocky man, prematurely grey and receding, with a small chin covered with untidy stubble, and cold, narrow eyes that reminded Conrad of a snake. His large belly stretched his T-shirt and hung over his belt. He glared at his wife, who retreated into the hall and scurried away like a mouse. When the men were alone, Jenkin drunkenly smiled at Conrad.

'Nice to see you, my boy. How's that father of yours?'

Conrad returned the smile. 'He's fine, thank you. How are you keeping?'

'Oh, you know. This damned leg gives me so much pain, but the doctors say there's nothing they can do about it. I'm sure if I had the money to go private it would be a different story, but there you are. That's life for you. It's one outcome for the rich, and another for the rest of us poor bastards.'

Jenkin belched, sending a cloud of acidic breath into Conrad's face. His smile began to waver.

'Your father's boat seaworthy yet?' Jenkin asked. 'Terrible business, that was. Must be costing Albert a pretty penny. And I suppose they ain't caught the bastard who did it.'

'Actually, that's why I'm here,' Conrad said. 'The insurance company paid up so Dad reckons the *Laura-Lynn* will be back on the water in a few days. I need to talk to Ewan about when he can come back to work.'

Jenkin grinned and chuckled to himself. 'I'm glad to hear it. Money's been tighter than a nun's cunt around here since your father's boat almost sank. We've barely been scraping by, seeing as how I can't work anymore. And with all the awful business occurring in this town right now, I think we're overdue some good luck, don't you?'

'That we are.'

Lance Jenkin continued to talk, recounting his days at sea with Conrad's father with a wistful look in his bloodshot eyes. Conrad tapped his foot impatiently on the doorstep. His hands curled into fists once again. Above him, the sky was growing dimmer by the second.

'Is Ewan here?' he asked, cutting Jenkin off mid-sentence.

The older man's face darkened at the interruption. He scratched the stubble on his chin, picked a crumb from it.

'He's in his room, probably playing with himself. If only he was more like you, eh? Maybe then I'd be a proud man.' Jenkin swayed in the doorway. He belched again. 'What was it you wanted to tell him?'

Conrad's fingernails dug into the palms of his hands. He could feel the violence coming, like the guts of a volcano threatening to erupt. He was running out of time. A frightened voice in his head told him to forget about Ewan, to leave town while he still had life and breath in his body.

But Conrad was going nowhere. Not until he had taught that little prick a lesson.

'The *Laura-Lynn*,' he reminded Jenkin. 'Getting your son back to work?'

'Oh, that's right. Forgive me. It's the painkillers the doctor's got me on. They play tricks on my mind.'

Nothing to do with the gallon of booze on your breath, Conrad thought.

'I'll call him down,' Jenkin said.

'No need. I'll go up.'

The man stared at him warily, then glanced over his shoulder at the open living room door. The call of an open bottle was no doubt singing to him like a Siren. 'Go on then. First door on your right. You tell that little shit to get downstairs after. I need him to go to the shop for me.'

Mr Jenkin stood to the side. Conrad entered the house, the smell of alcohol growing stronger with each step, as if the walls had been painted with it. He thanked Mr Jenkin and headed for the stairs. As he planted his foot on the bottom step, he glanced along the hallway and saw Mrs Jenkin in the kitchen entrance, her eyes burning into him. He smiled coldly at her then ascended the stairs.

Reaching the landing, he stopped outside Ewan's bedroom door. Blood rushed in his ears. The volcano inside him erupted and fury flooded out. Conrad opened the door.

Ewan was sitting on the bed with his feet up and his hands tucked behind his head. A pair of headphones was clamped over his ears, its long cord plugged into a record player that sat between two large speakers on a side table in the corner. He glanced up as Conrad entered. At first, a veil of confusion fell over his face. Then his complexion turned deathly white, and he froze.

A cruel smile spread across Conrad's lips as he silently closed the door.

'Hello, faggot,' he said. Then stepped towards the bed.

The room was tiny, with just enough space for a single bed and a couple of pieces of furniture. The only escape route was through the door, or if you were feeling plucky, through the window.

'I ought to kill you right now,' Conrad said, as Ewan stared in shock at him. 'You told someone, didn't you? You blabbed about what I told you and now everyone is dying.'

Ewan tried to retreat on the bed. The back of his head struck the wall. His headphones slipped from his ears and hooked around his neck. Tinny rock music filled the air. He shook his head violently from side to side.

'I—I didn't,' he croaked.

Conrad circled the bed until he was towering over the teenager. He stared down at him, his fists clenched so tightly that his tendons ached.

'You're a fucking liar. I told you, didn't I? I promised that if you told anyone I'd make you live to regret it. Except I don't think you should get to live at all.'

He lunged forwards, his left hand wrapping around Ewan's throat, his right pinning the boy's shoulder to the bed. In one swift movement, Conrad was on top of him, clamping Ewan's slim legs between his thighs.

Ewan grabbed Conrad's hand but he was too weak to remove it from his throat. He tried to kick and thrash, but the weight on top of him made it impossible. Instead, Ewan sucked in a breath to shout for help.

Conrad released Ewan's neck, drew his hand back and slapped the boy hard across the cheek. Then he clamped his hand over Ewan's mouth and drove a fist into his stomach.

The boy's eyes grew wide. His body went rigid. As Ewan struggled for breath, Conrad freed the headphones and quickly wrapped the cord around his neck. He pulled hard. Ewan's head came up from the pillow. Conrad looped the cord around again. Then he was strangling Ewan, his face inches from the boy's own.

Ewan's face turned scarlet. His eyes filled with fresh terror. He tried to get a grip on Conrad's hand again, digging nails into the man's flesh. But he was too strong.

Conrad pulled the cord even tighter, mashing his teeth together with the effort. Suddenly the headphone jack was torn from the socket on the record player. An explosion of drums and guitars blasted from the speakers, filling the room.

Ewan was purple now. Burst blood vessels were spreading across the whites of his eyes like splinters across cracked glass.

Madness had taken hold of Conrad. He was no longer in control of his body or his actions. He laughed maniacally. Tears sprang up in his eyes. The thundering music made his rib cage vibrate.

'I'm not going to die because of what happened ten years ago!' he yelled. 'It's not my fault!'

Ewan kicked his legs. His eyes began to roll in their sockets.

Over the music, shouting came from downstairs.

'Ewan! Turn that fucking music down or so help me God, I'll smack you into next week!'

Conrad blinked. He stared down at his hands. At Ewan's purple face and protruding tongue. What was he doing?

He released his grip on the cord and held up his hands in front of his eyes. Beneath him on the bed, Ewan clawed at the cord around his neck, loosening it, and gasped for air.

More shouting from downstairs. 'Don't make me come up there, boy! Turn it down or I'll break your arm!'

Conrad lowered his hands, memories from ten years ago flashing in his mind like a fractured nightmare. He stared at Ewan, who was still struggling for breath as tears streamed from his eyes. Slowly, Conrad reached out and gently patted the boy's right cheek, making him flinch. Then he climbed off him, picked up the headphones cord and plugged it back into the record player. The music vanished. Now the only sound in the room was Ewan's laboured panting and wheezing.

Conrad stood watching him for a moment. He pointed a finger at him.

'You shouldn't have told,' he said. 'Everything that's happening is on you.'

He left the bedroom and closed the door behind him. At the foot of the stairs, Lance Jenkin stood, staring up with a red face and fresh beer stains on his t-shirt. Conrad descended.

'What the bloody hell is going on up there?' Jenkin said, his words running together.

'I'd keep an eye on that boy of yours,' Conrad

told him. 'He's got a smart mouth. The things he was saying about you . . .'

He shook his head, smiled, then left through the front door. As he shut it behind him, he heard Mr Jenkin's angry voice bellowing from inside.

'Ewan! Get your bloody ass down here right now!'

Conrad stood in the dark street, looking left to right. Fear had returned to him, sinking its claws into his skin. He hurried through the darkness, checking every shape and shadow. He would not miss this place while he was gone. Perhaps he wouldn't even come back.

His father's furious face flashed in his mind, and he felt the sting of his open hand. No, he wouldn't miss this place at all.

'Fuck the lot of them,' he whispered to the dark. Then he melted into it and was gone.

29

His mother was slumped on the sofa, just like she always was, her heavy-lidded eyes transfixed by the television screen. There was an odious stink about her, of sweat and filth, of slow decay. Mason stood to her right, also watching the television. Usually, it was of no interest to him, but his mother was watching the ten o'clock news and a photograph of Martin Bennett was superimposed on the top right corner of the screen.

'The body discovered yesterday morning at Northcliffs beach, known locally as Dead Man's Cove, has been formally identified as Martin Bennett,' the middle-aged newsreader said. 'The thirty-six-year-old fisherman from Porthenev, Cornwall, had been previously wanted for questioning following the murder of his wife, thirty-three-year-old Sharon Bennett, who was found unresponsive at their home early Thursday morning. Police are treating Martin Bennett's death as suspicious. The

Bennetts leave behind six-year-old twins, who are currently being cared for by family members. The police are appealing to the public, asking anyone with information that could help with their investigation to call the following number . . .'

A dreamy smile slowly spread across Mason's lips. He shut his eyes for a moment, recalling his succulent first taste of Martin Bennett. His stomach rumbled in response. But there was an underlying panic lurking beneath the hunger. Displaying Bennett's carcass at Dead Man's Cove had initiated a countdown of sorts. The police would be working hard in their search for evidence and clues that would lead them to the killer. Mason had been careful to leave no trace of himself behind, using latex gloves and rubber boots that were one size too large for his feet. The mask he wore over his head prevented stray hairs being left at the crime scene. But he knew that no matter how careful he had been there was always room for accidents and errors of judgement. Because when the hunger came it was overwhelming. It was as if Mason left his body and Wrath took control. He had once watched a nature documentary about marine life, in which the waters turned black and bloody as a frenzy of sharks feasted upon a dead whale. Was that how he behaved when the hunger took him? Frenzied and ravenous, the rest of the world disappearing, leaving only flesh and blood and his snapping jaws?

'Where did you go last night?' His mother's slurred voice dragged him back to the room. 'You didn't come home until almost sunrise.'

'Fishing,' Mason said.

'You're always fishing. Yet you never bring any fish home.'

He stared at his mother, whose glazed eyes were still glued to the television screen. He tried to remember the last time she had looked at him.

'That's not true. I caught a big catch the other night. It's already filleted and in the fridge.' He waited for a response, for a blink of an eye, or a twitch of the lips. But there was nothing. His mother was slowly wasting away on that sofa, disappearing with the passing of each day. 'I'll make you something to eat now if you like. Then I need to go out again.'

'You have work in the morning,' his mother said.

'I know.'

'You're never home anymore. You're always leaving me alone. Sometimes you're as cruel as your father.'

Mason flinched as if he had been slapped. He did not reply, only shrugged his shoulders then left the room.

The kitchen was a cramped space, which made the piles of dirty dishes and cluttered counter tops look somehow worse. The only objects that were kept scrupulously clean were the heavy iron skillet sitting on the stove, a block of expensive-looking butcher knives, and a selection of chopping boards.

Mason opened the refrigerator door, which had no family photographs or takeaway menus attached to it by magnets, only a printout of tidal times for the next six months and a single bloody thumbprint in the bottom-left corner. The dreamy smile returned to his lips as he stared at the contents of the fridge.

Removing a plate from the middle shelf, he carried it over to the kitchen counter, where he pushed a tower of dirty crockery to one side, and set it down. Next, he fetched the butter dish from a wall cupboard, spooned some into the skillet, and depressed the stove's ignition switch. Petals of blue flames bloomed beneath the skillet.

As Mason waited for the butter to melt, he cast a glance at the kitchen floor and saw a thin trail of blood leading from the refrigerator to where he had set the plate down on the counter. There were no paper towels, so he took the dishcloth from the sink and used it to wipe the blood from the floor.

The butter had now melted in the skillet. The hunger returned in force, gripping Mason's stomach, filling his mouth with saliva. Using a wooden spatula, he scooped up a slab of fresh meat from the plate and dumped it in the skillet. Fat sizzled. Globules of blood began to bubble and blacken. Mason shut his eyes and inhaled deeply through his nose. This was the last of the meat in the fridge. He would savour every bite. And then he would go out and get more.

∼

With his belly full, he went upstairs to his bedroom, which, in comparison to the kitchen, was meticulously clean and organised. He was satiated for now, but he knew the feeling would not last long. The hunger went deep. It was about more than just feeding his physical needs. It was about feeding the darkness that lived within. It was about punishment and retribution. It was about filling the wretched void that tore at him in the quiet hours, and it was about drowning out his father, whose voice he could still hear to this day, even though his father was nothing more than a pile of bones in a shallow grave, his flesh devoured by maggots and worms, then excreted and returned to the earth.

The upstairs ceilings were lower than in the rooms of the ground floor, forcing Mason to stoop as he opened his wardrobe doors. He stood, staring at the shadowy interior, at the fearsome mask draped over a mannequin head on the middle shelf. Wrath was calling to him. Mason felt his desire to crush and tear and destroy like an overwhelming pressure in his chest. He stared at Wrath, and Wrath stared back. He wanted to take another of the men, to enjoy the terror in their eyes as they realised their time in this world had come to an end, and that the end was lingering white-hot pain. He would take another soon. But not tonight. Because hunger was calling him back to the cave, where a fresh calf was still hanging from a hook in the ceiling, starved and dehydrated and gone mad in the pitch darkness.

Mason carefully removed the mask. He took a black sports bag from the bottom of the wardrobe, unzipped it, and placed the mask inside, next to the cutting tools he had stolen from the abattoir. Slinging the bag over his shoulder, he returned downstairs, where his mother still sat on the living room sofa, the food he had cooked for her left untouched on the side table. Mason's eyes darkened. Ungrateful, he thought. She was lucky Wrath had not torn her apart. He gave her one last look, then opened the front door and slipped outside, where he melted into the night.

30

The staff of *The Cornish Press* had been at work for ten minutes when Blake strode in through the front door. The newsroom was a small area with a few desks spaced out as far as possible, which was not very far at all, so its trio of journalists could at least pretend to have their own private bubbles. In the far wall, a door on the right led to the newspaper's archive room, while behind the door on the left was the editor-in-chief's office. Blake had only met the man once and immediately decided he was a pompous ass who didn't appreciate Judy Moon's occasional visits from her private investigator friend. Nor did Judy's colleague Rod, who glowered at Blake as she drifted past his desk without so much as a hello.

Blake was thrumming with nervous energy and too much caffeine. The discovery she had made yesterday had kept her mind busy most of the night, robbing her of sleep. But she still only had a piece of the puzzle. She hoped that with Judy's help she would find more.

'Morning,' Blake said, as she perched on the edge of Judy's desk. 'Have you got a minute?'

Judy stared up at her then shot a glance towards the editor-in-chief's door.

She sighed. 'He's in, you know. And I've got a deadline.'

'Please, Judy. It's important.'

'It always is with you. What do you need?'

Blake leaned in and dropped her voice to a whisper. 'I saw on the news Martin Bennett's been positively ID'd.'

'The word is he was hacked to pieces. Looked like a carcass in a butcher's window. But I don't know any more than that.' Judy paused and glanced around the room. 'Have you heard another fisherman's gone missing?'

Blake froze. 'Who?'

'Terry Lawrence. Lives a couple of streets away from Martin Bennett. He vanished Saturday night from Porthenev while walking his dog.'

Colour drained from Blake's face. 'Saturday night? What time?'

'I'm not sure. Why?'

Because I was in Porthenev on Saturday night, Blake thought. Had she been that close to Martin and Sharon Bennett's killer?

Judy was staring at her intensely. Blake leaned in closer still. 'I may have a lead.'

Now Judy glanced in Rod's direction, who was doing an amateurish job of pretending he wasn't listening in.

'What kind of lead?' she asked.

'Before I can tell you that I need to access your archives. The article I found online was from a national newspaper. Just a little side piece, so the details were scant.'

'What article? What are you talking about?'

'I figured if *The Cornish Press* covered the story, which I'm certain they would have, there would be more details about what happened, including the names of those involved.'

She had caught Judy's attention, but not in the way she had hoped.

'Don't give me half answers, Blake. Remember our deal? Information for information. If you want access to the archive, you tell me everything.'

'I will, I promise. But I need to be sure I'm right before I say another word.'

Judy sank back on her chair and crossed her arms over her stomach. 'Remind me why I'm friends with you again. I can't just let you into the archive without good reason, especially with Rod watching like a hawk. Give me something.'

Glancing over her shoulder, Blake met Rod's gaze with a hard stare. He quickly returned his attention to his computer.

'Fine,' she said. 'I'm looking for an article from around ten years ago, about an accident that happened at sea. Someone died. Fell overboard and drowned. I think what happened back then is connected to what's happening now. But I can't be sure without confirmation. Once I have it, I'll tell you all I know.'

'God, you're annoying,' Judy said, slapping Blake's thigh. 'And get off my desk.'

She stood and walked towards the archive door. Blake followed her. Behind them, Rod cleared his throat and opened his mouth to protest.

'Can it, Rod,' Judy called, as she opened the door. 'You behave yourself and you just might have a fresh lead on the Porthenev case.'

Entering the archive room, Judy flipped the light switch and cold fluorescent strip lighting flickered on the ceiling.

'Welcome to the morgue,' she said, with a wave of her hand, 'Where old newspapers go to die.'

Blake looked around the room. 'Cheery.'

The space was tiny, the only furnishings a computer workstation in one corner and a row of extra wide filing cabinets lined up on the opposite wall.

'How far back did you say you're looking? Ten years?'

Blake nodded.

'Then you'll find what you're looking for over here.' Judy sat down at the workstation and entered her username and password on the computer. 'We keep digital copies of every edition of *The Cornish Press*, have done for years, except for papers from the early days, but we've almost finished scanning them in. I like to think we'll still keep those original copies; they're over a hundred years old, so it seems wrong to throw them away. It's history in the flesh.'

Pulling up a chair, Blake sat down next to Judy, who showed her how to operate the archive system. 'It's easy, really. Even you could do it.'

'I can use a computer,' Blake said, defensively. 'It's literally half of my job.'

Judy smiled but showed no sign of leaving.

'Haven't you got baby lambs to write about, farmer girl?' Blake said without looking up from the screen.

'You really are a piece of work, Blake Hollow. You know that, right?'

'It's why you love me so much.'

'Oh, piss off.' Judy flashed another smile and left the room.

Now alone, Blake focused her thoughts. Removing her phone from her jeans pocket, she opened a web browser, then her bookmarked pages, and located the news article she had discovered yesterday. The headline read: *Death at Sea Ruled an Accident*. Below the headline was the date the article had been published. Blake entered the date into the digital archive and began her search. It didn't take long to find what she was looking for. The story in *The Cornish Press* had been published a few days after the original article, and had made it to the front page with a more personal headline: *Local Parents Mourn Son's Death as Inquest Rules Out Foul Play*.

Blake read through the story, then read it again, feeling increasingly light-headed. There were more details here than in the national news article, including the name of the trawler that had been the victim's passage for one last, fatal trip. The *Persephone*. Named after the queen of the underworld and one of the many death deities from Greek mythology. More importantly, the article listed the names of the rest of the trawler's crew. Martin Bennett. Terry Lawrence. Conrad and Albert Roskilly.

Shock ran through Blake's body. This had to be it. The reason why Martin Bennett and his wife had been murdered. Why Terry Lawrence was now missing too. They had been there that day on the *Persephone*, along with the Roskillys, who were still alive for the time being.

'Why now and not ten years ago?' Blake muttered.

She had to tell someone. Judy, yes, as per their agreement, but not until Blake had informed DS Turner of her findings. She could already picture his angry face, could hear him complain that she had once again "interfered" with police business. At least this time she could argue it wasn't interference, that she was merely following up on the investigation that she had been paid to conduct. Turner didn't need to know that her investigation had officially come to end. But if he was going to take Blake seriously, she would need proof that went beyond the circumstantial, which meant she still had more work to do.

She glanced around the room, searching for a printer. Seeing none, she sprang from the chair and opened the door.

'Judy, how do I print off an article?'

But Judy was not at her desk. She was standing in the far corner, next to Rod, both hunched over and listening to a radio scanner as a static-heavy voice rang out from the speaker.

Blake drew closer. Judy looked up, her mouth half open.

'What is it?' Blake asked.

Judy glanced at Rod, then back at Blake. She shook her head in disbelief.

'The police are heading to Gwithian Towans,' she said. 'There's been another murder.'

31

Forming one three-mile section of glorious sand located within St Ives Bay, Gwithian Towans beach is golden and vast. The word 'towans' means 'dunes' in the Cornish language, and here at Gwithian, visitors can find huge swathes of sandy hills capped with wild grass serving as a backdrop for the beach, along with several impressive cliff faces. With the swell of the Celtic Sea and a strong breeze, the beach is a popular spot for surfers and kite flyers alike. At low tide, an intricate network of rock pools is revealed on the shore, rewarding children of all ages with hours of pleasure exploring tiny underwater worlds. Out in the bay sits a rocky isle on which stands Godrevy lighthouse, guardian of the local fishermen and inspiration for one of Virginia Woolf's most celebrated novels.

This morning, beneath a clear blue sky and an early spring sun, Gwithian Towans beach could have easily been mistaken as an idyllic brushstroke of pure paradise. But then there was the blood; a thick, gloopy trail leading from the water's edge, across the sand, and into the dunes, where the Crime Scene Investigation unit was already hard at work within the confines of a police cordon. A pristine white tent sat at the centre of the area, pitched over the victim's body to prevent the prying eyes of dog walkers and the nearby campsite and holiday guests from spying the horrors that lay inside.

Turner and Angove had arrived five minutes ago and dressed into sterile white coverings. They hovered outside the tent, both suffering the apprehension that came before viewing a dead body, especially one that had been so viciously treated. Turner gave Angove a quick glance.

'You all right to go in?' he asked.

Angove nodded stiffly. 'Yes, Sarge.'

'No more puking?'

'No, Sarge.'

They entered the tent. The smell hit them first, a heady mix of coppery blood and putrid intestinal gases. The body lay spreadeagled on the ground, naked, and in a familiar desecrated state. As with Martin Bennett, the victim's organs had been removed, the intestines wrapped around his neck, and the chest cavity crudely torn open. Both the heart and eyes were missing too. But unlike Bennett, the body was not crucified to the ground, confirming Turner's theory that Bennett had been nailed down to prevent his corpse from being washed away by the tide. Here, the dunes were too far from the water for the tide to be of concern.

There was another difference. Following the

post-mortem examination, the pathologist had confirmed Bennett's body had been drained entirely of its blood, and that it had been drenched over the body at the disposal site. It appeared this latest body had been drained of blood as well, except this time the blood had been used to create a trail from the tide to the dunes, as if the killer had left directions to ensure any early morning walkers would find the remains. Meaning the killer not only wanted to put his victims on display, Turner thought, he wanted them to be discovered. Why was that? To shame the victims? To show the world the power this maniac possessed? His disturbing ability to strip a human of its flesh and blood, until it was nothing more than a carcass?

Amanda Le Bretton was crouched over the dead man and currently examining his inner ear with a pen light and focused scrutiny.

'Good morning, Detectives,' she said, without looking up. 'I wasn't hoping to see you both again so soon. Yet here we are.'

Turner nodded grimly. 'What have you got for us?'

'Much of the same as before, I'm afraid. Little to no evidence. Although this is a fresher kill. Rigor mortis has started to set in, but the limbs are still somewhat malleable. See?' She paused to gently take the dead man's hand and wave it up and down at the wrist joint. 'So that would likely put the time of death at around four or five hours ago. Although I'm not a pathologist, so take my estimation for what it is.'

Detective Constable Angove let out a shuddering

breath. He was pale and queasy but managed to keep his breakfast in his stomach.

'Jesus Christ,' he said, bending his knees a little to get a closer look at the body. 'This has to be Terry Lawrence, Sarge. Look at the big scar on his left thigh. Lawrence's wife said he has a scar in the exact same place from an accident at sea years ago. Apparently, a hook tore right through his flesh.

Turner winced as he inspected the scar. It was half the length of the man's thigh, the scar tissue thick and uneven.

'Are we talking serial murder here, Sarge?' Angove's face was completely drained of colour.

'Let's not get ahead of ourselves,' Turner said.

He returned his gaze to the body, to the gaping black hole that once held the man's organs. *Why does he take them?* Turner thought. And was Angove right? Were they dealing with a serial killer? Turner's gut said no, at least not in the typical sense. Serial murderers usually selected their victims at random. But the two dead men were both fishermen who worked out of the same harbour. They were connected. This was not random.

As for Martin Bennett's wife, Sharon, Turner suspected she had been killed either as a way to get her husband's attention, or because she had stumbled upon the killer before Martin Bennett had arrived home. She had been spared the violence and desecration that the men's bodies had been subjected to, which likely meant she was of no importance to the killer, only a means to an end or an obstacle that had been in his way.

Turner's eyes slowly moved up and down the

length of the man's body. Both men had been drained of blood, which had been collected and used at each disposal site. How had the killer achieved such a feat? Turner grimaced. The easiest way would be to hang the victim upside down, with a bucket or container placed beneath him. Turner shut his eyes for a moment, picturing the act, seeing the terrified face of the man, watching a blade puncture his groin area then slice downwards, splitting him open and spilling his blood into the waiting bucket below. Turner opened his eyes again. The man would have been strung up like a carcass in a butcher's window. Or like livestock at an abattoir, ready to be slaughtered . . .

'What's our next move, Sarge?' Angove asked beside him.

Amanda casually glanced up from the body. 'Whatever it is, gentlemen, would you mind making it outside? It's all too cramped in here.'

Turner and Angove left the tent and signed out of the crime scene. They walked through the grassy dunes until they reached the edge and stared down at the sandy beach below, which was carved in two by the long streak of blood. Turner sucked in a breath of sea air, grateful that it cleansed his nostrils and lungs, freeing him from the stench of death.

The image of the dead man hanging upside down in a deep, dank place with a bucket of blood beneath him returned to Turner's mind. He stared at the long trail of blood discolouring the sand.

'Rory, how far away are we from Dead Man's Cove?'

Angove rubbed his chin and squinted a little. 'I'm not sure exactly. Five, six miles by road.'

'And by boat?'

'Maybe a little longer than that. It would depend on tidal times, plus you'd have to sail out and around Godrevy Point. But it's the same stretch of coastline. Porthenev Harbour is about ten miles from here, just past Dead Man's Cove.'

'We need a list of all the beaches, coves, and inlets along this coastline, and we need it today,' Turner said. 'I want you back at Porthenev Harbour. See if you can borrow a few uniforms to go with you. Gather up as many of the fishermen as you can and interview them again. We need to find a connection between Martin Bennett and Terry Lawrence that goes beyond the obvious. Were they friends? Enemies? Did they ever work together? Any history of bad blood? You know the drill.'

Angove nodded. 'I'm on it, Sarge.'

Glancing over his shoulder at the white tent and the investigators working around it, Turner let out an unsteady breath.

'I'm headed back to HQ,' he said. 'I need to talk to the boss, see if we can release a few officers to patrol the harbour tonight.'

A sudden gust of wind blew up from the beach to whip their clothes and hair.

Angove stared at his superior. 'You think he might strike again?'

Turner's gaze returned to the bloody trail. 'I don't know. But for now, we need to presume that's a given.'

32

Parking on the street of terraced townhouses, Blake switched off the car engine and sat in silence. The news that another body had been found sat like a weight on her chest. It had to be Terry Lawrence. Which meant two out of the four surviving former crew members of the *Persephone* were now dead. Not just dead but brutally butchered, their bodies ripped apart and dumped in the open for all to see. Two down, two to go, Blake thought, as the fine hairs on the back of her neck stood up.

She glanced at the house that she had parked in front of, at the white door and curtained windows. It hadn't taken her long to find the address, which happened to be in Redruth. Derived from the Cornish words "Rhyd-Ruth", meaning "Red Ford" in English, Redruth happened to be the next town over from Wheal Marow, and was located just a few miles inland from both Porthenev and Dead Man's Cove.

Like Wheal Marow, the town was known for its rich history connected to tin mining. Indeed, it was believed Redruth was named after the small stream that ran through it, which, by the fourteenth century, was so discoloured with iron oxide from the tin mines that the water was as red as blood. Today the river ran clear, but blood had been spilled elsewhere, and Blake knew answers were hiding inside the house with the white door.

Flipping open the glove compartment of the car, she took the can of pepper spray and slipped it inside her coat pocket. Not knowing whether she was right or wrong in her assumptions made her nervous. If she was wrong, she would walk away with a red face and no more leads. But if she was right, she was potentially stepping into the path of danger. Again. At the very least, she should have told someone where she was going. But her compulsion to find answers before talking to DS Turner had left her blinkered and impatient.

As she stepped from the car, she sucked in a cold breath. Above her, blue skies were turning grey. She walked up to the house and knocked on the white door. Thirty seconds tick by. She took out her phone and checked the time. 12:47 p.m. It was a weekday, so there was a chance no one was home. She knocked again. A flock of gulls swooped over the street, filling the air with a cacophony of screeches and cries.

Someone was coming to the door. Blake heard the chain lock being engaged. The door opened a few centimetres and the chain pulled tight. A woman in her late forties peered out from the shadows of the foyer. The first thing Blake noticed was how exhausted the woman looked. Dark circles bruised her haunted eyes. Her complexion was pale and drawn, as if the muscles beneath had withered and now the skin was wrapped tightly around the skull, like paper wrapped around a rock. Her lips, thin and colourless, were pressed together in a sharp line, while her lank hair fell lifelessly to her shoulders. Not just tired, Blake thought, but tired of life.

The woman stared coldly. When she spoke, her voice was cracked and brittle. 'Yes? What do you want?'

'Bonnie Thomas? My name is Blake Hollow. I'm a private investigator.' Blake fished out her licence card from her wallet and held it up for the woman to see. 'Could I speak with you for a moment?'

The woman leaned forward slightly, staring cynically at the licence. 'What does a private investigator want with me?'

Blake returned the licence to her wallet. 'I'd like to talk to you about your son, Perran.'

At the mention of the boy's name, an invisible portcullis slammed down between them.

'Why?' she said through clenched teeth.

'Perhaps I could come in and explain.'

'No, I don't think so. You can stay right where you are.'

'That's fine. We can talk right here.'

'My son has been dead for ten years,' Mrs Thomas said. 'Why are you so interested in him now?'

Blake had two choices. She could tell the woman the truth and risk having the door slammed in her face. Or she could make something up and try to get the answers she needed in a more roundabout way. But time was running out, and if there was one thing Blake had learned over the years about a situation such as this, it was that the truth, no matter how dangerous, would get you what you wanted much faster than a lie.

'Mrs Thomas, you must have heard by now about the murder of Martin Bennett,' she said. 'The same Martin Bennett who was on board the *Persephone* the day your son died.'

The suggestion of a cruel smile tugged at the woman's lips. But she remained silent.

Blake continued. 'And if you've heard about Martin Bennett, then you've likely heard about the disappearance of Terry Lawrence, who was also on board the *Persephone* when Perran fell overboard and drowned.' She paused. 'Mrs Thomas, the police have just found another body, which almost certainly belongs to Terry Lawrence. I've come here today because something terrible is happening, and I believe it's connected to the death of your son. So, if I could come in for a minute and talk to you about it, then maybe we can—'

'No.' Fire burned in Mrs Thomas's eyes. She was smiling fully now, but there was no joy there. Only hatred. 'I have nothing to say to you or anyone else for that matter. I don't know what's happening or who is killing those men, but I'll tell you this—I'd like to shake his hand. I'm glad Martin Bennett is dead. And if Terry Lawrence is dead too, then even better. I hope whoever killed them comes after Albert Roskilly and that bastard son of his next. Because they're all responsible for my boy's death.'

'The inquest ruled it was an accidental drowning,' Blake said.

'I don't care what the inquest ruled! And if you believe that you must be a truly awful private investigator.' The woman paused. Grief was welling, threatening to spill over and break her down. Yet somehow she resisted. 'I couldn't even give my boy a proper burial. He's still out there, you know. Floating through the ocean somewhere. I didn't get to kiss his sweet face one last time to say goodbye. So, you'll forgive me if I smile when you tell me those men are dead. Because there's only one thing I want in this world, and I can't have it. The four of them dying will have to do instead.'

Mrs Thomas moved to shut the door. Blake lurched forward.

'Please, Mrs Thomas. If you know something, or if you don't want to talk, at least let me speak to your husband.'

The woman stared at her. There was no emotion in her eyes now, only hardened emptiness. 'Wes hasn't lived here for years. As far as I'm concerned, he's just as guilty as the others. If you must see him, he works at the abattoir, but you'll be wasting your breath. He won't talk to you.' The woman paused, desolation crumpling her face. 'Please, just go. Don't you think I've suffered enough?'

Mrs Thomas shut the door, leaving Blake to stare at its chipped white paint. She stood there for a short while, her shoulders heavy with guilt. Then she returned to her car and pulled out her phone. A quick online search revealed there were three abattoirs in a ten mile radius. If Mrs Thomas wouldn't speak to her, then Blake would make damn sure Mr Wesley Thomas did. Lives depended on it. Starting the engine, she pulled away from the curb and headed towards the first abattoir.

33

Luck was on Blake's side. Wesley Thomas worked at the first abattoir she came to. Croft Meats was located at the end of a private country road flanked by tall hedgerows just a few miles east of Gwithian Towans. A collection of corrugated warehouse-like buildings huddled together on a concrete base. They appeared surprisingly clean, as if recently given a new coat of paint, but the smell of death was everywhere.

Blake had left her Corsa in a visitor's bay in the front facing car park and entered the reception area, where she had been greeted by a polite if somewhat wary receptionist, who had asked her to take a seat while she telephoned the manager and spoke quietly into the receiver. It was 12:57 p.m., just a few minutes away from the lunch hour. Ending the call, the receptionist told Blake that Wesley would be through in a few minutes. Now, Blake waited impatiently, her knee bouncing up and down, a sudden rush of anxiety increasing her heart rate. She tried to shut it out, drawing in a deep breath of air through her nose and expelling it through pursed lips. Even here within the sterile yet sparsely furnished reception area, she was convinced she could smell the coppery aroma of freshly spilled blood.

She was taking a risk coming here. Wesley Thomas was an obvious suspect for the murders, a grieving father who believed his only child's death had not been an accident. A man who had been let down by the justice system, whose marriage had broken apart like a ship crashing on rocks, who could not bury his boy because there was no body to bury. Add to that ten years of bitter resentment, of watching the men he held responsible for killing his son live their lives without recompense, while his own life had slowly fallen into ruin, it would be of no surprise if he had suddenly snapped one day and decided to take matters into his own hands. Now Blake had decided to meet him face to face, without telling anyone where she was, and with no means of protecting herself except for the can of pepper spray inside her left coat pocket. The man worked at an abattoir for God's sake! Hadn't Judy told her Martin Bennett had been hacked to pieces? Surely that spoke of rage and revenge, and of a killer who was used to handling a sharp blade.

Blake had a sudden urge to leave this place and return to her car, to call Rory and tell him all that she had learned. She was about to get to her feet and do exactly that when a pair of double doors to the left of the reception desk opened and Wesley Thomas stepped out.

He was a rough-looking man, weary and unshaven, with short wiry hair streaked with silver, and deep-set eyes that were dark and furtive. He was of average height with broad shoulders and very little paunch for a man in his early fifties. Blake had been expecting him to appear in a blood-drenched apron and carrying a meat cleaver in his hand, but he was dressed in worn blue jeans, a grey T-shirt, and a plaid over shirt. There was some sort of utility belt around his waist. Blake examined it, immediately saw the sheath resting against his right thigh and the hilt of a knife nestled within.

Her heart thudded in her chest as she slowly got to her feet. At least she was meeting him in a public place with at least one witness.

Wesley Thomas glanced at Blake, then leaned in towards the receptionist and muttered inaudible words. The receptionist whispered back and shrugged. Then Wesley was walking towards Blake, his eyes fixed on hers.

Blake propelled herself forward, meeting him halfway. They stood still for a moment, assessing each other. Then she reached for her wallet.

'Wesley Thomas?' she said, removing her licence card. 'My name is Blake Hollow and I'm a private investigator. I'm sorry to disturb your lunch hour, but I need to talk to you.'

Wesley's brow furrowed as he plucked the card from her fingers and carefully examined it. As he returned the card to Blake, she caught the aroma of antibacterial soap mixed with a faint scent of blood on his large and powerful hands.

'Are you sure you're not a journalist pretending to

be a detective?' Wesley's voice was deep and gruff, like that of a man who had just woken up. 'Because I was done talking to journalists years ago.'

'Now Martin Bennett has been identified I don't think it will be long before the press come looking for you again,' Blake said. She tried to keep her expression neutral as the man watched her closely. 'But I can assure you I'm not one of them.'

Wesley glanced over his shoulder at the receptionist, who quickly looked down at her desk. He nodded towards the glass entrance doors. 'Let's talk outside.'

Blake hung back for a second before following him outside to the forecourt. Making sure they were standing in front of the glass entrance door and in full view of the receptionist, Blake cleared her throat.

Wesley spoke before she could. 'So you're here because of what happened to Martin Bennett.' From his shirt pocket he removed a pack of cigarettes, took one out, and lit it. He inhaled deeply then blew the smoke out in a long steady plume.

'That's right.' Blake's gaze flicked down to the sheathed knife on Wesley's belt. 'But I'm also interested in hearing about what you believe happened to your son.'

The cigarette froze in front of Wesley's lips. His eyes narrowed slightly. 'Who hired you?'

'That's not important right now.'

'It is if you want me to talk to you.' Wesley sucked on the cigarette, his eyes never leaving Blake's.

Drawing in a breath, Blake quickly explained to him how she had been hired by the fishermen of Porthenev Harbour, and how an investigation into vandalism had quickly turned into one of murder.

'But I'm not working for them anymore,' she explained.

Wesley frowned. 'So you're here off your own back? I think that's strange.'

'Someone is killing these men in terrible ways, Mr Thomas. Whoever is behind it has to be stopped before he kills again.'

'And you think I can help? That I would be *willing* to help you? You've come to the wrong person if that's the case.' He laughed, snorting smoke through his nose like a dragon.

'Martin Bennett wasn't the only one to die though, was he?' Blake said. 'What about Sharon Bennett? What did she ever do to anyone? And what about her children? They've been orphaned. They'll have to live the rest of their lives knowing how their parents died. Those boys were in the next room when someone broke into their home and strangled their mother to death.'

Wesley nodded, blew smoke through his lips. 'That is unfortunate.'

'I suppose that's one way of putting it.' Blake was aware of the hostility in her voice. She took a breath and let it out. 'Please, Mr Thomas. I just need to ask a few questions then I'll be on my way.'

The man continued to smoke his cigarette. 'How did you find me anyway?'

'A little guesswork,' Blake said. 'And some help from your ex-wife.'

'Bonnie is still my wife. We never divorced, just went our separate ways.' Wesley smiled bitterly. It was an unpleasant smile, full of anger and betrayal. 'What did she tell you about . . . our boy?'

'Nothing. She wouldn't talk to me.'

'Sounds about right. Bonnie was never one for mincing her words.'

More silence. Wesley stared into the distance.

'Have you heard Terry Lawrence has gone missing?' Blake asked, trying again. She decided not to tell him that the police had almost certainly discovered Terry's body; if Wesley was responsible there was a chance he might slip up during their conversation.

'I heard about it,' Wesley said. 'And I suppose you're here because you think what's happening now is connected to what happened to my boy. That the men responsible for killing my son are getting their just deserts. And what? You think I have something to do with it?'

Glancing through the glass door, Blake caught the eye of the receptionist. 'You tell me.'

'You tell me . . .' Wesley repeated, musing over the words. 'If I were the killer, why would I tell you anything?'

'You probably wouldn't.'

'And if I'm a suspect, where are the police right now? Why aren't they here instead of you?'

'Because in all likelihood they haven't discovered the link yet.'

'But you have.' Finishing his cigarette, Wesley walked a few metres alongside the building and came to a halt beside a large rectangular planter box made of stone that contained a selection of depressed looking greenery. He stubbed the cigarette out then returned the spent butt to the packet. Behind the planter box was a row of windows. He peered through one for a moment before turning around and perching on the edge of the stone box.

Blake reluctantly moved up to him. Through the windows she saw groups of workers clustered around tables and eating their lunches. Two men on the nearest table were watching her. One flashed a leery smile and winked.

'Mr Thomas,' she said. 'In all honesty I don't know what leads the police do or do not have. I'm not working with them. But if I found a link between the killings and what happened to your son, they will too. You'll likely be their chief suspect.'

Wesley stared at her. 'Am I yours?'

'I don't know yet. But if you talk to me, tell me what you think happened with your son, then maybe it will give me a clearer idea of what to believe.'

Fishing out another cigarette from the packet, Wesley lit it and took a long drag. Blake remained standing.

'The inquest ruled Perran's death an accident,' Wesley said. 'Me and my wife don't believe that's true. We never have and we never will.'

'Why not?' Blake asked.

The man heaved his large shoulders and frowned, as if trying to make sense of his thoughts and feelings. 'Perran was always a sensitive boy, just like his mother. He was quiet, didn't have many friends. He liked to draw. He was never cut out for a life at sea. But I forced him into it anyway.' He paused. Blake noticed his fingers were trembling slightly. 'I thought working on the boats would toughen him up, like it did to me when I was young.'

'You used to fish on the trawlers?'

'Just like my dad did, and his dad before. A long line of Thomas fishermen that went back generations. Which was why I pushed Perran into it, otherwise that line would have died with me. It's funny. It took the death of my son for me to realise that none of that mattered. So you come from a family of fishermen. Big fucking deal. You could die tomorrow and that's the end of it.'

Blake stared across the car park. Wesley's story was beginning to feel eerily familiar. Hadn't Ewan Jenkin's father done exactly the same thing to his son?

'You know Bonnie blames me more than the other men,' Wesley said. 'Perran was scared, you see. He didn't want to work on the boats anymore. He kept making up excuses for why he couldn't go. Bonnie says if I hadn't marched him down to the harbour that morning Perran would still be alive. That's why she blames me. Why she hates me. The sad thing is she's probably right.'

Ewan's face swam in Blake's mind. 'What was Perran afraid of?'

'It was that son of a bitch Conrad Roskilly,' Wesley said through clenched teeth. 'He was always on Perran's back, making fun of him, pushing him around, trying to belittle him in front of the other men. Perran never told me about it, but Bonnie got it out of him. He'd been so withdrawn, spending more and more time in his room, barely eating a thing at meal times. Most of the time he wouldn't even look at me. Seeing him like that made me mad. He wasn't acting like a man is supposed to. When Bonnie found out about the bullying, I went to Perran and I told him he needed to toughen up. To fight back. How was he going to get anywhere in this world if he let people like Conrad Roskilly walk all over him? He didn't say anything, just sat on his bed nodding like one of those stupid toy dogs you see in the back of people's cars. Then, the next time he was away at sea, he came home with a black eye that was so swollen he couldn't open it. I asked him what happened. He told me he fought back, and all it did was make things worse. He wouldn't speak to me after that. My own son, ignoring me like I was the villain. So I went to see Albert Roskilly. We go way back, so I knew he'd listen to me.'

Blake looked up. 'You and Albert used to crew together?'

'In the early days. We'd been friends at school. Both left without much in the way of qualifications and ended up on the trawlers together. Then Albert met Jan and got her pregnant with Conrad. I met Bonnie a few years later and then came Perran. Me and Albert ended up on different boats, but we stayed friends, right up until . . .' The bitter smile returned, frozen to his lips in a grimace. 'Anyway, I told Albert to keep a tighter rein on Conrad because he was knocking my boy around. Albert said he'd have a word. For a while everything went quiet. Perran's bruises went away. But he didn't seem any happier. And he became even more determined not to go to sea, to the point he started pretending he was sick when clearly he wasn't.' A look of shame spread over Wesley's face. His gaze flicked up at Blake, then down at the ground. 'I'm not proud of what I did the day Perran died. But he was trying it on again, and I was sick of it. I'd fixed the Conrad problem and that boy wasn't showing an ounce of gratitude. So, when it was time for him to leave and he still hadn't got up, I went into his room and I dragged him out of bed by the scruff of his neck. I stood there, made him get dressed. That's when I saw the bruises on his back, when I realised the Conrad problem hadn't gone away at all. Perran had just got better at hiding it.'

Wesley shook his head, then hung it again in shame. 'I made him get on the boat that morning anyway. Took him down there myself and stood on the pier, watching the *Persephone* sail away, knowing that Conrad was still beating my boy. But at that moment, I didn't care. I can admit it to myself now. I didn't care because I was embarrassed. Instead of behaving like a man who could stand up for himself, he was acting like a coward. I couldn't have the other men laughing at me behind my back, shaking their heads, talking about how I hadn't raised my son right. That I'd raised him to be a queer.'

His voice cracked on those last words. Blake watched his shoulders crumple, his head hang lower.

'The last time I saw my son alive, he was staring at me from the stern of the *Persephone* with nothing but hate in his eyes. So, yeah, maybe Bonnie is right. Maybe I am responsible for Perran's death just as much as the others. Probably more.'

Blake's mind was reeling, her emotions fraught and confused by the man sitting before her. Wesley Thomas had knowingly sent his son to sea with his torturer because of outdated, toxic beliefs. Jesus Christ, she thought. It was hard to feel pity for the man despite his obvious grief and guilt. But she tried.

'Wesley, why are you so convinced Perran's death was not an accident?'

He looked up. 'Isn't it obvious?'

'I'm not so sure. If he was as depressed and frightened as you described then maybe—'

'My son didn't kill himself, if that's what you're thinking.' Wesley was glaring at her. 'He didn't jump overboard. Conrad killed him. Accident or not, he killed him, and his bastard father covered it up.'

'Do you have evidence of this?'

'Of course I bloody don't! Do you think if there was evidence the inquest would have ruled his death an accident? All I know is that what Albert told me doesn't make sense. He said Perran must have got up in the night, gone wandering in the dark, and fallen overboard. Because when they woke up in the morning, he was gone. No trace of him left.'

'Isn't that possible?' Blake asked.

'Have you been on board any of the trawlers down at Porthenev?'

Blake said that she had.

'Then you know how small and cramped the sleeping quarters are. You're practically sleeping on top of each other. You can't breathe without waking someone else up. So you're telling me that Perran was able to get out of bed and out of the sleeping quarters without waking a single member of the crew?'

'Maybe they were all heavy sleepers.'

'I know for a fact Albert Roskilly isn't. I crewed with him, remember? He's always had trouble sleeping, that one. So no, I don't believe his bullshit story. I don't believe my son got up in the night to piss over the side so as not to wake the others. I don't believe that at all. They killed my boy and they dumped his body out at sea. Evidence or not, that's the truth.'

Blake's gaze moved to the window of the staffroom. The men that had been watching her had lost interest and were now busy demolishing sandwiches.

'I assume you confronted Albert and Conrad?' she said.

Wesley smiled cruelly. 'I beat Conrad nearly half to death. I would have killed him too if Albert hadn't stopped me. He told me if I ever laid a finger on his son, he would end my life. You can imagine how I reacted. Later that evening, I got a visit from the police. They warned me to stay away from the Roskillys, told me I should be grateful that Conrad didn't want to press charges. No one would listen to me and my wife. Our accusations fell on deaf ears. Then the inquest came and it was all over. Accidental death. It broke Bonnie. She left me and Porthenev soon after. A few months later I left too. Seeing the Roskillys walk around every day as if they owned the town made me want to hurt them.' He paused, meeting Blake's gaze. 'And now someone is killing the men who killed my son, picking them off one by one, saving the best for last. And you think it's me. Which means you're either incredibly brave or incredibly stupid to come here alone.'

Wesley stood, his eyes growing as dark and fathomless as tar pits. Blake felt a chill run through her. Her left hand slipped inside her pocket and gripped the can of pepper spray.

'Is it you?' she asked. 'Are you killing these men?'

He smiled. 'I wish it was. I really do. But I haven't

got the strength in me these days. Even the anger has petered out. Oh, it's still there burning away under the surface, but it's not out of control like it used to be.' He extinguished the cigarette, returned the stub to the packet. 'Your next question will be, did I hire someone to do the dirty work for me?'

Blake watched him carefully. 'Did you?'

Wesley surprised her by laughing. 'You think I could afford to hire a hitman on my salary? As if there even is such a thing in Cornwall. I can barely cover my rent, let alone pay someone to kill Martin Bennett or the rest of them.'

'What about your wife?'

'Bonnie works in a bakery. She's no better off than I am. Now, if there isn't anything else, I've lost half my lunch break and I'm hungry.'

Blake was quiet. She wanted to believe Wesley Thomas was telling the truth, but she couldn't be certain.

'One last question, if you don't mind,' she said. 'Where were you the night Martin Bennett disappeared?'

Wesley turned to face her. 'I was home alone.'

'And on Saturday night, when Terry Lawrence disappeared?'

'The same again. If you'd like to question my dog, he can verify it.'

He brushed past her, bringing with him the faint aroma of freshly slaughtered livestock. Then he was heading towards the glass entrance door.

Blake called after him. 'If you're not killing these men and you didn't hire someone else to do it for you, then who is?'

Wesley paused, the door half open.

'I have no idea,' he said. 'But if you find out who it is, do me a favour and be sure to thank them.'

'You know I have to tell the police everything I've learned. They'll come for you.'

Wesley smiled one last time. 'Let them.'

Then he was gone, disappearing through the reception door, back inside the abattoir.

Blake was paralysed with indecision. She watched the door swing shut with a soft click, then her eyes returned to the staffroom window, distracted by sudden movement. But whoever had been standing there, watching her, had gone.

Was Wesley Thomas responsible for the killings? How could it not be him? Yet Blake's instincts said no. His wife, then? Could a woman in her late forties be capable of such brutal, violent murder? When Blake had met Bonnie earlier that morning, she had thought the woman too thin and weak to possess the physical strength required to kill a man twice her size. Wesley on the other hand . . .

Blake was confused. She had to speak to Rory. Even better, Detective Sergeant Turner. But whether Wesley was guilty or not, the killer was still out there, and with Martin Bennett and Terry Lawrence dead, it was only a matter of time before he came for the Roskillys. Blake had to warn them.

Heading for her car, she quickly devised a plan. She would go to the harbour first, speak to Albert and Conrad. Then she would go to the police, perhaps even convince the men to come with her for their own protection. Because Wesley Thomas had been right about one thing. Whoever was killing the crew of the *Persephone* was saving the best, or worst, until last. Getting in her car, Blake shut the door, inserted the key into the ignition, and started the engine. She paused, staring up at the abattoir through the windscreen. Judy had told Blake that Martin Bennett had been ripped apart, that his corpse had been reduced to a carcass hanging in a butcher's window.

Pulling her phone from her jeans pocket, Blake found Rory's number and tapped the call button. She would still go to the harbour and warn the Roskillys, but first she had a duty to pass on everything she had learned. Because unlike Wesley Thomas, she didn't want any more blood on her hands.

34

Mason Kitto stood frozen in the centre of the staffroom, his attention drawn to the windows and the two figures outside. Wesley Thomas was talking to a woman Mason had not seen in the flesh before but had recognised almost instantly. It was the private investigator from the newspapers. Blake Hollow. She had first come to Mason's attention shortly after the arrest of the serial killer Dennis Stott, whom Mason greatly admired. A murderer of eighteen women, Stott had gone about his business undetected for years, until the private investigator had finally caught up with him. What was she doing here?

There could only be one answer. She was close to uncovering Mason's identity, thereby putting an end to his retribution. Panic washed over him. How did she find him? Had he been foolish enough to leave a trace of incriminating evidence behind? He was sure he hadn't. If he had been that stupid, it wouldn't be just a lone private investigator standing outside right now. It would be the full force of the law. Which meant Hollow must have found another way, another thread that had led her right to him.

Mason drew closer to the window, flames of anger igniting inside his chest. The private investigator was talking to Wesley. That meant the thread she had pulled on was the death of Wesley's son. How had she learned about it so quickly when the police had not? Mason narrowed his eyes. The police were smart. Clearly, Blake Hollow was smarter. And she was standing right outside, just metres away from him.

Panic returned. He had to do something. To move quickly before she put an end to it all.

Voices from behind him broke his concentration.

'Hey Dolittle. What's the matter? Missing your boyfriend?'

'Don't worry, he'll be back soon. Why don't you go to the toilets and wank over him like you always do? Or will Mummy get jealous?'

Laughter ricocheted around the room. Mason clenched his fists. Mickey and George were up to their usual tricks again. He shut them out, pictured his hands wrapped around their necks, crushing their windpipes, squeezing until their eyes burst inside their sockets.

He stepped forward until he loomed in front of the window. Wesley was walking away from the woman, heading back inside. She was going to leave at any moment.

Turning on his heels, Mason hurried from the room. Mickey and George's taunts trailed behind him. When this was all over, he would come for those two. He would kill them slowly, pull them apart piece by piece, until they begged him for a quick death, which they would be denied. Heading down the dingy corridor, he took a right and stopped in front of the abattoir manager's office. He rapped on the door with a great fist and waited impatiently to be called in. When the invitation came, he threw the door open and stepped inside.

Colin Wharton was a thin, wiry man with rat-like features and unfriendly eyes. He sat behind his desk with his back to the wall and his gaze fixed firmly on his computer screen.

'Yes, what is it?' he said, without looking up.

Mason paused, then said, 'My mother is sick. I need to go home.'

His voice sounded rusty, unused.

Colin Wharton continued to type in silence. Finally, he glanced up. A startled look passed over his face as he took in the hulking figure standing in front of his desk. Then, as if remembering his position of authority, his expression hardened.

'What's wrong with her?' he asked.

Why was Wharton asking questions? If Mason had told him his mother was sick, then Wharton should have granted him immediate leave, with a wish that his mother recovered soon. Yet the manager was sitting behind his desk, daring to question the validity of Mason's request. It left Mason flustered.

'She's . . .' he began.

'Yes?'

His face was heating up. He could feel his cheeks turning red. 'She's sick.'

Wharton picked up a pen and tapped it impatiently on the desk. 'We've already established that, Mason. So, unless your mother is seriously ill, as in rushed-to-hospital ill or on-her-deathbed ill, I'm afraid you'll have to wait until the end of your shift. We're short-staffed today, as you know, so we need all hands on deck.'

Wharton attempted a withering stare, which fell flat, then returned his attention to the computer screen.

Mason was paralysed, his feet cemented to the ground. Blake Hollow was getting away. This impotent, pathetic excuse of a man was allowing it to happen. Panic took hold of him. He glanced around the windowless room. He had to do something. Now.

Freeing his feet, he stepped towards the desk. Wharton looked up.

'My mother is seriously ill,' Mason said. 'I need to take her to the hospital.'

Wharton leaned back in his chair and crossed his arms over his stomach.

'Oh, come on. If that were true, you would have said so in the first place. Please don't lie to me, Mason. You're a hard worker, but I won't stand being lied to.'

His hands were curling into tight balls. Fear was subsiding, anger burning through his veins like rivers of lava. The sudden urge to commit violence was all-encompassing. Mason took another step forward, until he felt the front of the desk pressing into his knees.

'What do you think you're doing?' Wharton said.

The smug tone of his voice was gone, replaced by wariness.

'I have to leave,' Mason said. 'Now.'

'And I said no. I'm sorry, but if you choose to leave now without my consent that's your job finished. Do you understand? You're replaceable, Mason. All of you are.'

Slowly, Mason unfurled his fists and placed his hands on the desk surface. He leaned forward, until his face was inches from Wharton's. His vision was turning red with rage. He wanted to tear the man's head from his shoulders. To put fingers inside Wharton's mouth and tear off his jaw with his bare hands. But to do so would be the end of all things. Mason would be arrested, his task left incomplete.

'Well done,' Wharton said, fear never leaving his eyes. 'You just got yourself fired. Now leave before I call the police.'

Mason smiled. Straightened up. Without taking his eyes off Wharton, he backed away to the door, then turned and left the room. He hurried along the corridor, until he reached a row of lockers. Finding his own, he opened it and removed a set of keys and a black sports bag. Crouching down, he unzipped the bag and stared at the glistening blade of the machete that lay inside. Then he was slinging the bag over his shoulder and marching towards the exit.

As he stepped outside, he caught a glimpse of Blake Hollow driving away in a battered blue Corsa. Mason hurried towards his white minivan that was rusting in places and covered in dirt. Climbing inside, he started the engine, performed a U-turn, then followed after the private investigator. The blue

Corsa was just visible in the distance, reaching the end of the private road then taking a right. As Croft Meats shrank in Mason's rear view mirror, he suddenly became aware that losing his job meant not seeing Wesley on a daily basis. His heart fractured. It would be worth it, he told himself. Because once Wesley had seen what Mason had done for him, he would take Mason into his arms and thank him for doing the work that Wesley was incapable of doing himself. He would thank Mason and he would call him 'Son'. Mason would call him 'Father'. He would finally have a parent who, despite his failings, would love him unconditionally. Who wouldn't hurt him like his biological father had done. And Mason wouldn't have to hurt him back.

The white minivan sped up, shortening the distance between it and the private investigator.

35

Adrenaline coursed through Blake's veins as she stepped from her car and raced towards Porthenev Harbour. There were a few workers around, all pale faced and muttering nervously to each other. As Blake hurried past a trio of men gathered on the quayside, she caught the words "body" and "Towans". So, word had reached this group of already terrified fishermen. And they were right to be afraid. But only if they had once been crew members of the *Persephone*.

Moving on, Blake conducted a quick sweep of the harbour interior. The *Laura-Lynn* was still resting at the top of the slipway, the large hole punched in its side on full display. The *Seraphine* was still docked in the water below the north pier. There was no sign of Albert or Conrad, and no one had seen them. A sinking feeling pulled at Blake's stomach as she headed for the harbourmaster's office and entered without knocking. Jasper Rowe was behind his desk.

He glanced up as Blake came towards him. His face was pallid and he looked exhausted, as if he had barely slept all night.

'Blake,' he said. 'I wasn't expecting to see you today.'

Blake wasted no time. 'Albert and Conrad Roskilly. When did you last see them?'

The harbourmaster shook his head. 'I was here Saturday and saw Albert then. As for Conrad, I haven't seen him since last Friday.' His expression turned grave. 'I suppose you've already heard about the body at Gwithian Towans. And the police showed up at Terry Lawrence's house about an hour ago. I suppose that means . . .'

'I know,' Blake said. She was still standing in front of his desk, unwilling to sit down for fear of wasting precious seconds. She had called Rory on the journey to Porthenev, but had been redirected to his voicemail. Leaving a message, she had next called the police station at Truro to be told Detective Sergeant Turner was unavailable. She asked that he call her as a matter of urgency. So far, her phone had remained stubbornly silent, both detectives clearly preoccupied with the murder of Terry Lawrence.

'I'm sorry about Terry,' she said. 'But right now I need to find Albert and Conrad. I think they might be next.'

Jasper's eyes widened. 'Why would you think that? What's happening?'

Blake fixed the harbourmaster with a steely gaze. 'Why didn't you tell me about what happened to Perran Thomas on the *Persephone*. I asked you to tell me anything you knew, no matter how unimportant it might seem. You should have mentioned it.'

Confusion clouded Jasper's eyes. 'Perran Thomas? But that was years ago. How is that relevant now?'

'Oh, it's very relevant. Someone is killing off the former crew members, one by one. First Martin Bennett, then Terry Lawrence. Which leaves Albert and Conrad. I need their addresses and phone numbers now, Jasper.'

The little colour remaining in Jasper's face slowly drained away. He opened his mouth then shut it again. Locating a small black box on his desk, he opened the lid with a trembling hand. Inside was an old-fashioned index card system containing all of the fishermen's contact details, which he began to thumb through.

As Blake waited, she tapped the carpet with her right foot and chewed her lower lip, hoping that she was right about her theory, that she could save the men before death came for them.

Jasper removed two of the index cards and glanced up at Blake. 'Here they are. I'll write them down for you.'

'No time for that.' Blake plucked the cards from his hand, placed them on the desk, and took photographs of the men's details with her phone camera. She thanked Jasper, who struggled to hold her gaze. 'If either of them turn up here before I can get to them, you keep them here and you call me right away.'

'Will do. And Blake? I'm sorry I didn't mention Perran Thomas. It honestly didn't cross my mind.'

Blake tried to offer him a sympathetic smile, but

found she couldn't. Instead, she turned and hurried from the harbourmaster's office, then raced towards the car park. Sliding to a halt, she opened the map application on her phone and, one by one, typed in Albert and Conrad Roskilly's addresses.

Conrad's home was closest, just a few streets up the hill to the right. Albert lived at the top. Leaving her car behind, Blake got moving. If Conrad refused to listen to her, which was entirely possible thanks to his arrogance, she would have to abandon him and go straight to Albert, who would surely be able to convince his son that his life was in danger. If Wesley Thomas really was the killer, which Blake was still unsure about, she would have time to get to the men before he did.

And if he wasn't the killer?

Blake had to hope that either Rory or Turner called her back, sooner rather than later. She had already risked her life more times than she cared for, and had paid the price for it as well. It was time to let the police detectives do their job, just as soon as she got the men to safety.

36

Turning onto Bocox road, Blake quickly located Conrad's home and knocked urgently on the door. She waited, aware that her breathing was thin and hurried. When there was no answer, she knocked again and tried calling Conrad's phone. The call went straight to voicemail. The door remained firmly closed. Panic fluttered in Blake's chest. Pressing her ear to the front door, she listened but heard nothing. Conrad was not at sea and hadn't shown his face at the harbour since last week. Perhaps he was visiting a friend or his parents.

Blake glanced at the other houses in the street, wondering if one of his neighbours might be able to provide her with Conrad's location. But time was running out. A sudden thought struck her, sending a chill through her body. If Wesley Thomas was the killer, had he abducted Conrad before Blake had even shown up at the abattoir?

She stepped back into the road and peered up at

the house. All of the curtains were open. There were no signs of movement.

Turning on her heels, she left the street and continued climbing the hill. Perhaps she would have better luck tracking down Conrad's father. But Albert wasn't answering his mobile phone either, and when Blake tried his landline, it rang until the automated voice of the answer machine was triggered. There was another number to try on Albert's contacts card, a number listed as "in case of emergency". Blake punched the numbers into the keypad and hit the call button. The phone rang and rang. Finally, a recorded message played. 'Hi this is Jan. I can't take your call right now, but if you leave your name and number, I'll get back to you.'

Blake hung up, quickened her pace. The gradient of the hill was steep, making her thighs burn and her lungs heave. Neither Conrad, Albert, or Albert's wife Jan had picked up. Something was wrong. Blake felt it like a fist closing around her heart.

Finally, she reached the crest of the hill. She was panting hard and beads of sweat had formed on her forehead and the back of her neck. Albert Roskilly's home was located on St Michael's Street, the entrance of which lay up ahead on the right. Another road on Blake's left led to the housing estate where both Ewan Jenkin and Terry Lawrence resided. Blake wondered if a police car was still parked outside Terry Lawrence's home, if officers were still inside, comforting his shell-shocked wife. She turned her head, eyes returning to the mouth of Albert Roskilly's street.

What was she doing? Had she not learned

anything from her encounter with Dennis Stott? Or the Trezise case at Saltwater House last year? On both occasions she had put her life at risk. On both occasions she had encountered violent and depraved individuals who had wanted to hurt her, who had succeeded even if they hadn't killed her. Was she really about to put herself in a situation where that could happen again?

If police officers were still present at Terry Lawrence's house, wouldn't it be better to go there now and ask for their help? But what if she were raising a false alarm? What if by doing so she only made matters worse for Terry's grieving and distraught wife?

Blake swore under her breath. She continued on, entering St Michael's Street and checking Albert Roskilly's address on her phone. A minute later, she stood in front of a modern looking, two-storey, semi-detached house with a tidy front garden, where daffodils and snowdrops were in full bloom. The front door of the house was ajar. Blake stared at it. Her mouth ran dry.

Opening the gate, she quietly advanced along the garden path until she reached the door. Slipping her hand inside her left coat pocket, she removed the can of pepper spray and rested her index finger on top of the nozzle. With her other hand, she pushed the door open wider.

'Hello? Albert? It's Blake Hollow.'

Silence. A smell, thick and metallic, that permeated the air and invaded her senses.

'Mrs Roskilly? Hello?'

Nothing. Only the smell and the pounding of

Blake's heart. She pushed the door open to its fullest extent. Then stepped inside.

The smell grew stronger, more pungent, reaching down into Blake's stomach. The hallway was dimly lit, but she could make out family photographs hanging on the walls, a side table with a telephone on top, and a set of carpeted stairs ascending into darkness on the left.

Blake was about to call out again when, from an open doorway on the right, she heard a strangled whimper. Her hands trembling, she rounded the corner and entered the living room.

A middle-aged woman was lying in a pool of blood in the centre of the room, next to an upturned coffee table. Her floral print dress was soaked scarlet and had ridden up, exposing her bloodied thighs. Her hands clutched her stomach. She peered up at Blake with glassy eyes. A moan escaped her lips.

Slipping the pepper spray back inside her pocket, Blake rushed forwards and dropped to her knees. The woman had lost a lot of blood, which appeared to be flowing from beneath her hands.

'Mrs Roskilly?' Blake said, with a gasp. 'It's going to be okay.'

She scrabbled for her phone, dropped it in the woman's blood, then scooped it up again and dialled 999, asking for an ambulance. With the phone pressed between her ear and shoulder, she gently eased the woman's hands away from her stomach and saw a ragged puncture wound through a tear in her dress. The wound was clean, no weapon still inside her. An emergency call handler came on the line. As Blake returned Mrs Roskilly's hands to the wound and pressed down firmly, she answered the handler's questions quickly.

Mrs Roskilly writhed and moaned beneath her.

'Please,' she said, as fresh blood oozed.

'Is there somewhere you can wash your hands?' the call handler asked. 'We don't want to infect the wound.'

Blake shook her head. 'She's losing a lot of blood. I can't leave her.'

'Then we need a clean cloth or towel to apply pressure with. An ambulance is on the way, but we need to get the blood clotting as soon as possible.'

Blake's gaze swung wildly about the room. Finding nothing, she removed her coat, then her pullover, and rolled it into a tight ball. Removing Mrs Roskilly's hands again, Blake pressed the pullover tightly over the wound.

The woman wailed in agony. Her clammy skin turned whiter.

'I'm sorry,' Blake said. 'But we have to stop this bleeding.'

'The ambulance is five minutes away,' the call handler said. 'Keep applying as much pressure as you can.'

Five minutes. Blake wondered if the woman would last that long.

The call handler asked another question, but Blake didn't hear it. Because suddenly Albert's wife was reaching up to weakly grasp her arm.

'He . . . took him,' Mrs Roskilly croaked, her words slurring as if she were drunk. 'He took my Albert.'

Blake leaned in closer and saw blind terror in the woman's eyes.

'Who took him?' she asked. She could already feel blood seeping through the pullover to wet her skin.

'Hello?' the call handler said. 'Can you hear me?'

Mrs Roskilly drew in a ragged breath.

'Who took him?' Blake repeated.

And then the woman was shrieking hysterically. 'A giant! A giant broke into our home and took my Albert!'

Blake stared in horror. Blood ran between her fingers as the call handler spoke in her ear, while Mrs Roskilly continued to scream.

37

Thirty minutes later, the police had cordoned off the street and were busy patrolling the crime scene while shocked and concerned neighbours gathered in growing numbers. Paramedics had come and gone, stabilising Mrs Roskilly as best as they could before hurrying her into the back of an ambulance and hurtling away to Royal Cornwall Hospital in Truro. The Crime Scene Investigation unit was on its way. Turner and Angove had arrived on scene two minutes ago and were now standing in front of the Roskilly house with Blake, whose clothing was soaked with Jan Roskilly's blood. One of the paramedics had given her antiseptic wipes, which she had used to remove the blood from her hands, but there were still scarlet coloured crusts beneath her fingernails.

Turner did not look happy to see her.

'How are you?' he asked. 'Are you hurt?'

Blake shook her head, gave Rory a brief glance. He stared back, worry lining his brow.

'I'm fine,' she told Turner. 'A little shaken but fine.'

She looked down at her hands, then at her stained clothes. It never ceased to shock her how much blood could come out of a human being.

'I'm glad you're okay,' Turner said. 'What I'm not happy about is why you're here in the first place. Did you not receive my message? To stay out of police business? This case is already complex enough without civilian interference.'

Blake glared at him. 'It's not my fault that our two individual cases happened to cross paths. And thank goodness I *was* here or you'd be dealing with four dead bodies instead of three.'

Turner's expression froze. 'How did you . . .'

He shot an accusatory glance at Rory, who quickly held up his hands in defence.

'It wasn't me, Sarge. I swear.'

'Word travels fast in these parts, Detective Sergeant,' Blake said. 'You've lived here long enough to know that by now.'

Turner relented, giving a slow nod. 'I suppose I can't argue with you there. And yes, I'm glad you were there to save Mrs Roskilly. Although I'm not sure if she's out of the woods just yet.'

'I suppose we'll have to wait and see.'

'What were you doing here, anyway?'

More people had gathered at the police cordons. Word truly did travel fast in Cornwall, especially in a close-knit community like Porthenev. It wouldn't be long before the press arrived. Then the circus would really begin.

Blake stared at Turner, knowing his bad mood

was about to get worse. 'Before I tell you, I need to ask you a question. The body found at Gwithian Towans, is it Terry Lawrence?'

A startled look passed between the two detectives, confirming Blake's suspicion.

'Then this is everything I know,' she said.

Drawing in a breath, she told Turner about the alleged accidental death of eighteen-year-old Perran Thomas, ten years ago on board Albert Roskilly's trawler, the *Persephone*. She told him that, excluding Sharon Bennett, Turner's murder victims were both former crew members of the *Persephone*, which left only Albert and Conrad Roskilly alive and very likely next to die. Finally, she told him about her encounter with Wesley Thomas, who was highly skilled with a butcher's knife but denied any involvement in the murders.

As she told Turner all these things, the creases on his forehead and the lines around his eyes grew like fissures. He looked deeply troubled, almost angry.

'So, you're telling me,' he said, 'that you confronted your chief suspect, this Wesley Thomas, alone and unarmed?'

Blake smiled wryly. 'As a mere civilian, it would be against the law for me to be armed, Detective Sergeant.' There was no need for Turner to hear about her can of pepper spray; with the mood he was in, he was likely to charge her with possession of an illegal weapon. 'Anyway, I met him at his place of work, in front of plenty of witnesses.'

Turner stared at her. 'That's quite a theory. Do you have any hard evidence to back up your claim?'

'Not yet. But I would say there's enough circumstantial evidence to warrant further investigation. Wouldn't you?'

'Perhaps,' Turner replied. 'Angove, get out your notebook and pen. Ms Hollow is going to give you the contact details for Mr and Mrs Thomas.'

Rory did as he was told. Blake took out her phone and relayed the information. When she was done, she slipped the phone back inside her trouser pocket, got caught off guard by the blood again, then stared at Turner.

'There's one more thing. After speaking to Jan Roskilly, I'm not sure Wesley Thomas is the killer.'

The detective sergeant stifled a laugh. He suddenly looked exhausted. Blake couldn't blame him. Juggling three homicides, an attempted murder and a probable fourth victim in the shape of the missing Albert Roskilly, while tied down by bureaucracy and red tape, did not sound like a fun day at work. Blake decided to treat Turner more gently.

'So you're telling me,' he said, 'that even though you believe avenging the death of Perran Thomas is the motivation behind these killings, and even though he fits the suspect profile perfectly, that Wesley Thomas, father of Perran Thomas, is not responsible?'

'I know I sound insane,' Blake said. 'But Jan Roskilly told me she was attacked by a giant. That was the exact word she used. A giant.'

'She's clearly in a state of shock.'

'Possibly. But she said a giant broke into her home and took her husband. What if she was referring to someone very tall and powerful? I've met Wesley Thomas. He's five foot nine at most. He's in good shape for a man in his early fifties but he's by no means a giant. Far from it in fact. And Albert Roskilly is no fading flower. I don't believe Thomas could have overpowered him so easily.'

'So they hired someone to do the dirty work for them,' Turner said.

'I thought the exact same thing. But Wesley Thomas works at an abattoir and Bonnie Thomas works in a bakery. Both minimum wage jobs. Where on earth would they get the money to hire a professional killer, if such a person even exists in Cornwall? And why take ten years to do it?'

Turner was quiet. Next to him, Rory frowned and gave Blake a confused look.

'None of it makes sense,' Blake said. 'But isn't it worth looking into? Even if it's just to rule it out.'

At last, Turner spoke. 'Rory, get someone to give you a lift up to Royal Cornwall and check on Mrs Roskilly. If she's up to it, see what she has to say about this giant. I'm going to collect the Thomases and bring them into HQ for questioning. Let's see what *they* have to say.'

Good, Blake thought. At last Turner was listening to her. 'What do you want me to do?'

He smiled. 'You? I would like for you to go home. I'm grateful for the information, and if it leads somewhere, I'll make sure people know where it came from. But in the meantime, this is police business. As far as I'm aware, you were hired to find out who sabotaged the harbour, not to entangle yourself in an active murder investigation.'

For once, Blake could not disagree with him. She realised she still had not mentioned Ewan Jenkin's role in the sabotage down at the harbour, but decided it could wait. 'Fine. I need to get out of these clothes anyway. But I'll wait for the Crime Scene Investigators. They'll want to take my prints for elimination.'

'No need,' Turner said. 'We already have your prints on file from the last time you showed up at one of my crime scenes. Go home, Blake.'

He heaved his shoulders as he walked away, then stopped in the near distance to talk to a uniformed officer. Rory glanced around, searching for a colleague he could ask to give him a lift to the hospital.

Blake stared at him. 'You need a ride? I can drop you off on my way home.'

'I'm not sure that's a good idea,' Rory said.

'Then enjoy the walk. It should only take you three or four hours.'

Turner had finished talking and was now signing out of the crime scene. Blake watched him head down the street.

Rory sighed. 'Okay, fine. Just don't tell Turner.'

Despite the blood and the horror of the day, Blake managed to smile. 'The only thing I'd tell Turner right now is to learn some damn manners.'

38

Familiar hospital smells swam around Blake as she shifted position on the uncomfortable plastic chair in the waiting area of the Accident and Emergency department. There were other people here, some old, some young, some injured or seriously ill. A few seats along from Blake, a toddler was sobbing on his mother's lap, his complexion both pale and blotchy. The reception desk was up ahead, where two poker-faced receptionists sat and a nurse in blue scrubs was busy filling in paperwork.

Blake had been here for almost four hours. After giving Rory a lift, she should have gone home to shower off the blood and wash it out of her clothes. But no matter what Detective Sergeant Turner thought, Blake was involved now, and she wanted to help see it through to the end if she could. At first, Rory had protested at her presence, saying he didn't need or want a chaperone. What he really meant, Blake thought, was that he didn't want her causing any more tension between him and Turner. She had simply shrugged and told him it was a free country, and she could sit where she pleased. But as the hours ticked by while Rory waited to hear from the doctors about Jan Roskilly, he gradually relaxed and appeared almost grateful for the company. Ten minutes ago, one of the nurses had informed Rory that Albert's wife was now out of surgery and stable, and that the doctor had reluctantly allowed Rory to ask the woman a few questions.

'Five minutes and you're out,' the nurse had said. 'Mrs Roskilly is still very fragile.'

Tapping her foot on the floor, Blake tried to shut out the moans and cries of the A&E waiting room. She wondered if Rory was getting anywhere with his questions, if the woman was indeed in any sound state to be answering them. The only reason the doctor had agreed to the short interview was because of the life or death nature of the situation. But Jan Roskilly would be drowsy from the surgery and the painkillers they would have given her. She may have even been sedated.

A wave of frustration washed over Blake. If only she had the authority and resources that the police force had access to she would be out there right now, tracking down Conrad Roskilly, perhaps even rescuing Albert before he became another mutilated corpse dumped on a beach. But Turner was right. Despite Blake's private investigator licence, she was still just a civilian, which meant there was only so much she could do within the confines of the law.

That's why you investigate cheating spouses and insurance fraud, she thought. Not murder.

Her phone buzzed in her hand. Judy was calling.

'I heard what happened. Are you okay?' Judy's voice was tense with worry.

Standing, Blake walked away from the chairs and towards the entrance doors. 'I'm fine. Just a little shell-shocked.'

People were staring. Rory had given Blake his jacket to wear, but it failed to cover all of the blood stains, especially the ones on her jeans. The glass entrance doors slid open and Blake stepped out into the cold. It was just past five p.m. The sun was sinking, searing the steel sky with red flames.

'Thank God you were there,' Judy said. 'Or that would have been body number four.'

'Body number four is still very much a possibility. The killer took Albert Roskilly. His son Conrad's also missing.'

'Bloody hell.'

People milled in and out through the doors. A few smokers huddled to one side, staring listlessly into space. A blast of a siren startled the air as an ambulance hurtled away from the forecourt, its blue lights spinning and flashing.

'Why are you at the hospital?' Judy said, suddenly alarmed. 'I thought you said you were fine.'

'I am. I gave Rory a lift and decided to wait with him. He's talking to Jan Roskilly now. She's the only one to survive so far. Rory's hoping she can describe her attacker.'

'Jesus, this is why I stick to the farming news. Rod told me the police have taken in a couple of suspects for questioning.'

The Thomases, Blake thought. One day, that

illegal police scanner was going to get the staff of *The Cornish Press* into serious trouble.

'I heard that too. But I have a feeling the real killer is still out there.'

'Blake, you're not thinking of going after him, are you? It's just that after everything that happened with Dennis Stott—you almost died.'

Shivering in the cold, Blake turned and peered through the glass double doors.

'Don't worry. I've learned my lesson.'

'Are you sure about that?' Judy fell silent for a moment. 'Anyway, I just wanted to check in with you, make sure you're not hurt. Oh, and Rod says he wants to interview you when you're up to it. A "Local Private Eye Saves the Day Again" type headline.'

Blake laughed. She was surprised by the tiredness in her own voice. 'Yeah, I don't think so.'

'That's what I told him you'd say.'

At the far end of the waiting area, a pair of double doors swung open and Rory came walking out. His brow was furrowed and his eyes were troubled. Blake felt an old, familiar spark. But it was fleeting, quickly put out. She stepped forward and the entrance door slid open. The pitiful sounds of the sick and injured swarmed towards her.

'I've got to go,' she told Judy. 'Rory's back. I don't want him to think I'm leaking information from an active investigation to the press.'

Rory had spotted her and was making his way over.

'How very responsible of you,' Judy said, with a smile. 'Call me tomorrow, okay?'

'I will.'

'I love you, Blake Hollow.'

'Love you too.'

Blake hung up as Rory reached her.

'Your mum?' he asked.

'She's worried. You know how she gets.' Blake paused. 'How is Mrs Roskilly?'

'She'll live because of you.'

'I'm not the one who sewed her back up.'

'No, but the doctors wouldn't have been able to do that if you hadn't got to her in time. Credit where credit's due, Blake.'

Blake shrugged.

'As for Mrs Roskilly, she hasn't said much so far,' Rory continued. 'I think the doctors have got her on the good stuff. She does, however, want to see you.'

'Me? What for?'

'To thank you. If Turner was here he probably wouldn't allow it. But he's not. Besides, maybe having another woman in the room will make it easier for her to talk. But I'm asking the questions, Blake. This is still police business.'

Blake saluted him. 'Yes, Detective Constable. Understood.'

Rory turned on his heels. 'Well, come on then. Before the nurse comes back and throws us out.'

∽

They walked along a quiet corridor, heels squeaking on the recently polished floor. Halfway along, they stopped outside a private room, where a male uniformed officer sat on a plastic chair. He stood as they arrived, gave Rory a nod and Blake a wary look.

'She's with me,' Rory explained. 'If the nurse comes, keep her distracted for a couple of minutes.'

The officer nodded again and resumed his position on the chair.

Rory opened the door, then stared at Blake. 'Remember what I said. I ask the questions.'

She followed him inside, shutting the door behind her.

The hospital bed in which Jan Roskilly lay was the centrepiece of the clinical-looking room. Next to it, a machine attached to an IV pole flashed and beeped, while a bag containing sugary liquid dispensed a dose of painkiller via a cannula inserted into the back of the patient's hand. The window blinds had been pulled down, and the overhead fluorescent lighting switched off in favour of a small lamp perched on the bedside table. A chair had been positioned on the other side of the bed, while two more were stacked in the corner.

Jan Roskilly lay on her back with her head propped up by pillows and the bed sheets pulled up to her neck. She was conscious. Her eyes, which were glazed and sluggish, drifted in their sockets and found Blake. A crinkle appeared on her forehead. Her lips quivered.

'Mrs Roskilly, this is Blake Hollow,' Rory said softly. 'The one who found you.'

He hung back a little as Blake stepped forward.

Tears slipped from the woman's left eye as she slowly lifted her arm and reached out a hand.

Blake glanced over her shoulder at Rory then awkwardly grasped it.

'Thank you,' Mrs Roskilly said in a cracked voice. The effort to speak was clearly great.

'How are you feeling?' Blake asked. Still holding the woman's hand, she sat down on the chair next to the bed.

Mrs Roskilly did not answer. More tears squeezed from her eyes. She opened her mouth and drew in a shuddering breath.

'He took my Albert,' she moaned. 'Why did he take him?'

Blake glanced back at Rory, who shot her a warning look.

'I don't know,' she said gently. 'But the police are doing everything in their power to find your husband.'

She pulled a tissue from the box on the bedside table and used it to dab Mrs Roskilly's eyes.

'You're not with the police, are you? You're the private investigator my husband hired. Did you find out who tried to sink his boat?'

Rory, who remained standing, cleared his throat.

'Not yet,' Blake said, avoiding the woman's gaze.

'Mrs Roskilly, I know you're just out of surgery,' Rory said, 'and the last thing you want to do is answer questions, but we need your help to find your husband.'

Albert's wife started crying again. 'He took him. He came into our home and took him away. Picked him up like he was a child.'

'Who did?' Blake asked.

'The giant!' Mrs Roskilly wailed loudly.

Blake squeezed her hand, reached for another

tissue. Rory peered through the door glass at the corridor outside.

'What do you mean when you say "giant"?' Blake asked. 'Do you mean that the man was tall?'

'His head almost touched the ceiling. He was huge. Like a mountain. And he was wearing a mask.' The woman sobbed. 'That horrible mask!'

Rory moved closer, his notebook and pen at the ready. 'Can you describe it?'

Mrs Roskilly grimaced. 'It was like the face of an ogre. A monster.'

The sound of pen on paper filled the room. 'Did he ever take the mask off? Did you see his face at all?'

The woman shook her head. Then her eyes widened slightly. 'But he had blonde hair. When he attacked my husband, Albert managed to get hold of the mask and pull it up at the back. The man had blonde hair.'

'Short? Medium length? Straight or curly?'

'Short. Very short.'

'That's good, Mrs Roskilly. Very good. Is there anything else you can remember? Did he say anything?'

Blake dabbed at more of the woman's tears while nodding encouragement. Mrs Roskilly shut her eyes as she tried to remember.

'He called himself Wrath,' she said.

Rory's pen hovered above his notebook. 'Ralph?'

'No, Wrath. Like the word meaning anger. And he was very angry.' She squeezed Blake's hand as she wept. 'Please, Detective. You need to find my husband before this man hurts him.'

A sudden realisation dawned upon Blake. The

entire time they had been in the room, Mrs Roskilly had not asked for or enquired about her son, Conrad. Which was strange. When people experienced trauma, they almost universally wanted their loved ones close by to comfort them, especially when they had been stabbed in the stomach and their husband had been abducted. And their son was nowhere to be found. Did it mean Conrad was not missing after all? That Mrs Roskilly knew exactly where he was? Even if that were true, why hadn't she asked for him?

Because she knows something, Blake thought. Because she's trying to protect him from being taken like his father.

Rory was busy writing in his notebook again. Blake knew he had warned her not to ask questions, but she couldn't just sit there when there was a chance to at least save Jan Roskilly's son from a terrible, violent death.

'Jan,' Blake said. 'I need to ask you a question.'

Whether it was the tone of her voice or a preternatural sense borne from years of knowing her and how she operated, Rory looked up and eyed her sharply.

'Blake . . .'

Ignoring him, Blake focused her attention on the woman in the bed. 'Your son Conrad may be in danger. We believe he might be a target, just like your husband.'

Mrs Roskilly's face crumpled with horror.

'Jesus, Blake!' Rory said sternly.

'Why?' Mrs Roskilly cried. 'What does this monster want with my family?'

'I can't tell you that,' Blake said, hoping her

discretion would keep Rory happy. 'But he's coming for your son. If you know where Conrad is, you need to tell us so the police can bring him into protective custody. It's the only way to keep him safe.'

Rory swore under his breath and snapped his notebook shut. 'That will be all, thank you, Blake. Could you please wait outside?'

'Custody?' Mrs Roskilly said. 'You mean they'll arrest him?'

'No. It means they'll protect him. They'll make sure no one can hurt him.'

'Blake, did you hear me? Outside. *Now.*'

Blake shot a glance over her shoulder. She stood, gave Mrs Roskilly's hand one last gentle squeeze, then let go of it.

'Conrad's gone away for a few days,' Mrs Roskilly said, her eyes wide with alarm. 'Albert told me yesterday.'

'Where has he gone?' Rory asked.

Lying on the bed, Mrs Roskilly looked like the shell of a person, her skin as white as the bed sheets. 'I don't know. But he sometimes takes off to our cabin near Coverack. It's been in my family for years. Please, you have to bring my son back to me. And Albert. You have to bring them both home.'

Blake and Rory stared at each other, the knowledge that it was probably already too late for Albert Roskilly lurking between them like a monster in the shadows.

'We'll try, Mrs Roskilly,' Rory said. 'I promise you, we'll try.'

39

Evening fell, bringing cloying darkness and a constant drizzle of rain. Blake sat behind the wheel of her Corsa driving along winding country roads, windscreen wipers shifting back and forth, headlights pushing back the shadows. In the passenger seat, Rory wore a heavy frown as he stared silently through the side window. He had already radioed in to say he had a lead on Conrad Roskilly's location and was on his way there now to bring him in. He had deliberately omitted the fact that Blake was his designated driver.

'You okay?' Blake asked him, without taking her eyes off the road. 'You haven't said a word in five minutes.'

Rory let out a heavy breath. 'I'm not happy you're here. I don't want to risk you getting hurt.'

'I can take care of myself. Besides, it's more like you don't want Turner to find out I'm with you.'

'I'm being serious, Blake. We don't know how

Roskilly will react to us showing up. He could resist, try to run. Maybe turn violent. If he's responsible for the death of Perran Thomas—and that's a big "if" without evidence—then it could get ugly.' Rory paused, glanced in her direction. 'But yes, if Turner discovered you were with me right now, I'd probably be out of a job.'

'If he does find out all you have to do is tell the truth. That with the force stretched to capacity and no time to get back to Wheal Marow to pick up your car, I was your only option. You can even tell him I stayed in the car like a good girl.'

'Oh, you *will* be staying in the car.'

'We'll see.' Blake smiled. The automated voice of Google Maps told her to take a right. She spun the wheel, turning onto an even narrower road. The Roskilly cabin was located close to Stithians Lake, the largest body of inland water in West Cornwall, which was eleven miles south-west from the hospital, and six miles west from Blake's home. It was a fairly remote area, surrounded by both farmland and moorland, with a distinct lack of traffic on the roads that left Blake's headlights fighting through the darkness alone.

'Why does Turner dislike me so much?'

Rory shrugged. 'It's not that he dislikes you. Turner just likes things done by the book. There are rules to follow, procedures to abide by. You know, all those codes of conduct you choose to ignore.'

'I take my investigations very seriously, thank you very much. I'm just not hindered by red tape and chains of command. Anyway, from what I've learned about Turner, he's broken a few rules in the past for the greater good. Breaking protocol helped him save lives.'

'True. But he's in a position of authority now. And reading between the lines, I think some of those past actions have left him with emotional scars.' Rory glanced at his phone screen, checking the time. 'I know you probably don't believe it, but Will is actually one of the good guys. And you're a civilian—his words, not mine. That's what it's really about.'

Blake considered Rory's words as the wheels of the car rolled in and out of potholes. The windscreen wipers screeched against the glass as they swept away the drizzle.

'I suppose,' she said, with a shrug. 'As for Conrad Roskilly, once he's learned his father's been taken, his mother's in hospital with a knife wound in her gut, *and* he's next on the kill list, he'll come in easily enough. Better to be in the safety of police custody than out here by himself.'

'I hope you're right. I really do.'

The road twisted and turned, the tarmac becoming more uneven. The car's passengers fell silent for a while, each of them contemplating the day's events. Blake checked her phone screen. They were five minutes away from their destination.

'Do you think Turner has the Thomases in custody by now?' she asked.

Rory heaved his shoulders. 'They have to be behind the murders. If everything you've told me is true, even if they're not the ones doing the actual killing or they don't have the money to hire someone, they have to be responsible. Because who else would be?'

Google Maps instructed Blake to take a left down a thin, muddy track flanked by rows of skeletal trees that formed a tunnel with their branches.

'The Thomases being guilty is the obvious answer,' Blake said. 'But it feels too easy.'

'Wait a minute. Didn't you say Perran Thomas's body was never found? What if he didn't die? What if he managed to swim to shore and he's the one doing the killing?'

'The thought crossed my mind. But why wait ten years to take revenge? Why stay away from your family all that time? Anyway, how many people lost at sea have ever made it back to shore? I'm betting close to zero. If the cold doesn't get you first, you'd drown from exhaustion before the shore ever appeared on the horizon.'

Rory tapped the dashboard impatiently. 'Then grandparents maybe? Or brothers and sisters.'

'Perran was an only child. As for grandparents, it's possible—to hire someone, not to actually kill anyone. But again, why wait ten years?' Blake glanced at Rory, could see frustration etched in his features. 'We don't have the whole story yet. But Conrad Roskilly can fill in the gaps.'

The track was growing even thinner, hedgerows closing in and tree branches reaching down to scrape the roof of the car.

'Wrath . . .' Rory said.

'What?'

'Mrs Roskilly said her attacker called himself Wrath. Why does that sound so familiar?'

'A giant called Wrath,' Blake said. It did sound familiar.

And then the track was opening onto a small clearing that was surrounded by evergreens. A two-storey wooden cabin stood at the far edge, a downstairs window emitting a soft yellow glow. Parked in front of it was a motorbike.

Blake immediately killed the headlights and switched off the engine.

'We're here,' she said. 'Conrad probably heard us coming a mile off.'

Rory unbuckled his seat belt and opened the passenger door.

'Stay here,' he said.

Blake gaped at him. 'I thought that was a joke.'

'It wasn't. If Turner finds out you were here and actively involved in a police investigation it's my head on a plate.'

'But what if Conrad tries to run? Or tries to fight you?'

'Then it's a good job I'm trained in self-defence and that I'm armed.'

He opened his jacket to reveal his modular harness, and tapped the pocket containing an expandable police baton.

'What if he has a knife?' Blake said. 'Conrad knows who I am. A familiar face might put him at ease, instead of a strange man breaking into his cabin and swinging a baton. As far as he knows you could be the killer.'

Rory considered it for a moment, then shook his head. 'I can't risk it. That you came along for the journey was more than enough. This is police business now.'

A spark of anger shot through Blake's veins.

'Came along for the journey? If it wasn't for me, you'd still be stuck at the hospital with no idea of where Conrad was hiding out.'

Avoiding her gaze, Rory said, 'I know that, and I'm sorry. But you need to stay here.'

Blake slumped in the driver's seat. 'Fine, you win. But let the record show I'm not happy about this. And if you're not back in five minutes I'm calling the police.'

As Rory got out of the car he flashed her a wry smile. 'I *am* the police.'

He quietly shut the door. Then he was hurrying towards the cabin, while keeping his footsteps light.

Watching him through the side window, Blake felt a wave of anxiety wash over her. Rory was ascending the porch steps. Now he was at the front door. He shot a glance over his shoulder in Blake's direction, then reached inside his jacket and took out the baton. With his free hand he knocked on the door. When no one answered, he tried the door handle. The door swung open. Rory stood for a moment, head cocked, listening for signs of life. Then he disappeared inside, leaving Blake alone.

She heaved her shoulders, clenched her teeth together. This was a mistake. If Conrad reacted badly to Rory's intrusion there was no telling what could happen. Rolling down the side window, Blake stuck her head out and listened. All she could hear was the rain softly drumming on the body of the car and forming puddles on the ground.

A minute passed by. Then another. Still no sounds or movement from the house.

Blake gnawed on the inside of her cheek. She

didn't want to jeopardise Rory's career, but she couldn't just sit there when all kinds of trouble could be occurring inside that cabin.

Removing her can of pepper spray from the glove box, Blake climbed out of the car and shut the door. The rain was cold on her skin, the darkness like a swarm of flies around her. She glanced at Conrad's motorbike parked in front of the cabin, then up at the windows. She stepped forward. Adrenaline pumping into her limbs, Blake darted forward and climbed the steps to the porch, quietly opened the front door, and stepped inside.

40

The first thing to hit Blake as she entered the cabin was a welcome rush of warmth. The front door had opened directly onto the living area. A narrow wooden staircase on the right led to the upper floor, while a wood burner sat in the fireplace of the opposite wall, bright flames dancing and sparking. Faded rugs and simple rustic furniture decorated the space in between, while a kitchenette stood in one corner, a large black coal oven at its centre. Rory was sitting slumped against the pantry door, a trickle of blood running from a gash in his right temple. His police baton had been fully extended and was lying next to the coffee table in the lounge space.

Blake rushed over to him, dropping to her knees to examine his head wound. It wasn't deep enough to require stitches, but it would certainly give him a painful headache for the next couple of days.

Conrad was nowhere to be seen.

'Hey, wake up,' she said, gently slapping Rory's

right cheek. His eyes fluttered open and took a moment to focus on her. 'How badly are you hurt?'

Rory groaned and reached for his temple, wincing as his fingertips probed the wound.

'I'll live,' he said. 'Conrad was waiting for me as I came in.'

'Where is he now?'

Movement from behind her made Blake freeze.

'I'm right here,' Conrad said.

He stood in the centre of the room, a poker from the fireplace clutched in his hand. He was dressed in filthy jeans, work boots, and a black hoodie. Dark circles haunted his eyes.

'How did you find me?' he asked, his grip tightening on the poker.

Blake remained crouched. 'We're not here to hurt you, Conrad. We're here to help you.'

Conrad stepped forward, raised the poker. 'Answer the question.'

Slowly, Blake got to her feet. 'Your mum told us you'd be here.'

She quickly told Conrad about what had happened to his mother, that she was safe now and recovering in hospital. Then she told him about his father.

Conrad paled, his features growing slack.

'Someone broke into your parents' home and took him. Your mother unfortunately got in the way.' Blake paused, glanced down at Rory, whose expression was slowly gaining clarity. 'Conrad, the reason we came here tonight is because we believe you're next. The last one to die.'

Suddenly the man looked like a scared little boy,

lost in the dark without his parents. But the moment passed and his face hardened like stone.

'No. I'm not going to die because of something that happened years ago.'

Blake watched him carefully. 'You mean Perran Thomas?'

'How the hell did you . . .' Some colour returned to Conrad's cheeks. 'It was that prick Ewan, wasn't it? He told you.'

'Actually he didn't. But that explains why he's so afraid of you. You told him about what happened to Perran. You used it as a threat of what would happen to him if he ever told anyone about the bullying.'

Conrad said nothing, only glared.

Blake continued. 'I know Perran's mother and father blame you and the others for his death. That they believe the outcome of the inquest was wrong and you all got away with it.'

'If you know that, then why are you here? Why haven't they been arrested?'

Rory stirred, cleared his throat. 'The Thomases have been taken in for questioning. They'll be at the station right now.'

Hope sprang up in Conrad's eyes. 'Then you can get that bastard to tell you where he's taken my dad.'

'I'm not sure he'll know where Albert is,' Blake said. 'Your mother's description of the attacker doesn't match Wesley Thomas at all. She said he was huge, like a giant. Muscular, with blonde hair. Does that sound like anyone you know?'

Conrad shook his head. 'He must be working for them.'

Rory tried to stand, then quickly decided against

it. 'Whoever this man is, he took your father. He murdered Martin Bennett and Terry Lawrence. We don't know whether he was hired by the Thomases or if he's working on his own. Either way, if you come with me now, I promise you we'll find out. I'll make sure you're protected. He won't be able to get to you.'

'You need to be out there looking for my dad! That's what you need to be doing.'

'Conrad, you're the only surviving crew member of the *Persephone*,' Blake said, taking a tentative step towards him. 'What happened on that boat? How did Perran die?'

A tear slipped from Conrad's left eye and glided down the contours of his cheek. He remained silent.

'Please, Conrad. Your father is running out of time. If you tell us what happened, we might be able to figure out who's behind this. Your dad needs your help. Now.'

The poker slipped from Conrad's hand and clattered noisily on the floorboards. He stared desperately at Blake.

'It was an accident,' he said. 'It's not my fault.'

Blake took another step towards him. 'Tell me.'

'Careful, Blake,' Rory warned.

She ignored him. Took another step forward. Reached out a hand and gently placed it on Conrad's forearm.

'It's okay,' she said softly. 'You don't have to hide it anymore. Let it out.'

Conrad stiffened, stared at Rory. 'No. Not in front of him. I'm not going to prison for something that was an accident.'

'There's no time for this,' Rory said. 'We can question him at the station. We need to leave now.'

Indecision pulled Blake in opposite directions. Outside, the rain began to fall harder, hammering loudly on the windows. The fire in the hearth flickered and sparked. She glanced at Conrad, then down at Rory.

'He may not talk at the station,' she said. 'This might be our only chance. I'm sorry, Rory, but we have to take it.'

'And if he attacks you?'

'He won't. Will you, Conrad?'

The man hung his head. Slowly shook it.

Carefully, Rory pushed himself to his feet. The blood from his head wound had started to congeal.

'Fine,' he said. 'But let the record show *I'm* not happy about this. I'll wait in the car.'

'Sorry about your head,' Conrad said quietly.

Rory said nothing as he moved towards the door. He reached for the handle, then paused.

'One more thing,' he said to Blake. 'When Turner finds out about this, you're going to keep quiet and say nothing. If he questions you, you'll go along with exactly what I say. I'm not losing my job.'

'Scout's honour,' Blake said, feeling a stab of guilt. 'We won't be long, I promise.'

'No, you won't.'

She turned to Conrad, who stared at her like a lost puppy. 'Talk to me.'

Rory let out an exasperated sigh as he opened the front door.

A hulking shadow loomed in front of him, filling the door frame, blocking out the rain and the clearing beyond. Rory gasped, instinctively reached for his baton, which was still lying on the floor.

'Blake!' he cried.

Blake looked up.

An enormous hand emerged from the darkness and wrapped around Rory's throat, lifting him from the ground with such ease it was as if he were made of feathers. The hand grew an arm, then a powerful torso. Then came a face. A monstrous rubber face with yellow eyes that burned into Rory's.

Next to Blake, Conrad began to whimper. Blake was frozen, index finger hovering over the nozzle of the pepper spray.

Rory kicked and thrashed in midair. Threw a punch that landed on his attacker's right shoulder. Grabbed at the hand that was throttling his neck.

Wrath burst into the cabin with a bloodcurdling roar and threw Rory onto the wooden staircase.

The back of Rory's head collided with the hard steps. Then he was tumbling and rolling, collapsing into an unconscious heap on the floor.

Blake raised the can of pepper spray, noted how minuscule and ineffective it appeared when faced with a giant.

Conrad swept down to grab the poker.

Then Wrath was thundering towards them.

41

Despite the coldness of the evening, the cramped interview room in which DS Turner sat was stiflingly hot. In the chair next to him was Detective Constable Collins, a woman in her mid-twenties whom he had worked with upon occasion and who he believed demonstrated great aptitude and astuteness for someone so early on in her career. On the opposite side of the table, Wesley Thomas still smelled of animal blood despite having left work three hours ago. He stared at the police detectives while bouncing his right knee nervously up and down. He did not look afraid or particularly worried, Turner thought. If anything, he looked inconvenienced. He had also turned down the offer of legal aid, claiming he had nothing to hide, which was either incredibly bold or incredibly ignorant. Turner had yet to decide which.

He glanced down at the tape recorder on the table. The interview had now been active for forty-two minutes and twenty-six seconds; not so long in the grand scheme of things, but with the killer still on the loose and having absconded with another victim, those minutes were beginning to feel like hours. Turner briefly wondered if Rory had caught up with Albert Roskilly's wayward son and was now ferrying him to the station.

'Let's go over the events again, shall we?' Turner said to Wesley. 'This time in more detail.'

Wesley let out a deep, undulating sigh. The jigging of his knee intensified.

'I've already told you,' he said. 'I don't know anything about the murders. And you can't pin what happened to Albert and Jan Roskilly on me because I was at work, with plenty of witnesses who can back me up.'

'But there are no witnesses to corroborate your whereabouts on the night Sharon Bennett was murdered and Martin Bennett was abducted,' Turner said. 'Nor on the night Terry Lawrence disappeared.'

'Since when was living alone and staying in for the evening considered a crime?' His eyes instinctively searched out the recording device on the table. 'Even if I don't have an alibi for those nights, I do for today. Which means you've got the wrong man.'

Turner smiled. 'Plenty of killers have worked in pairs over the years. Myra Hindley and Ian Brady. Fred and Rose West. Why not Wesley and Bonnie Thomas?'

Wesley's expression darkened. 'My wife has nothing to do with this. I can tell you that for free.'

'How would you know? From what Bonnie told me, she hasn't spoken to you in years.'

The man's face paled. 'When did you speak to her?'

'She's here right now, in a holding cell waiting to be interviewed.'

Next to Turner, DC Collins shifted on her chair. As per Turner's instructions, her hardened gaze remained fixed on the suspect, never once wavering.

Wesley suddenly laughed. 'You really think me and my wife killed those men? You think that while I was at work today, Bonnie broke into Roskilly's house, stabbed his wife, and somehow grappled a man twice her size and carried him off over her shoulder? This is some sort of joke.'

Leaning forward, Turner pressed his lips together. 'Tell me about your son, Wesley. Tell me about Perran.'

The man's smile quickly faded. His knee came to a standstill as he regarded the detective.

'My son has nothing to do with this.'

'Doesn't he?' Turner said. 'To me, it seems your son's death has everything to do with the crimes being committed right now. Talk to me about the inquest into your son's death. How did the ruling of accidental drowning make you feel?'

Storm clouds were gathering in Wesley Thomas's eyes. He glared at Turner, lowered his head.

'You know how it made me feel,' he growled.

'All the same, if you could say it out loud for the tape.'

Wesley leaned back on the chair, folded his arms across his chest. 'The inquest was wrong. How can some coroner, or whatever they are, come to a conclusion like that without any evidence to back it up? How could he possibly know Perran's death was an accident when they never even recovered his body?'

'That must have torn you apart, not being able to bury your son,' Turner said, not without sympathy. 'But I have to ask you, how can you be so sure the inquest was wrong? You just said there was no evidence and your son's body was never recovered. Wouldn't that mean, by your interpretation, that you couldn't prove what happened either way?'

'I just know, that's all.'

'How?'

'Because that bastard Conrad Roskilly had been giving Perran a life of hell for months. Beating on him, humiliating him in front of the other men, making him a laughing stock. It went on and on. It got so bad that Perran was too scared to go to sea. That's how I know his death wasn't an accident. Because Conrad Roskilly killed him and the others covered it up.'

'That's what you believe?' Turner asked. 'That these men murdered your son?'

Wesley shook his head. 'It's what I know.'

'Why didn't you go to the police?'

'I did. I told them, over and over, until I was blue in the face. I said it to you lot, to the court, to anyone who would listen. But no one ever did. My boy is dead. He's never coming back. And like I said to that investigator who came to see me at work this afternoon, I didn't kill Martin and his wife, or Terry, and I didn't stab Jan or kidnap Albert. But I'd like to shake the hand of the man who did.'

Turner was quiet for a moment, absorbing

Wesley's anger and grief. He felt great pity for the man. To lose a child had to be the greatest heartbreak of all, but did it give you the right to take a life in exchange? Especially when your actions were based on circumstance and conjecture, not irrefutable proof?

Was Wesley Thomas involved in the killings? He still didn't know.

'Here's what I see,' Turner said, clasping his hands together. 'I see a man tortured by the death of his son. A man unable to bury his child, with no satisfactory explanation of how his child even died. A child who was bullied and humiliated on a daily basis by someone he had to share a cabin with, night after night, miles from land, too far from his father, who could do nothing to help.'

'I tried to help,' Wesley said, defensively. 'I warned Conrad. I talked to Albert, told him to make his son back off.'

'But that didn't change anything, did it? As a father you must have felt like a failure.'

Wesley flinched. His face flushed scarlet.

Turner continued. 'I see a man who has been carrying the weight of guilt around his neck for years, anger growing inside him as he watches the men who he believes are responsible for his son's death live their lives freely and without recompense. Until one day he can't take it anymore. Until one day he snaps.' Turner paused. Beside him, DC Collins held her breath in anticipation. 'Including your son, the fishing trawler called the *Persephone* had a total crew of five. Including your son, three of those crew members are now dead. One has been abducted and one is still unaccounted for. It's interesting to me how you hold Conrad Roskilly accountable for Perran's death above the others, because it's Conrad Roskilly who's been saved until last. How do you explain that, Wesley? Is it all just a strange and terrible coincidence? Or is there something you want to tell us?'

Wesley had turned a sickly colour. He licked his dry lips as he stared, unblinking, at Turner.

'I would like to go home,' he said.

'And I would very much like you to stay because I'm not done asking questions.'

'Am I under arrest?'

'As stated earlier, although conducted under caution this is a voluntary interview. You're free to leave at any time.'

Wesley stared at the door but did not move. 'I didn't do anything.'

Turner smiled. 'Then you have nothing to worry about.'

But Wesley *was* worried. Turner could see it in the pallor of his skin, in the constant bobbing of his Adam's apple. In the way his eyes could not rest for more than a second. Was he afraid because they'd got the wrong man? Or because they hadn't?

'I want to talk to a lawyer,' Wesley said.

Turner's heart sank. 'You waived your right to a lawyer.'

'I changed my mind.'

The two men locked eyes. Turner heaved his shoulders. The only conclusion he could make was that Wesley Thomas was either harder to break than he had anticipated or he was completely innocent.

'Very well,' he said, leaning back. 'Is there a solicitor you have in mind?'

Wesley sneered. 'Do I look like I can afford to have a solicitor in mind?'

Turner leaned towards DC Collins, who was still glaring at the suspect with unbridled commitment.

'See if the duty solicitor is free,' he said. 'If not, contact the DSCC and arrange for a solicitor to represent Mr Thomas.'

DC Collins gave a brief nod, stood up and left the room. Turner spoke into the recorder, formally ending the interview.

'That's it?' Wesley asked.

'Once you've requested legal aid we're not allowed to question you until your solicitor arrives.' Turner glanced at the door, then back at Wesley. 'Regardless of your feelings towards the other crew members of the *Persephone*, I would like to ask you something.'

'I thought you said the interview was over.'

'It is. This is just me being curious. What about Sharon Bennett? Do you think she deserved to die? Or what about her young twin boys who have been made orphans? They now have to grow up knowing that both their parents were brutally murdered. Their mother, strangled to death while they slept in the next room. Their father, gutted and left out to dry, much like the animals at your abattoir, I imagine. Those little boys will now have to live the rest of their lives with that knowledge burned into their brains, and it's going to utterly destroy them. Do you think they deserve it?'

Across the table, Wesley dropped his gaze. 'I didn't do it.'

Turner glanced at the door again. 'Then tell me who did.'

'I can't.'

'Can't or won't?'

'I didn't kill anyone! It's the truth.'

'Then maybe you can help me with something else,' Turner said. He took out his notebook from his jacket pocket and rifled through the pages. He knew he was breaking protocol, that if Wesley Thomas admitted to anything now it would be inadmissible without being recorded by the tape. But time was running out for Albert Roskilly. Turner couldn't just sit there and let him die. 'Jan Roskilly saw her attacker. She's given us a description. Perhaps you might recognise him. A white male, around six-foot-eight tall. Muscular. No facial description because he was wearing a mask, but his hair was blonde.' He looked up from the notepad, stared at Wesley, willed him to admit something, anything.

Wesley frowned, his eyes shifting from side to side as he lost himself in thought. Then a change came over him. The muscles of his face loosened. His eyes grew wide and confused.

'What is it?' Turner said.

'Well, it's just that it sounds like—but it can't be because why would he . . .'

Turner felt a rush of adrenaline as he sat up straight. 'Who is it? Who are you thinking of?'

Wesley shook his head. He looked utterly confused. 'Blonde hair you say?'

Turner nodded. 'And tall. Mrs Roskilly said his head almost touched the ceiling.'

He waited as Wesley wrestled with his thoughts. Finally, the man looked up.

'I could be wrong, but that sounds a lot like Mason. Which doesn't make any sense.'

A sudden chill made the hairs on the back of Turner's neck stand up. 'Mason who?'

'Mason Kitto,' Wesley said. 'He works at the abattoir. An absolute giant of a man, but quiet. Keeps to himself. The other men are always winding him up, making fun of him. I've stepped in a couple of times, told them to grow up and leave him alone, because he never fights back.' He shook his head and frowned. 'No, there has to be a mistake. It can't be him. I barely know the man.'

Turner was tingling all over now. Was this the breakthrough he had been waiting for? Because how many other giant blonde-haired men associated with Wesley Thomas could be living in the area?

He quickly flipped his notebook to a clean page. 'I need his address, Wesley.'

Wesley was still perplexed. 'I don't know it. But my boss will.'

Turner slid his pen and notebook across the table, just as the door opened and DC Collins re-entered.

'A solicitor's on the way, Sarge. Should be here within an hour.'

Finished writing his employer's contact details, Wesley passed the notebook back to Turner, who snatched it up and motioned to DC Collins to follow him outside.

Once they were in the corridor and the interview room door was shut, he said, 'Collins, jump on the

PNC and run a search for Mason Kitto. Pull up everything you can find.'

Collins opened her notebook. 'How am I spelling that?'

'I don't know. You're Cornish, I'm sure you'll figure it out. We need a home address and any background details. I have his employer's contact number right here.'

The detective constable copied the details, then glanced up at Turner.

'I think we have a lead,' Turner said, unable to hide his excitement.

Collins narrowed her eyes. 'So it's not Wesley Thomas?'

'Undetermined. Just get me the information ASAP.'

'Yes, Sarge.'

Collins took off along the corridor.

'Oh, and Collins?' Turner called after her. 'Any word from Rory yet?'

'I don't think so. I'll check and get back to you.'

As Turner watched her go, his mind raced uncontrollably. Mason Kitto. If Wesley Turner was telling the truth, that he had no connection to the man except for being a work colleague he barely knew, why would Mason Kitto take revenge on Wesley's behalf?

He opened the door to the interview room. He hoped DC Collins and the Police National Computer would have an answer for him soon.

42

At first there was only unending darkness. Then a light, bright and singular, shimmering at the edges. The light became pain, sharp and throbbing, all-encompassing. A pain that, once it had started, refused to let go. A wave of nausea rose up and crashed back down. A thumping began in the chest, soft at first then growing louder, until it sounded like a mallet punching a hole through the skin of a timpani drum. The nausea grew more intense, threatening to spill from the throat. Panic took hold, wide eyed and desperate like a bird with a broken wing.

'Wake up,' a voice whispered. 'Wake up before you die.'

It sounded just like Blake Hollow.

Eyelids fluttering, fingers twitching, Rory woke up.

He was lying at the foot of the stairs inside the Roskilly family cabin. The lights were out, leaving him in the shadows. He tried to turn his head, felt a shooting pain in the back of his neck. He tried to sit up, was almost there when he pushed his left hand against the floor and was rewarded with white hot agony. He screamed, then quickly lay back on the floor and clutched his wrist, which was almost certainly broken. He sucked in a trembling breath, expelled it. Drew in another, expelled it.

He tried to rise again, this time putting his weight on his right hand. Now sitting up, he glanced around the room. The fire had gone out. Only a few amber ashes lay dying in the hearth. How long had he been unconscious?

He was answered by a dizzying sensation that felt like falling. He anchored himself to the ground with his right hand and waited for his brain to re-balance itself.

A minute passed. The dizziness subsided. Using the bannister for balance, Rory managed to get to his feet. His right ankle complained bitterly. Unlike his left wrist, it didn't feel broken. More like a sprain.

Rory hobbled forward, reaching inside his jacket to retrieve a small penlight from his harness. Depressing the power switch, he directed its bright beam of light around the room. Furniture lay in pieces in the lounge area. A broken coffee table. Shattered glass. Droplets of blood spattered among the debris. Blood that he was sure wasn't his own.

'Blake?'

Fear betrayed his voice. The rain, still falling heavily against the windows, was his only reply.

Locating his police baton, Rory stooped with some difficulty to retrieve it. Not that the baton would have been much use against such a powerful man. Now he understood why Mrs Roskilly had described him as a giant. The mask had made him all the more terrifying.

'Blake?' he called again. 'Are you here?'

He already knew the answer. Panic threatened to overwhelm Rory as he shuffled towards the front door, which was ajar and letting in the rain. He opened it to its fullest extent and cautiously peered out.

Blake's car was still sitting where she had parked it. Conrad's motorbike had been knocked over and lay on its side in the weeds. Wincing as he limped across the porch and down the steps, Rory shone the torchlight over the tyres of Blake's car. He had expected them to be slashed, but they were still intact. Not that it was any good. Blake would have the keys on her person, and Rory knew you couldn't hotwire a car in real life as easily as you could in the movies. He shifted the torch beam across the ground, saw a fresh set of tyre tracks from another vehicle.

Why had Wrath taken her? It was Conrad he wanted, not Blake.

A terrible dread racked Rory's body, making him shiver even more. He could not go after Blake. Even if he was able, he had no idea where she had been taken. Which meant Blake was on her own.

He absentmindedly wiped the rain from his eyes with his left hand. A bolt of lightning shot from his wrist and made him howl.

Had Wrath followed them to the Roskilly cabin? Had he been at the hospital, watching them, waiting for them to make a move? Whatever the answer, it was too late now.

Wrath had taken Conrad. And he had taken Blake.

Rory doubled over and vomited on the ground. His head seemed to detach from his body and spin around it like the moon orbiting the earth. It was a concussion. It was what happened when you'd been knocked unconscious twice in one evening.

He waited for the spinning to dissipate. When it had, he reached inside his jacket and grabbed his radio. He looked up into the night sky, hoping to God that Blake wasn't dead. That somehow she had escaped from Wrath and she was somewhere safe.

He pressed the push-to-talk button and radioed for help.

43

Mason Kitto's house was shrouded in darkness. The only lights came from a small table lamp in the living room and the washed out flickering of the television. Mason's mother sat in her usual position on the dogeared sofa in front of the TV, her milky yellow eyes reflecting the images playing on the screen. The volume had been muted, but she did not appear to mind. It was 11:57 p.m. Almost midnight and all was quiet.

A sudden ear-shattering eruption of noise destroyed the silence as both the front and back doors of the house imploded. Police officers rushed in, dressed in black Kevlar vests and wearing protective helmets, Glock 17 pistols in their hands and pointing at the shadows.

Shouting. Chaos. A rush of cold air as the night swept in. Yet Mason's mother did not stir. Not even when an authorised firearms officer entered the living room and trained his gun on her.

'Armed police!' he yelled. 'On the ground. Now!'

Mason's mother remained seated, unblinking.

'I said on the ground!'

The officer circled the sofa, weapon still aimed at the woman, only now becoming aware of the acrid stench and the buzzing sounds.

Then, as he positioned himself to face her, his eyes grew wide and he tasted bile in the back of his throat. Outside the living room, he heard his fellow firearms officers moving from room to room and shouting, 'Clear! Clear!' Slowly, he lowered his pistol and reached for his radio.

He cleared his throat, which had become impossibly dry, then pressed the talk button.

'Sarge,' he said, aware his voice was trembling slightly. 'You'd better get in here.'

∽

Turner entered the house three minutes later. With no sign of Mason Kitto, the all clear had been given. Dressed in a Kevlar stab vest over his shirt, he passed a few of the armed officers, whose adrenaline was quickly wearing off, and headed into the living room. He could smell the decay, could hear the hum of the flies, before laying eyes on the body. Turner grimaced as he drew closer. It was difficult to determine the woman's age or what she had once looked like, so decayed was her body. The only discernible feature was that, like Mason Kitto, she had blonde hair, but with tinges of grey that had begun to show. She sat on the sofa in a heavily soiled nightdress, flies crawling over her ruined skin. A dark stain spread out from beneath her to cover the seat cushions, which looked like black mould. Her face had already turned to rot. Her eyes were the colour of sour milk, still pointed at the TV screen.

Turner peered at the ragged black hole at the top of her forehead and wondered what she had been watching when Mason Kitto had killed her.

'How long do you think she's been dead, Sarge?' The armed officer who had discovered the body was covering his nose with the back of his hand. His complexion had taken on a sickly hue.

'Hard to tell.' Turner said. 'Definitely a while.'

His gaze moved to the mantelpiece, where framed photographs were collecting dust. Captured in the centre frame, Turner saw a young blonde-haired boy sitting on the lap of his equally blonde mother. The child's gaze was distant, never reaching the camera. His mother's smile was blank and lifeless. Next to them stood a powerful looking man with dark hair and dangerous eyes that seemed to pierce through the picture frame and penetrate Turner's soul. He looked back at the body.

'Let's get this room sealed off. No one in or out until the CSI team arrives.'

'Yes, Sarge.'

Someone else was calling to him from the rear of the house, requesting his presence. Turner backed away from the corpse on the sofa, returned to the hallway, and followed the voice into a small and filthy kitchen. The officer who had summoned him was standing by the refrigerator, holding onto its open door with a gloved hand and looking as if he might vomit.

'What have you found?' Turner asked.

The officer did not speak, just nodded towards the contents of the fridge. Steeling himself, Turner peered inside.

Sitting in a bowl of blood on the centre shelf was what appeared to be a human heart. The top right section was missing, neatly sliced off. Turner's gaze wandered over to the oven and the used skillet sitting on top of the bottom left hob. Nausea twisted his gut. He thought of Blake Hollow, who, according to Rory's report, had been taken by Mason Kitto along with Conrad Roskilly.

The officer by the fridge door suddenly clamped a hand over his mouth and made an unpleasant gurgling sound.

'Outside now,' Turner barked. 'Stay out there and watch the back.'

Grateful, the officer scurried across the kitchen and exited through the open rear door.

'Sarge!' The voice was calling from somewhere upstairs. 'I found something you should see.'

Turner left the kitchen, passed the living room door, where one of the officers was busy sealing off the room with police tape, and took the stairs two steps at a time, his gloved hand gripping the banister. Reaching the landing, he saw one of the officers poking her head out of a doorway.

'In here, Sarge,' she said quietly.

Turner followed her inside. Stopped. Looked around.

'Jesus Christ,' he muttered.

He was in a bedroom, which was surprisingly neat and clean compared to the rest of the house. If not for the stench wafting up from downstairs or the severed lamb's head sitting on the windowsill, Turner could have forgotten for a moment that he had stumbled upon a house of horrors and was instead attending a minor incident at an ordinary family home.

His eyes fixed on the lamb's empty sockets, on its shrivelled, dried-up skin. I think we've got our man, he thought, and almost laughed hysterically.

'Over here, Sarge.' The officer who had beckoned him in was standing next to a desk, above which a collection of maps and images plastered the wall. She waited for him to join her, then tapped a map of Cornwall with her index finger. 'Take a look at this.'

Turner leaned closer. Three locations had been marked with a red 'X' along the west coast of Cornwall. One 'X' marked the beach at Gwithian Towans, where Terry Lawrence's body had been discovered among the dunes. Another marked Northcliffs beach, otherwise known as Dead Man's Cove, the spot Martin Bennett had been found crucified to the rocks. Further along the coast, in the direction of Porthenev, the final X marked a location Turner didn't recognise.

'Ralph's Cupboard,' he read aloud. 'Is that a beach?'

'It's a cove,' the officer said. 'It's small, inaccessible by land. It used to be an old sea cave until the roof collapsed in.

'Strange name. Who the hell is Ralph?'

'A giant, from an old Cornish folktale.'

Turner felt a chill slip under his Kevlar vest. 'Ralph is a stupid name for a giant.'

'Well, the giant was also known as Wrath. But Ralph seems to have stuck. Anyway, the story goes that Ralph the giant lived in the sea cave. When passing ships and fishing boats sailed by, he would emerge from the cave and attack them, smashing the boats on the rocks, stealing their loot and dragging the sailors back to his lair, where he would store them for his food. That's why it's known as his cupboard.'

Nausea climbed Turner's throat. 'We need a team there now.'

'Just a minute, Sarge. Here's something else.'

With gloved fingers, the police officer removed a smaller hand-drawn map from the wall.

'What is it?' Turner asked.

'Looks like a section of the west coast. The same stretch where the bodies have been found. But there's different markings on these ones.' She frowned. 'I think they might be sea caves.'

'How could you possibly know that?'

'Because I recognise some of the locations. My mum works in marine science. I spent a lot of my youth exploring the coastal waters with her.'

Turner was silent as his mind sifted through facts and findings, while his body fought off rising panic.

Why a map of sea caves?

Think, man. Think.

He looked up. Martin Bennett and Terry Lawrence had not been murdered at the sites where their bodies had been found. They had been tortured and killed elsewhere. Not here, in this house, where neighbours would have heard them screaming. But somewhere else.

Was Kitto using one of the sea caves as his killing ground?

Plucking the map from the officer's hands, he studied it closely. There were four caves marked along the coast. Four sites where Mason Kitto could be right now, sharpening knives, separating flesh from bone. Blake Hollow's face flickered in Turner's mind. He glanced at the wall, at the bright red 'X' hovering over Ralph's Cupboard.

Ralph. Or *Wrath*.

He had a decision to make. Devon and Cornwall police did not have enough human resources on hand to cover all the locations at once. The DCI was waiting at headquarters to hear back from Turner, so a decision could be made about what to do next. Time was running out. If it hadn't run out already.

Ralph's Cupboard or the sea caves? Catch the bastard dumping another body? Or catch him in the act of butchering one of his abductees?

They would need both air and marine support, armed response, even the coastguard to help with the search from a distance. It would be a huge operation with little time to organise it. But he had to at least try.

Reaching for his radio, Turner contacted HQ and asked for his boss. While he waited, he hoped that Blake had managed to escape from Mason Kitto. That somehow she was still alive.

44

She was dreaming of being smothered. One hand crushing her windpipe. Another clamped over her mouth and nose, cutting off her airways. And she was cold, as if lying on a sheet of ice while her killer slowly choked the life from her. Cries of seagulls competed with the rush of blood pounding in her ears. Her heart throbbed dangerously inside her chest, swelling with pressure, close to bursting. And then something strange happened. From out of nowhere came a wave of freezing water that crashed over her face and into her eyes. Blake gasped.

And woke up.

She had just enough time to draw in a deep gulp of air before another wave of icy water slapped her about the cheeks. This time she cried out in shock. Realised she was lying face down, skin pressing into soft wet earth. Not earth, she thought. Sand.

Dizzy and disoriented, she managed to push herself up and roll onto her back. Water cascaded over her, cold and stinging. With another cry, Blake hoisted herself up into a seated position, arms splayed behind her back, palms pressed into the sand, wet hair plastered to her skull. She shivered uncontrollably. A dull pain began to radiate from her right temple.

She heard the rush of water coming towards her. Instinctively, she scrambled backwards, saw the white foam of the incoming tide illuminated in the darkness. She was on a beach. Could have easily drowned in the shallow tide if she hadn't woken up.

Panic took hold. How did she get here? She sat, panting and trembling, trying to shut out the growing headache. She focused on the water in front of her, watching it ebb and flow, listening to it drag over pebbles.

Memories returned to her. The cabin near Stithians Lake. Rory. Conrad Roskilly. *Wrath*. He had thrown Rory onto the stairs as if he were a rag doll. Then Wrath had come at Blake, hands outstretched, that awful rubber mask like something out of a nightmare. He had knocked the pepper spray from her hand before she could press the nozzle. And then . . . nothing. She couldn't remember any more.

Her eyes were adjusting to the dark. She could just make out the sea, with walls of darkness all around. Above her head, seagulls swooped and cried, disturbed by the presence of the stranger on the beach.

Where was Rory? She hoped he wasn't dead. Why had Wrath brought her here? Why hadn't he just killed her back at the cabin?

Blake tried to stand, felt a surging wave of dizziness, then slumped to the ground again. She waited a minute for the nausea to pass. She tried again, this time managing to stay on her feet. She couldn't feel her toes. Couldn't feel much of anything. If she stayed there on the beach she would freeze to death.

She turned her back on the water and began heading up the sand to discover exactly where she was. After just two metres of walking, she slid to a halt. There was no more beach. Only a sheer cliff that blocked her path. Blake looked up, following its trajectory until her gaze reached the top, which was capped by a starless night sky.

Turning back to face the ocean, she realised with dawning horror that what she had previously thought to be walls of darkness were in fact two walls of rock that reached out into the water and slanted inwards to almost touch, leaving a narrow channel in between for the ocean to come and go. Three sheer cliff faces forming the shape of a broken arrowhead.

Terror gripped Blake by the throat and refused to let go. Wrath must have dumped her here by boat. But why? As a sick joke? As some sort of test? And why this exact place?

She turned full circle, staring up at the towering cliff faces, her teeth chattering, hopelessness draining the life from her. Wrath, she thought. Wrath the Giant.

'Why does that sound so familiar?' Rory had asked.

Suddenly Blake knew why. And she knew where Wrath had left her stranded. Walls on three sides like a cave without a roof. She was inside Ralph's Cupboard. Home of Wrath the Giant, borne of local myth and Cornish legend, immortalised in a story that Blake had enjoyed as a child, along with all the other tall tales of giants and piskies and spriggans and changelings. Wrath, who wrecked ships and stole their loot and sailors, taking them back to his cupboard. Was that what he had done to Blake? But was she for coveting or consumption? She would not be staying around to find out.

Fumbling with numb fingers, she attempted to retrieve her phone from her jeans pocket. The Coast Guard could rescue her from here, either by boat or helicopter. But her phone was not in her pocket. She checked the others, found them empty.

You're going to die, a voice whispered in her mind. *Right here on this beach, inside Ralph's Cupboard.*

Tears welled in Blake's eyes. Fear snatched the breath from her lungs. How could she escape? The cliff faces were too sheer and too high to climb, growing at sharp, impossible angles that even the most experienced of climbers would find deadly.

Which left her with two choices. The first, to stay here and wait for help that might never come, and hope it arrived before she either froze to death or Wrath returned for her. The second, that she attempted to swim. There were several coves dotted along this stretch of coastline, most of them accessible by land. If she could make it to the closest one there was a chance she might survive.

Blake stared at the water lapping the shore. The rain had stopped and there were no strong winds to whip the sea into a frenzy. The best conditions she could hope for. Except it was barely spring, which meant the water would be bitterly cold. Blake had been a strong swimmer in her youth, but she hadn't entered a pool or the ocean for years. How was she going to do this?

Because you have no choice, she thought. *Not if you want to live.*

She began by removing her boots and socks, allowing her numb feet to sink into the wet sand. Then she removed her jacket and knitted pullover, decided to leave her skinny jeans and T-shirt on. She stood, staring at the sea, at the narrow open channel between the walls of rock. Her heart thumped erratically in her chest, looking for escape.

You can do this, she told herself. Plenty of people have swum across the English Channel in much harsher conditions.

Yes, said the voice, *but those people train for months and swim in teams, and slather themselves in layers of goose fat for insulation. You have nothing.*

'I do,' she said aloud. She had stubbornness and a strong will to survive.

Blake drew in a thin and ragged breath. She tried to open up her lungs and sucked in another. Quaking with terror and cold, she stepped towards the tide and entered the water.

45

Conrad had awoken a short while ago to find himself slumped against a cave wall with his arms strapped to his body with rope, and his knees and ankles tied together. His head hurt. He could taste blood in the back of his throat. His right eye was so swollen he could no longer open it. An orange glow from an LED lantern illuminated the cave, creating ominous shadows and revealing the horror that had made Conrad piss himself and cry out in terror. His father, naked and bound, hanging upside down from the cave's ceiling. He was still alive but drifting in and out of consciousness. He could not speak, the thick strip of tape over his mouth preventing him from begging for release. His eyes fluttered open now and again but refused to focus on this world, as if he had already chosen to depart it. Conrad stared at the bucket that had been placed beneath his father's head. A whimper escaped him.

In the left corner of the cave, Wrath's imposing

mass loomed over a workbench as he sharpened the long blade of a filleting knife against a whetstone, the awful grating of quartz against steel amplified by the cave's acoustics. He was unmasked, his back turned on Conrad, temporarily lost in his own trance-like state.

Conrad stared at Albert's limp body, feeling hysteria rising inside his own.

'Dad!' he hissed. 'You've got to wake up.'

Albert did not respond, just hung there, frozen like a stalactite.

'Dad, please!'

The noise of the sharpening blade felt like hot needles piercing Conrad's eardrums. He thrashed on the ground, trying to loosen his bindings but only succeeding in burning his skin. His panic was gathering mass, building pressure. Soon, it would explode and he would lose his mind, just like his father. Tears came, shamefully squeezing from the corners of his eyes and rolling down his cheeks.

'Why are you doing this?' he wailed at the hulking shape in the corner. 'I don't even know who you are.'

Silence fell over the cave.

'Whatever Wesley Thomas is paying you, we'll give you more. I promise. Just let us go.'

Wrath set the whetstone onto the workbench and slowly turned the filleting knife, examining the sharpness of its blade.

'No one is paying me,' he said. 'Wesley doesn't even know what I've done for him.'

Conrad stared incredulously at his captor. 'Then who are you? Why are you doing this to us?'

'Because I know how it feels to live a life filled with pain and suffering. My father taught me that. I know what it's like to be a child and have your innocence stolen. Your light snuffed out. Wesley is the only person to have ever shown me kindness. When others try to tear me down, he steps in to raise me up. I see the pain he carries with him every day, as if he's holding his dead son in his arms. The pain *you* caused him. Yet in spite of his pain, his loss, he still looks out for me. He makes me feel I'm not alone in this world after all. Which is why when I heard him talking to the others one day about what you and your crew did to his son, I decided that I would repay his kindness. I would give him what he dreams about, night after night.'

He stepped into the light, revealing his face and glittering eyes.

He's just a man, Conrad thought. *Younger than me. But still dangerous. Still deadly.*

'Killing you won't bring Wesley his son back,' Wrath said. 'But knowing the people who murdered his son are dead, that they suffered, might bring him some peace.'

Unhinged, hysterical laughter erupted from Conrad's throat. The man was insane beyond all sense and reason, which meant there was little chance of escape.

'This is all because Wesley was nice to you?' he cried. 'What are you to him? Not family. A friend? Someone he works with? A complete fucking stranger?'

The dreaminess in Wrath's eyes flickered and died. 'He knows who I am. He sees me.'

'For Christ's sake, you didn't even know what happened to his son until you overheard him telling someone else. But now you're killing for him? You need locking up in the loony bin!' Conrad stared wildly at him. Felt shreds of his sanity falling away. 'The inquest into Perran's death ruled it an accident. You're killing us without any proof.'

Wrath stepped towards him, the blade of the filleting knife glimmering in the orange light.

'The only proof I need,' he said through clenched teeth, 'is your refusal to admit what you've done.'

He pulled his rubber mask from his back trouser pocket and slipped it over his head.

Conrad stared at the monstrous face, unable to comprehend what was about to happen.

'Please,' he said, eyes flicking towards his father's semi-conscious, hanging form. 'Please don't hurt us.'

Wrath was beside Albert now, the knife poised and ready.

'Watch,' he said, a wicked smile in his voice as the blade touched skin. 'Listen to your father scream.'

46

Ice cold water rushed around Blake's waist, robbing her of breath. She was immediately paralysed, her body's natural survival instinct fighting to take back control. The ocean surged forwards, threatening to knock her off her feet, then pulled at her as it retreated from the shoreline. It called to her like a Siren, tempting her into its depths. And she had to go deeper. There was no choice.

She willed her body forwards, telling herself that the sooner she was submerged, the sooner this nightmare would be over. That she would get to live.

The water rose to her rib cage, the cold biting into her flesh. She pushed herself onwards, the sea swelling, currents tugging her from side to side like dogs fighting over a carcass.

It was getting too hard to walk. She had to go under.

But the cold, she thought. It's too cold!

No, you have to do it. If you stay here you'll die.

Sucking in a trembling breath, Blake plunged into the water, fully submerging her body, then resurfacing with a shocked cry. It was like swimming in liquid nitrogen. She floundered, limbs flailing, mind panicking.

Swim, damn it! Swim like your life depends on it!

Blake swam, the backs of her hands pressed together out in front of her, then her arms slicing through the water in wide arcs as she kicked her legs out. Seawater splashed her face, stinging her eyes and filling her mouth with salt. Her breathing was out of sync with her limbs. If she carried on like that she would drown in a matter of minutes.

She slowed her movements, expelled the air from her lungs as she cut through the water, then inhaled as she drew her limbs back in. The cold was unbearable, like needles piercing her skin. But she had to ignore it because to succumb was to die.

A few minutes of steady swimming, Blake passed through the rocky channel of Ralph's Cupboard. She paused, treading water, her body trembling as she glanced back at the beach, which was now barely visible in the darkness.

Which direction did she swim? Left or right? She tried to remember the geography of this stretch of coast, but the cold had entered her mind, leaving it damp and foggy. Left or right? Which way was life? And which was death? Damn this cold, she couldn't think!

She spun around, turning her back on the open water and training her gaze on the coastline that stretched out in both directions. Which way was Porthenev? Would it be the closest village? What about the coves that led to land? It was as if the cold had wiped her memory.

Left or right? Right or left? Dizziness took hold. Spun her around. Confused her.

It doesn't matter which direction, a voice whispered in her mind. *You're going to die anyway.*

Blake chose left. Keeping the coastline in full view, she started swimming again. She could barely feel her limbs now. Tiredness was already creeping in. But she swam, leaving Ralph's Cupboard behind her. Moving in the opposite direction of Smuggler's Cove and its beachside cottages. Away from the seaside town of Portreath. Away from the fishing village of Porthenev, where a seemingly innocuous investigation had cast her into living hell.

Disoriented, Blake swam on, flanking the rugged, impenetrable cliff face that stretched out as far as the eye could see.

47

Conrad could not watch as Wrath brought the knife to his father's skin. Instead, he squeezed his eyes shut, shook his head violently from side to side. How could he stop this? How could he make this raging psychopath let them go? He could tell the truth about Perran and hope the monster would reward his honesty with freedom, or at the very least spare his father. Because Conrad had a feeling that for him there was no letting go, no matter how much he begged or pleaded. But he didn't want to die! He didn't deserve that. Would it be better then to try to escape? One last try for survival while his father was butchered alive? He thought of the beatings Albert had given him over the years. Of the verbal diatribes designed to strip him of his ego and remind him of his position in the family. Albert Roskilly had always been a hard man to love. And yet it was Albert Roskilly who had saved Conrad from a life behind bars, who had risked everything to protect his only son. Surely that had to mean something. That Conrad's father loved him even though he had never once said it to his face.

A horrible, smothered shriek filled the cave. Conrad snapped his eyes open. He saw his father, now fully awake, bucking and writhing on the end of the rope. He saw Wrath's blade puncture his father's flesh and sink deep into his stomach.

Albert Roskilly screamed in agony, the tape over his mouth doing little to mute his pain.

'It was all me!' Conrad yelled.

Wrath looked up. Slowly, he removed the blade. Blood began to pour from the wound in Albert's gut.

'My dad did nothing wrong. He didn't hurt Perran. I did. All Dad ever tried to do was protect me. To try and make it all go away. Because it was an accident. I didn't mean for it to go that far. It was a stupid, horrible accident.' Conrad searched out his father's terrified gaze. 'I'm sorry, Dad. I'm so sorry for everything.'

Wrath remained completely still, his monstrous face tilted to one side.

'There are no accidents,' he said at last. 'Only choices.'

He rammed the blade deep into Albert's stomach again, and thrust it downwards towards his sternum. Albert began to convulse, his eyes rolling back in their sockets..

Conrad screamed loud enough for both of them, his tortured voice bouncing off the walls as he watched Wrath open up his father, and saw blood run over his face and into the bucket below.

Madness came. Conrad was glad for it, because

now he knew there was no escape. He was going to die, naked and hanging upside down in this godforsaken cave. And he knew he would die slowly. Wrath would take his time with him, first torturing Conrad until he blacked out, then again when he woke up. At some point, the giant would tire of playing with his captive. Then he would kill him. But it wouldn't be quick and painless, even after all that torture. No, he would make Conrad feel every cut and slice and tear. Because Conrad was the one he really wanted. The one who, accident or not, had taken the life of an innocent boy. That was why Wrath had saved Conrad for last. So he could look forward to inflicting more pain than a human being could withstand.

Somewhere, deep down, Conrad knew he deserved it. So he closed his eyes and waited.

48

Blake had been swimming for what seemed like hours, but in reality had been just minutes. Her limbs felt unnaturally heavy. The coldness of the water had numbed her to her core. Exhaustion held her in its grip. Yet the coastline continued to stretch on in the darkness, no sparkling lights from towns or villages to illuminate the way.

She didn't know how much longer she could keep this up, swimming through what felt like frozen black treacle. She had slowed down considerably, limbs paddling limply through the water. The voice was calling to her again.

Give up. Let yourself sink. You're never going to make it.

She willed it to go away. But she was beginning to wonder if the voice was right.

She should have seen lights by now, or a welcoming cove leading to a path back to civilisation.

But there was nothing. Only darkness and the icy Celtic Sea.

Blake stopped swimming and turned to treading water as she tried to clear her mind.

Had she chosen the wrong direction? The mounting evidence only seemed to confirm it. She scolded herself.

Idiot! A life or death situation, and you royally fucked it up.

What did she do? Did she keep going or turn around? The truth was she didn't think she had the energy to make it back to Ralph's Cupboard then journey beyond. But if she kept moving forward on her current course, what were the chances of making it to safety before she finally succumbed to cold shock and sank into the depths?

No. She had to turn back. She could make it to Ralph's Cupboard, rest for a while, and then head back out, this time in the right direction. She just had to hope that Wrath did not return in the meantime.

Blake started swimming again.

Minutes later, her movements had become sluggish and clumsy, doing more to hold her back than propel her forward. Her clothes felt as if they were made of lead. She was trembling uncontrollably, her breathing growing more erratic by the second. Dizzy and disoriented, she rested for a moment, treading water while she tried to remember on which side the coastline was meant to be. She got moving, then felt a sudden debilitating stab of pain in her left calf that made her scream.

Cramp.

She immediately sank beneath the waves, water

rushing into her mouth, then re-emerged and flipped over onto her back. She let the waves carry her as she squeezed her eyes shut and waited for the cramp to subside.

It's the cold, the voice whispered in her ear. *It's going to kill you.*

The pain faded. Blake began swimming once more, feeling as if she were wading through mud. Was she even moving?

She sank again. Resurfaced.

Another wave of cramp bit into her leg. Shrieking, Blake rolled onto her back. Went under. Pushed herself back up, choking and spluttering.

The voice was right. She really was going to die.

She lay on her back, the pain refusing to leave her, the ocean cradling her in its arms. Hopelessness washed over her.

She did not want to drown. Despite the myth of it being a peaceful, hallucinatory experience, she knew it was a terrifying and agonising way to die. The drowning itself was quick, transpiring in mere seconds. It was what happened before that she feared. It could take up to three minutes for you to lose consciousness underwater. During that time, you would desperately hold your breath for as long as you could to stop the water from getting in. Pressure would build, along with excruciating pain, until your head felt like it might explode. An overabundance of carbon dioxide and a lack of oxygen in the blood would then trigger an overpowering, desperate need to draw in breath. And you would do it; your body would not entertain any other choice. That first faltering breath would suck in huge amounts of water. Your larynx would snap shut in an attempt to prevent the water from rushing into your lungs. But it would only be a matter of time before you became unconscious, and your larynx relaxed, and your lungs flooded and quickly collapsed. No more oxygen for your starving organs, which would quickly start to fail. Your heart would continue to beat for a while, albeit at an accelerated rate. But then it, too, would cease to be, and finally you would die.

Blake could not bear the thought of it. Could think of a hundred different ways she would rather go. And so, with the last dregs of her energy, she rolled over onto her front and tried again.

She had progressed no more than a few metres when she heard a distant humming above the lapping of waves. It grew louder, closer. Her first thought was that Wrath had returned. Then, on what she thought was the horizon, she saw a beam of light appear in the night sky and reach down to touch the ocean.

At first, she was convinced she was hallucinating. But as the light and sound drew closer, she saw what they were coming from. A helicopter, roaming the sky, its searchlight moving back and forth as it scanned the water below.

Was it here for her? How could anyone possibly know where she was?

The helicopter drew closer, hugging the coastline, bringing hope with it.

Blake waved a hand, called out even though she would never be heard. A third cramp hit, this time in her right leg. She went under, sucking in water, coughing it back out as she resurfaced.

The helicopter was closer now, the roar of its

rotor blades filling her ears. And then the searchlight was upon her, blinding and brilliant. Blake waved manically, screamed at the top of her lungs. The searchlight seemed to hover for a moment. Then it was gone as the helicopter moved on, leaving her in darkness once more.

She spun in the water, screaming in frustration as it continued on its journey.

Desolation returned. Her eyes grew heavy. Her limbs flailed and flopped like dying fish. All she wanted to do was sleep. To surrender to the voice that was telling her to give up.

But then the helicopter was turning full circle. Racing back towards her. Once again, she was enveloped in staggering white light. Waves were whipped into a frenzy by the air being pushed down by the helicopter's blades.

There were other lights now, on the peripheries and closer to the water. Glowing red lights like the eyes of a ravenous giant emerging from his cave.

The helicopter turned one last time and flew away, still hugging the coast. But this time, Blake had not been abandoned. She heard voices. Saw startled faces and barrels of guns pointed at her.

Then darkness as she sank below the water. And in the darkness, she saw a hand reach towards her with outstretched fingers. She let it take her, but couldn't tell if it was pulling her up or dragging her down. She was too broken to care either way.

49

Wrath dropped the knife onto the workbench with a clatter as he casually glanced at the blood-soaked corpse hanging lifelessly from the hook. Only moments ago there had been a look of pure terror in the man's eyes as Wrath had torn into him and removed his internal workings. It had taken him a surprising while to die, much longer than the others, which meant he had endured more pain. This was good, Wrath thought. How it should be. What had been more exciting to him was the unadulterated horror and madness that had gripped Conrad Roskilly as he had watched his father die right in front of him. That had been worth the wait.

He glanced at the man slumped in the corner, who was deathly pale and broken beyond all sense and reason. His eyes had taken on a glazed, distant look, as if he had seen enough horrors to last him a lifetime and had officially checked out from reality.

But only for a moment, Wrath mused. Because he would soon bring him back, kicking and screaming.

Returning to the father's corpse, Wrath carefully removed the full bucket and set it down to one side. Next, he produced a pocket knife and severed the ropes that secured the body to the hook, cutting through the threads like butter. The body fell to the ground with a sickening snap. Some bone or other had broken. Wrath glanced over at Conrad, hoping for a reaction. But his eyes remained empty.

Frustration overcame Wrath. He wanted to see fear return to the killer's eyes. He wanted to hear him beg for forgiveness. He didn't want this . . . nothingness.

As he picked up Albert Roskilly's body and dumped it next to the bucket, he briefly wondered if he should present Conrad's head to Wesley Thomas as an offering. That way Wesley would know with absolute clarity that his son's death had been avenged, and that Wrath had been the one to do it.

He stared at Conrad's catatonic form. It was time.

Crossing the cave floor in five large strides, he stooped to grab the rope binding the man's ankles, then began dragging him towards the centre.

Conrad came back to the world of the living. Realising what was about to happen, he started to scream.

Beneath his monstrous mask, Wrath smiled. There he is, he thought. The snivelling, cowardly child killer.

Reaching the centre of the cave, Wrath effortlessly hoisted Conrad up by the ankles and hung him upside down on the hook. He stood back, watching with glee as the man jerked and thrashed about, wailing, begging, crying like a baby.

The pleasure Wrath felt was indescribable. It was not sexual. It never had been. It was more like when a child had been given his most wished for birthday present and had just removed the wrapping paper. Some killers took no pleasure in their work, he knew. But Wrath did. Had always done so. Even his first kill, as messy and bungled as it had been, had brought him significant joy. These days, killing those who deserved to die was about the only thing that did.

He went to the workbench, selected a large pair of shears and a particularly rusty blade, then returned to Conrad. With the shears, he began to remove the man's clothing, cutting through trouser legs and underwear, then his T-shirt and jacket, peeling it all away like layers of skin.

When Conrad was finally naked and still pleading for his life, Wrath dangled the blade before him.

'I've been saving my bluntest knife for you,' he said. 'It's going to really hurt.'

'Please,' Conrad managed to say, but then he was crying again, his words turning into unintelligible garble.

Wrath pressed the tip of the knife against the soft skin of Conrad's stomach, letting him feel the coldness of it, the dullness of the blade. Then he moved it slowly along the contours of his body, down his chest, to his throat, where he let it rest for a moment, before sliding it back up and eventually coming to a standstill beside Conrad's left nipple. He waited a second, listening to the man's rising hysteria. Then he applied pressure to the blade, which easily pierced the skin in spite of its bluntness. A single drop of blood appeared.

Conrad screamed as Wrath smiled.

And then the giant froze. Underneath the man's frenzied shrieking, he could hear something. Cocking his head, he listened carefully. But Conrad's wailing continued.

Irritated, Wrath drew back a fist and punched him in the throat, immediately silencing him. He listened again, felt his heartbeat race a little.

He could hear the outboard engine of an approaching boat that was getting closer by the second.

Wrath looked towards the narrow tunnel that connected the cave to its entrance, where his boat was currently moored.

He glanced down at Conrad, who was gasping and choking, his larynx convulsing from the impact.

Wrath raised the knife once more. He lowered it again. It sounded like the boat was heading right towards him. Which was highly unusual. He never heard passing boats at this time of night.

Conrad was breathing a little easier now and finding his voice again.

'Help,' he managed to whisper. 'Please—'

Wrath struck him in the throat again. Then, with a look of sheer frustration in his eyes, he went to the workbench, swapped the filleting knife for a machete, and ducked into the tunnel.

50

Blake sat within the cramped wheelhouse of the police boat while the pilot navigated the waters in silence and an authorised firearms officer stood watching over her. Three more AFOs sat on seats at the stern of the boat, dressed head to toe in body armour and armed with Heckler & Koch G36c assault rifles and Glock 17 semi-automatic pistols.

The foil blanket that Blake had been wrapped in was slowly beginning to generate a semblance of heat, yet she continued to shiver uncontrollably. She was still wearing her sodden clothes. She was exhausted, aching, her fine motor skills reduced to clumsy fumbling, the nerve-damaged fingers of her right hand smarting with sharp pain.

'How are you feeling?' the officer next to her asked. He had introduced himself as Daniels, and had been the one to give her the blanket.

'Nothing some dry clothes wouldn't fix,' Blake said through chattering teeth.

'It's safer for you to change once you're in a warmer environment,' Daniels said. 'We've contacted the coastguard. They're sending someone to rendezvous with us. They'll take you to the hospital.'

'I don't want to go to the hospital. I just need a hot shower and to go to bed.'

Daniels smiled. 'A shower? Really? I'd have thought you'd had enough of being doused in water after tonight. How long were you out there?'

'I don't know. Twenty minutes, maybe.'

The wind had picked up and was churning the ocean. The police boat crested a wave then came down with a bump. Blake winced.

'Honestly, lady luck is on your side tonight,' Daniels said, shaking his head. 'It's a miracle we found you, considering we were just passing through. What happened to you?'

'A police boat and helicopter just passing through?' Blake said, ignoring the question. 'You're looking for him, aren't you? You're looking for Wrath.'

The officer failed to hide his surprise. 'How did you know that?'

Taking in a shaky breath, Blake told him in as few words as possible about her involvement in the case, and about the events at the Roskillys' cabin that had ended with her swimming for her life.

'Do you know Rory Angove?' she asked. 'He's a detective constable. Do you know if he's—if he's all right?'

'I'm sorry, I don't. All I know is we've been instructed to search this network of caves for the suspect, and that he's likely armed and extremely dangerous.

'I need to talk to DS Turner. I need to find out about Rory. Can you contact him?'

The pilot suddenly looked up and over his shoulder. 'Approaching the next location.'

Daniels expression changed instantly. He held up a hand to his fellow officers. The boat began to slow down, the roar of the engine quietening to a soft purr. The pilot turned the boat ninety degrees.

'Fifty metres ahead,' he called.

Blake peered through the windows of the wheelhouse and saw the imposing coastline looming up ahead.

Daniels called to his team. 'Someone get on the searchlight.'

A moment later, a bright beam lit up the night and shot out across the water. Blake watched as the spotlight moved slowly from right to left across the cliff face. Everyone fell silent, eyes tracking the light as it searched every crack and crevice.

'There,' the pilot said, pointing a finger. 'Looks like a boat.'

Blake fought to keep her eyes open as the searchlight fell upon the cave entrance.

Next to her, Daniels spoke into his radio. 'Approaching final location. We have eyes on a boat moored at the entrance. Looks like a dinghy, two-seater. No passengers.'

The radio crackled and a disembodied voice replied. 'Stand by.'

Blake's pulse had begun to quicken. She stared at the boat floating in the narrow mouth of the cave, wondering if it was the same one that Wrath had used to ferry her to Ralph's Cupboard. She wondered if Rory had been on that boat too, or if he had been left to die back at the cabin. She shuddered, suddenly tasting blood. Pressing two fingers to her mouth, she examined the tips and was shocked to find she was bleeding. She had bitten her lip and hadn't felt a thing.

The police boat was swaying idly to and fro, its engine quietly puttering, waves splashing against its hull. There were no other sounds or movements. The police officers were standing to attention, assault rifles gripped pensively in their hands.

Daniels' radio crackled. Excusing himself, he left the wheelhouse and joined the others, nodding as the disembodied voice returned with instructions. Blake could not hear the words being spoken, but she saw the immediate shift in Daniels' body language. Tense and alert, shoulders back, eyes open, ready for action.

Raising a hand, Daniels signalled to the pilot, who got the boat moving again in the direction of the cave. They travelled at an unhurried pace, keeping the engine noise at a low level.

They were thirty metres away. Then twenty. Then ten.

Blake stood on wobbly legs and stared through the wheelhouse windows at the cave entrance. Darkness emanated from within, thick and impenetrable. The dinghy was moored just outside, tied to an iron stake that had been rammed into the stone of a naturally formed jetty. This had to be it. Wrath's killing ground.

'You need to sit down right now.'

She turned to see Daniels standing beside her, a troubled expression on his face. Blake did as she was instructed. She was feeling a little warmer now, but still lacking energy.

'You shouldn't be here,' Daniels said. 'We shouldn't be doing this with a civilian on board. But I have my instructions. And here are yours: no matter what happens, you stay right here. Do not move. Understood?'

Blake gave a nod. 'Don't worry, I've seen what he can do. He's all yours.'

Her words brought no comfort.

They reached the cave.

On Daniels' signal, one of his team moved forward to the bow and took hold of the mooring line. The pilot switched off the engine. The searchlight was deactivated. The remaining officers quickly checked their weapons one last time and tested the torches attached to their rifles. The officer at the bow leaned out over the water and gently pushed the moored dinghy to one side so that he could tie the police boat mooring line to the stake. With the boat secured, he gave Daniels a nod.

The team advanced, passing Blake and the pilot in the wheelhouse, weapons pointing dead ahead.

Blake stood up again and joined the pilot, who gave her a sideways glance before returning his gaze to the team. They reached the bow, with Daniels leading.

From the mouth of the cave came a bloodcurdling roar.

Blake saw the police officers momentarily freeze.

Then, emerging from the darkness like a demon from a nightmare, came Wrath.

He charged forwards, huge and fast, machete swinging in one hand. With one powerful shoulder, he ploughed into the officer who had moored the boat and sent him spinning and flailing into the water with a loud splash.

He was on the boat before a single trigger could be squeezed. He drove the machete down, sinking the blade into one of the officer's arms, who screamed in agony and lost his grip on his rifle.

Gunfire exploded in Blake's ears. Muzzle flashes lit up the dark. Then a scream of rage filled the air as bullets tore into Wrath's left arm. He was knocked backwards, almost went overboard, then managed to anchor himself at the last second. He sprang forward again.

Daniels was in front of him. He raised the rifle. Wrath swung at him with the machete. The machete sliced into Daniels' helmet and he went down fast and hard.

The pilot suddenly abandoned his station, pushing Blake to one side while drawing his sidearm. Another round of gunfire shattered the air, this time missing its target.

Wrath attacked, grabbing a police officer by her throat, then lifting her off her feet and hurling her at the wheelhouse. Her body crashed into the windows.

Blake gasped as she jumped back, one hand protecting her face from the flying glass.

The pilot reached the starboard bow and fired his pistol with trembling hands. The bullet lodged in

Wrath's shoulder, instantly paralysing his arm. The machete clattered to the floor.

Wrath bellowed, smashed his right fist into the pilot's face, who stumbled backwards and fell.

And then Wrath was staring at Blake through the shattered windows. She met his gaze, terrified and spent, no energy left to fight back.

A mouth full of bloody fangs grinned as he reached for her.

And then the air filled with red mist as Wrath's chest exploded. He flew forwards, slamming into the wheelhouse with an earth-shattering thud.

Horrified, Blake watched the fury die in his eyes. He stared at her sadly. Then his body slid to one side. Wrath toppled over the edge of the boat and plummeted into the black water below.

Blake was on autopilot, her feet moving of their own accord, leading her out of the wheelhouse and towards the bow. One of the officers was slumped on the floor, blood seeping from a wound in his arm. Both the pilot and another of the police officers lay unconscious, while a third was busy hoisting himself out of the ocean and onto the boat. Daniels sat at the tip of the bow, his rifle still pointed at the wheelhouse and his helmet almost split in two. Blake staggered to the starboard side and stared down at the water.

Wrath's huge form was floating face down with his limbs spread out like the points of a star. His monstrous mask had come loose. It stared at Blake as it bobbed up and down. Then a wave washed over it and the mask was gone, sinking down into the ocean's watery depths.

Shocked silence hung over the boat for a long

time. Then from the darkness of the cave came a far-off strangled cry. The officer with the injured arm immediately gripped his pistol.

Blake held her breath and listened.

'Someone's calling for help,' she said.

Daniels slowly staggered to his feet, stood swaying slightly for a moment, then removed his helmet. He stared at its two halves in wonder before dropping it to the deck.

'Well then,' he said, sounding dazed and distant. 'We should probably go and help them.'

51

A clear blue spring sky hung above Falmouth Harbour. The air was cold and crisp, with a gentle breeze that teased the pristine white sails of the yachts on the water. A few people milled up and down the Prince of Wales Pier, colourful strings of bunting fluttering over their heads. All seemed well. It had been three days since Mason Kitto had been gunned down in front of Blake. Three days since she had almost lost her life in the freezing Celtic Sea. She had spent one night on a ward at Royal Cornwall Hospital for observation then had been released home with orders to rest. And she *had* rested for a while, staying with her parents until this morning, when she had felt well enough to go home and her mother's inordinate fussing had started to overwhelm. With her beloved Corsa finally returned Blake had driven directly to her office, where she now sat behind her desk nursing a cup of black coffee, while Rory sat on the other side, his broken arm in a sling and his left eye still bruised and swollen. Sitting next to him was Will Turner, who for once was dressed in civilian clothing. Blake stared at his blue jeans, white T-shirt, black boots, and charcoal pea coat, and decided he could almost pass as a regular person.

Turner had called that morning and asked if he could see her. At first Blake thought it was so he could further berate her for interfering with his case. But it turned out his reason for meeting was quite the opposite.

'I thought you might like to know more about Mason Kitto,' he told her on the phone. 'I think you've earned that much.'

Now he sat, staring dubiously at the strong black coffee Blake had made him while he gathered his thoughts.

'Mason Kitto,' he began, 'was twenty-six years old and had worked at Croft Meats alongside Wesley Thomas for the past three and a half years. On the day you went to visit Mr Thomas, Kitto was relieved of his duties after threatening his manager, who had denied his request to go home early. He left almost immediately after you did. I believe your presence spooked him, that he thought his time was running out and he needed to accelerate his activities.'

"Activities" was a strange word to apply to cold-blooded murder, Blake thought. Nevertheless, she nodded for Turner to continue.

'It's likely that Kitto then followed you to Porthenev Harbour, where he abducted Albert Roskilly but failed to find Conrad Roskilly. '

'How is Mrs Roskilly, by the way?' Blake asked.

'Still in hospital but recovering. Of course, now

she has to deal with the murder of her husband. Anyway, after abducting Albert Roskilly, Kitto either tortured Conrad's location out of him, which I doubt —who would give away the whereabouts of their only child if it meant their death?—or he followed you and Rory to the cabin at Stithians.' He paused to shoot a disapproving side-eyed glance at the detective constable. Rory carefully avoided his gaze. 'Over the past few days, we've been piecing together Kitto's history, which is patchy at best. It looks like he had an abusive childhood. Social services were called out a number of times during his infancy, and we've uncovered a few drunk and disorderly charges brought against his father around the same time. When Kitto was twelve years old, his family home was burned to the ground with his father inside. An inquest ruled that Kitto senior fell asleep while drunk and dropped a cigarette. I guess we'll never know if that's the truth or if Kitto junior lent a hand.'

'More like a match,' Blake said.

'Following his father's untimely death, Kitto's mother went off the rails for a while and he was taken into foster care, where subsequent reports of violence followed. He was arrested at fourteen years of age and then again at sixteen, both times released without charge. At some point, Kitto reunited with his mother. We don't know when. We did, however, find her body at their home address. She had been murdered and, judging by the level of decomposition, had been dead for quite some time. Neighbours say the Kittos kept themselves to themselves, and that the mother was rarely seen.' Turner paused, as if deliberating whether to share what was on his mind. Then relented. 'We also found other human remains at the house, although these were fresher. On account of being kept in the fridge.'

Blake stared at him in horror. 'He *ate* them?'

'We'll have to wait for test results to come back, but it certainly looks that way. Other than that, there's not much else to tell.'

A sickened silence fell over the room.

'What about Wesley Thomas?' Blake asked. 'Did he hire Mason to kill the crew of the *Persephone*?'

Turner placed his mug of coffee on the desk, untouched, and let out a sigh. 'We're still investigating. There's no evidence so far, and both Wesley and Bonnie Thomas emphatically deny any involvement. In fact, I'd go as far as to say they both seem utterly perplexed by it all. Wesley claims he barely knew Kitto, that he'd helped him out at work a few times when some of the other men had taken to bullying him. He says that despite the man's size, Kitto was always shy and quiet, barely making eye contact with anyone. Which made him a target. We spoke to his manager and some of his colleagues, who've all corroborated Wesley's description. Some of the men admitted to teasing Kitto and claimed he had a strange infatuation with Wesley Thomas, always staring at him from across the room like a lost puppy. But Wesley swears he never once mentioned his son to Kitto. As far as he's aware Kitto didn't even know he had a son. Wesley had, however, shared his suspicions about his son's death to other colleagues.'

'So it's possible Mason Kitto either overheard him or some of the others talking about it?'

'If Kitto and Thomas were not in cahoots that

might be the only other explanation. As bizarre as it seems.'

Blake was quiet for a moment. But she slowly shook her head. 'Maybe Wesley was one of the few people in Mason Kitto's life to ever show him kindness. And that somehow compelled Kitto to repay the favour by avenging Perran Thomas's death on Wesley's behalf.'

'Without any real proof those men were guilty,' Rory said. It was the first time he'd spoken since he had sat down.

The three of them were quiet for a moment.

'How's Conrad Roskilly doing?' Blake asked.

'Physically he'll live,' Turner said. 'Psychologically, well, he watched Mason Kitto dissect his father right in front of him, and narrowly escaped dying himself. Needless to say he's a bit on edge. He did confess to killing Perran Thomas, however. Swears it was an accident.'

'I knew it,' Blake said. 'What happened?'

'He'd been bullying Perran for a while, although he phrased it as "having a laugh" with him. Mostly it was childish games. Humiliating the boy in front of the others, roughing him up, playing pranks, typical school bully type behaviour. But sometimes he took it too far. On the day Perran died, Roskilly thought it would be funny to dangle him over the side of the trawler by his ankles. You know, with his head under water.'

'Christ.'

'Unfortunately for Perran, Roskilly claims to have lost his grip on the boy's ankles. Perran went under the trawler and directly into the propeller. When they recovered his body, his neck and face were cut to ribbons. Rather than turn his son into the police, Albert persuaded the rest of the crew they would all be incriminated and so it was better to cover the whole thing up. They were all young at the time, in their early to mid-twenties. Which meant Albert's authority and a fear of prison would have helped to convince them. They weighted Perran's body, threw him overboard, and let him sink to the bottom of the sea.'

Blake was horrified. Perran Thomas had done nothing to deserve such a horrific death. She felt a spark of anger ignite in her chest. The irony was not lost on her that out of all the people Mason Kitto had targeted, the sole survivor happened to be the guiltiest.

'What will happen to Conrad now? I assume he'll be charged?'

Turner shifted on his seat then pulled at the collar of his T-shirt. 'I'm afraid it's a little more complex than that due to Perran's death having already been ruled an accident. It's a closed case and, unfortunately, to open a closed case we need hard evidence.'

'I would think Conrad's confession was hard evidence, wouldn't you?' Blake said, aghast.

'It would be if we had caught it on tape, but unfortunately he blurted it out before we'd even stepped into the interview room. He hasn't spoken a word since on advice of his solicitor.'

'But even so—'

'I'm sorry but it's not up to us, Blake. The Criminal Cases Review Commission has to sanction a review of a closed case. A request for their involvement has to come from the victim's family, not the police.'

Blake sat back on her chair, mouth ajar. 'Except the victim's family is currently under investigation.'

'If we find the Thomases are innocent,' Turner said, 'then of course we can encourage them to apply to the CCRC, who will then decide whether the case should be reopened and a new investigation started. But it will still come down to there being enough evidence to warrant it.'

'So Conrad's going to get away with it?'

'Maybe he'll confess again. Hopefully the responsibility of his father's death, along with Perran's and all the others, will weigh heavily on his shoulders.' He stared sympathetically at Blake, then slowly got to his feet. 'Anyway, like I said on the phone, I thought you had a right to know, considering your help was integral to identifying Mason Kitto.'

Blake was lost in thought, shocked by how unfair the justice system sometimes seemed.

'You're welcome,' she said softly.

Turner glanced at Rory. 'I'll give you a lift home. See you downstairs.'

He nodded at Blake, went to say something, changed his mind and left through the door. Quiet resumed.

Rory leaned forward, catching Blake's eye.

'How are you doing?' she asked him.

'I've been better. How are you?'

'Oh, you know. Mum's been driving me mad with worry. Dad wants to install iron bars on my windows and a safe room in my loft. I can't wait to get back home.'

'They mean well.'

'I know. Anyway, what about you? When can you return to work?'

'Next week. It's desk work for me until I'm fully healed.'

'You didn't get into trouble with Turner for bringing me along to the cottage?'

Rory shrugged. 'Turner says a broken arm and weeks of admin is punishment enough. I told you Will was one of the good guys—that could have been the end of my career.'

Blake smiled. 'He's all right, I suppose. For a cop.'

Rory stood up. 'Well, I'm glad you're okay, Blake. After what you went through out there in the water . . . I've been worried about you.'

'You didn't get off too lightly yourself, Detective Constable Angove. But at least we're both still here to tell the tale.' They were both quiet for a moment, processing all that happened. Then Blake looked up and said, 'Well, I'll see you around.'

Rory walked to the door. Hovered for a moment. Then said goodbye and left.

Now that she was alone, exhaustion returned to taunt Blake, leaving her on edge. She shut her eyes for a moment, and saw Wrath staring at her from the darkness. Heard gunfire. Felt blood splash over her face.

She snapped her eyes open. It was time to go home.

Gravel crunched beneath Blake's tyres as she pulled into the front yard and switched off the engine. She did not exit the car straight away but sat for a while, peering through the windscreen at the stone cottage with its slate roof and overgrown lawn that she called home. At last, she climbed out of the car, locked it, and made her way along the garden path. Halfway to the door, she froze. It was quiet. No birds in the trees. No traffic on the country road she lived next to. She stared at the ground floor windows of the cottage, saw herself reflected back, vulnerable and alone.

Removing her phone from her pocket, Blake called Kenver and waited for him to pick up. When he didn't, she left him a voicemail message. 'Hey, it's your favourite cousin. Just wondering if you were free tonight and wanted to come over. Call me back.'

She hung up, got moving. Stopped again. She glanced over her shoulder at the empty road, then back at the cottage. Mason Kitto lunged at her behind her eyes. Blake flinched. She called Judy Moon.

'How are you feeling?' Judy asked as soon as she picked up. 'Warmed up yet?'

'Well, I haven't frozen to death, if that's any comfort,' Blake replied, scuffing her right heel on the path. 'Do you have any plans for tonight? Want to come over?'

Judy gasped. 'Is Blake Hollow finally inviting me to her home? The one that she's lived in for the past two months?'

'Yes, it is. But any more of your cheek and I'll rescind the offer.'

'In that case, I would love to. Charlie can babysit

the girls for once. They've been teaching him to braid their hair, you know. I think he secretly enjoys it.'

'Lucky man,' Blake said.

'Every father should know how to braid their daughters' hair.'

'I don't disagree. You want to get here for six-thirty? I'll cook.'

Now Judy laughed. 'You? Cook? Are you sure you didn't bang your head when you were out there swimming to Ireland?'

Blake tried to smile, but the thought of entering her house alone was draining her of all humour.

'I'm hanging up now,' she said.

'Wait. Before you go, Rod wanted me to ask one last time if you'd consider being interviewed for the paper.'

'Tell Rod he can blow me.'

'It might be good for you, Blake. It might lead to new clients.'

'Right now, I'd rather have my privacy.'

Blake said goodbye and hung up. She stared at the cottage, sucked in a breath and let it out. Then she went inside.

Closing the front door, she realised that she still hadn't done anything about the broken lock. She slid the deadbolt across at the top then called a locksmith in Falmouth and asked for someone to come out today, or, if that wasn't possible, first thing tomorrow. The locksmith told her that she was in luck, he would be there within two hours.

Returning her phone to her pocket, Blake hovered in the hallway, standing perfectly still as she listened to the house. She could hear the ticks and creaks that haunted old homes, but nothing more. And while she stood there, she thought about Mason Kitto, about the horrific acts of savagery he had committed. She thought about the terrible death of Perran Thomas, his life snuffed out by a pathetic bully who stood a strong chance of getting away with it. She thought about Ewan Jenkin and his vicious, drunk of a father, and the destruction Ewan had caused at Porthenev Harbour. All of these violent acts went in circles, igniting flames under each other, creating a chain of fires that burned dangerously bright, incinerating all that they touched. Violence begets violence, Blake thought. If that were true, when would the cycle ever end?

Blake had no answers. Only crushing exhaustion and a sense of vulnerability that felt both alien and familiar. Giving the front door one final wary glance, she entered the kitchen, made a pot of coffee and brought it to the table, where she sat down and stared into space while she waited for the locksmith to come.

A Note from Malcolm

Dear Reader,

I hope you enjoyed *The Dark Below*. If you did, please consider leaving a short review at the online store you purchased it from. Just a few words can go a long way to help new readers take a chance on my books.

While I include many real Cornish locations in the PI Blake Hollow series, it's important to note that some of my towns and villages are made up. In the case of this book, Wheal Marow and Porthenev are both very much works of fiction. I've been asked a few times why I include fictional towns in my writing, and the simple answer is that, if there's going to be lots of murder and mayhem occuring, as well as a plethora of unsavoury characters, I'd rather avoid painting a real place in a negative light—I don't think the residents or the local tourist board would appreciate it.

To that end, I should also mention that Croft Meats, the abattoir where the deeply disturbed Mason Kitto spends his working hours, is also fictional. Incidentally, the research I did on abattoirs left *me* so disturbed that I've since stopped eating meat altogether.

If you ever visit Cornwall, do make sure to spend an afternoon at Gwithian Towans. It really is a beautiful place, and I assure you there are no mutilated dead bodies waiting to greet you. If you're feeling particularly brave and can stomach heights (I can't), a trip to Ralph's Cupboard is highly recommended—but don't step too close to the edge or Wrath the Giant might get you!

Finally, if you're looking forward to more Blake Hollow books, you're in luck. She'll be back very soon.

Malcolm Richards

Acknowledgements

Thank you to my editor, Natasha Orme—and congratulations on publishing your first novel (*Murder in the Fast Lane*—it's great, everyone go read it). Thank you to Patrick O'Donnell and the team at *Cops and Writers* for answering my landslide of questions. Thank you to my family and friends, and to my constant companions, Xander (my love) and Sebastian (yes, I just thanked my dog). Thanks also go to my wonderful readers, including my Read & Review team—you're the best.

As well as turning to the *Cops and Writers* team, I used a few books to help research the police procedural scenes in *The Dark Below*, including *The Crime Writer's Guide to Police Practice and Procedure* by Michael O'Byrne, published by Robert Hale, and *The Crime Writer's Casebook: A Reference Guide to Police Investigation Past and Present* by Stephen Wade and Stuart Gibbon, published by Straightforward Publishing.

Printed in Great Britain
by Amazon